Across the Lake

A Novel of the Holocaust and Ravensbrück

PATRICK HICKS

Author of *THE COMMANDANT OF LUBIZEC*
and
IN THE SHADOW OF DORA

STEPHEN F. AUSTIN STATE UNIVERSITY PRESS

Parts of this novel originally appeared as "A Woman's Place" in *Wrath-Bearing Tree*

For more information:
Stephen F. Austin State University Press
P.O. Box 13007 SFA Station
Nacogdoches, Texas 75962
sfapress@sfasu.edu
www.sfasu.edu/sfapress

Managing Editor: Kimberly Verhines
Editorial Assistants: Awele Ilusanmi and Meredith Janning
Cover Design: Meredith Janning:
Distributed by Texas A&M Consortium
www.tamupress.com

ISBN: 978-1-62288-243-4

OTHER BOOKS BY PATRICK HICKS

Fiction
In the Shadow of Dora
The Commandant of Lubizec
The Collector of Names

Non-Fiction
City of Hustle (co-editor)

Poetry
Library of the Mind
Adoptable
This London
A Harvest of Words (editor)
Finding the Gossamer

PREVIOUS PRAISE FOR PATRICK HICKS

"This is a vividly detailed, terrifying, convincing, and completely spellbinding story rooted in those murderous events we now call the Holocaust. [...] Patrick Hicks has accomplished a very difficult literary task. He has given a believable and fresh and original face to barbarism. What a fine book this is."

> — Tim O'Brien, author of *The Things They Carried,*
> Winner of the National Book Award

"In *The Commandant of Lubizec*, Patrick Hicks imagines the unimaginable and thus gives us a glimpse into the terrible complexity of the human heart. This is a fascinating and important book."

> — Robert Olen Butler
> Winner of the Pulitzer Prize

"Fiction at its highest register—creating inroads into the past so that we might hear those murdered in the extermination camps of the Holocaust, so that we might better recognize the world we have inherited. Profound and trenchant, *The Commandant of Lubizec* is a brave and unflinching book."

> — Brian Turner, author of *Here, Bullet* and *My Life as a Foreign Country*

"Hicks' prose is clear and unflinching [...] Thought-provoking and gut-wrenchingly powerful."

> — *Kirkus Reviews*

"The fictional presentation here measures up to any factual account of the Holocaust this reviewer has ever read. Highly recommended, especially for general readers who wish to know more about this unspeakable chapter of human history. Even specialists will be taken in by its human-interest dimension."

> — *Library Journal*

"The stories in Patrick Hicks's *The Collector of Names* haunt me the way that Joyce's 'The Dead' haunts me. And for the same reason: the precision of the evocation of our mortality, set against the different music of our lives."
— Bruce Weigl, author of *Song of Napalm*
Winner of the Lanan Literary Award

"Patrick Hicks has managed to bring two of history's greatest events down to the molecular level in the extraordinary character of Eli Hessel, a survivor of the Holocaust and a member of the vast team of scientists that put a man on the moon. This story is gripping in its tragedy, thrilling in its detail, and unforgettable for its protagonist, whose will to not only survive, but thrive, live, and love is a testament to the human spirit. *In the Shadow of Dora* is tenacious, just like its hero. I'll never forget it."
— Peter Geye, author of *Northernmost* and *Wintering*

"*In the Shadow of Dora* is an astonishing novel. With a poet's eye and meticulously lyric prose, Patrick Hicks unspools a harrowing tale that begins in a Nazi concentration camp and ends on the Apollo 11 launch pad. It is between these two extremes—the most base of the basest of evils and the highest of all human achievements—that Eli's story unfolds. Hicks' novel is fundamentally a narrative of inquiry and self-interrogation: Is the past what defines us? Does the future redeem us? How can you know if you're dead? This is a profoundly moving book."
— Jill Alexander Essbaum, *New York Times* Bestselling author of *Hausfrau*

The mission of women is to be beautiful,
to bring children into the world.

—Joseph Goebbels,
Reich Minister of Propaganda

CHAPTER ONE

A Bright Future

Anna applied lipstick and studied herself in the mirror. She opened her mouth and made sure she hadn't accidentally stained her front teeth. Another daub of firecracker red to her Cupid's Bow (the salesgirl in Berlin had called the top of her lip that) and she took a step back. She let her arms hang at her sides as she turned to the left. To the right.

The mouse-grey uniform looked good on her, she had to admit that. It was designed to make them all look the same of course, but there was no denying that the button-up jacket, skirt, and peaked cap brought out her best features. Waist. Hips. Chest. She smiled and cocked her head. Why, she could be a poster for the perfect Aryan woman. Blonde hair. Blue eyes. Straight nose. Dimples. Men found her attractive, she knew this, and when she hit puberty she found them watching her as she crossed the street or boarded a tram. Whenever she entered a pastry shop, their eyes lingered on her legs as if she were a sweetness behind glass.

Anna did a slow turn and made sure her hair was pinned just right. She touched it with both hands and adjusted her cap to a jaunty angle.

"There," she said to her reflection. "Ready for your first day?"

She capped her lipstick and placed it into a small pocket. Soon she would be on display for the prisoners—yes, of course—but there were also men in the camp to think about. Good men who had been with the SS for many years. Career men. Men who liked boxing, hiking, and shooting. Perhaps if she…

Anna let the thought evaporate and she looked at some paperwork on the night table. When she arrived into camp late last night, she spread out her orders to convince herself that this new life was really happening. She stared at the top lines.

Aufseherin. HARTMANN, JOHANNA R. b.1924, Berlin.
Post of Duty: FKL-Ravensbrück, 19 May 1943

Was she doing the right thing? Surely it was okay to be nervous, maybe even a little bit scared, on her first day. What would it be like to guard prisoners? What would it be like to hit them? Could she do it? Was she tough enough?

She pushed the thought aside. She had worked too hard and she would just have to trust in her training. She *was* tough, she nodded to her reflection. Not every woman was accepted to be an Aufseherin and it was an honor to wear the uniform of a female guard in a concentration camp. Anna picked up her rubber truncheon and saw her eyes narrow in the mirror. Her dimples sank.

It had all started in a bakery. That's where she saw the sign—next to the honey rolls—asking for female guards. There was a swastika and a young woman who looked out at a golden horizon. *Healthy female workers between 20-30 wanted for a military site. Good pay, clothing, free room and board. Single women only.*

And here she was. The sun was just beginning to rise and a cool breeze was coming through the window. It fluttered the orders on the night table and she went over to place a paperback onto them. It was a romance novel. The heroine was on the French Rivera and she had just had her luggage stolen in a train station. She was stranded and alone in a foreign country. Anna wondered what would happen next. That, however, would have to wait until the evening when she returned to barracks.

Barracks, she thought, looking around. It didn't look like the kind of place that housed soldiers, though. These were more like medieval houses or villas or cute mountain chalets. Each one was painted white and they were decorated with wooden shutters. There were eight villas in front of the main entrance to the camp and each one had ten single bedrooms. A small communal kitchen was down the hall and each floor had a bathroom. There was an open space with chairs in the middle of each floor and there was a fireplace. It was cozy. And since these villas had only been built a few years ago, everything was fresh and clean. The smell of new wood was still in the air.

Anna studied her corner room and smiled. It was tidy and everything had its place. Her bed was made to regulation standard— the duvet folded, just so—and outside her window she could hear ducks landing on Lake Schwedt. The horizon was turning pink. Across the lake, in the town of Fürstenberg, church bells chimed the hour. 0500. When the wind picked up, waves shushed against the shore.

The lights of the Administration building cast panes of yellow on the gravel, and she watched a black Mercedes roll up to the front door. The world was full of blue morning shadow and, almost against her will, she looked at the tall chimney on her right. She knew exactly what it was but didn't see the point in dwelling on it too much. There was a low rumbling sound as tarry black smoke spilled up into the sky. Sometimes there were sparks and licks of fire. Last night, as she tried to fall asleep, the constant low thundering kept her awake. She'd get used to it, she told herself, turning away.

"At least it's better than working in a factory," she said aloud.

Anna studied the laces on her boots and then, with both hands, she snapped the front of her jacket against her chest. She liked the grey color. It made her skin look more milky. She also liked what the culotte-style skirt did for her waist and hips.

Yes, a new life, she thought, reaching for her orders. She was an adult now and she had a good job, good pay, meals that someone else cooked, and laundry that someone else washed. She even had an allowance for travel. She looked around her room. *Her* room. Inside the wardrobe were old civilian clothes that she didn't need anymore. When she officially became an Aufseherin a few days ago, they had given her two pairs of leather boots, three blouses, several stockings, a cap, and respect. Not bad for a girl who came from nothing.

She glanced at a framed photo of Hitler bolted to the wall. He wasn't exactly a handsome leader, but he was a strong father to the nation. Why not follow him? He had created the largest empire since the Kaiser and now all of Europe was like wax in his hands. He came from humble beginnings, too. Born in a stable, she had been told. And he promised the two things any society needed for safety: guns and butter. She remembered the day when he seized power—the church bells rang for hours all across Germany. She looked at his toothbrush moustache and took it as a sign that he was a true man of the people, that he had come from the lower classes, and that he enjoyed beer halls. Thoughts of her own father scuttled into her head, but she turned her back on them and went over to the window. She closed it, flipped the lock, and snapped the drapes neatly back into place.

National Socialism had given her much. Not only was it an escape from a life she didn't want, but the Nazi movement was exciting because it was a youth movement. Her generation was working hard to create a new Germany, they were agents of change in a corrupt world, and they were sweeping away all that was unwanted and dirty. She had learned all of this on camping trips with the League of German Maidens when she was a girl. In a blue skirt, white blouse, and a kerchief that was held in place with a leather knot, they played tennis, swam in a pool, and went on long marches in the woods. At night, they sat around a bonfire and talked about what it meant to be a woman. Frau Pfeiffer asked them questions about proper breeding and who had the right to call themselves a citizen. They read parts of *Mein Kampf*. They talked about the virtue of bearing children.

Anna looked down at the orders in her hands. Imagine that. An entire generation devoted to the Führer. It felt good to swap her girlish uniform for something more powerful, more adult, more womanly. Wearing her mouse-grey jacket and dress wasn't about conformity; it was about uniformity. They were in this together.

A voice called from behind. "Anna? You coming? It's time for roll call."

It was her floormate and new friend, Ruth. She was also from Berlin, and she was also excited about becoming a guard that would protect the Reich.

"Coming!"

Anna smiled, squared her shoulders, and walked across her room. Her culotte skirt swished around her knees and her heavy boots thumped on the wooden floor. She liked the feeling. She left her door unlocked and hurried down the stairs. A bright future awaited.

CHAPTER TWO
Under the Clock

Svea leaned against the triple-layered bunk and jabbed a sewing needle into her pinky. A bubble of red appeared and she smeared it on her left cheek, then her right. Another squeeze. She daubed her lips. It was a way to hide her pale grey skin and appear vital, necessary. It could mean the difference between being selected or not selected. Her fingertips were getting badly calloused from this morning ritual and she wondered if she would need to start jabbing her toes.

She nudged her friend, Julienne, and offered the needle. They had stolen it from the sock factory several months ago and kept it hidden in a crack in the wall. If there was a random search by the Aufseherin, they were reasonably sure they wouldn't find it.

Julienne took the needle and pricked her thumb. She winced and smeared several drops of blood onto her cheekbones. Julienne— young, pretty, dark-haired, from France—handed the needle back.

"Let me see," Svea said, stepping closer. She licked her finger and smoothed out the red on Julienne's cheeks until they were a healthy salmon pink. Putting on makeup was a matter of life and death. "One more drop, I think," Svea said, using her own blood. "There. Perfect. You're the picture of health."

They both laughed at the lie and Svea hid the needle in the wall. She glanced over her shoulder to see if anyone was watching. No, she half-smiled. Good.

It was 0500 and the barrack was bustling with ragged skeletal women. No one spoke above a whisper and all the prisoners went about the business of arranging their beds, tiding their blue-grey striped uniforms, and pulling the freshly dead out into the sunrise. The sound of wooden clogs clattered against floorboards. The walls had been white-washed and a sign had been painted above the door. *Verhalte dich ruhig.* Remain calm and quiet.

A second siren sounded. It meant it was time to gather in the

Appellplatz, the roll call square. They were expected to stand in neat rows, at spiky attention, and their bodies would be counted off. The whole camp would do this every morning and evening, and they had to stand there, quietly, silently, until every last soul had been accounted for.

Svea grabbed her steel mug. She fastened the handle into her belt and made sure that Julienne did the same. Although winter had melted into the tufting greenery of spring, it was still cold. Svea looked at the other prisoners around her and saw everyone's breath. It reminded her of horses in a stable. That's all they were to the National Socialists. They were bodies to be worked, bodies to be watched over and controlled. No, she reconsidered, they weren't like horses. Animals were at least cared for and considered valuable. Animals could be sold. They were more like moving parts on a sewing machine. They were things to be oiled, and used, and thrown away.

The second siren continued to wail as they moved in a clattering mass over the cindery gravel. Svea had discovered long ago that it was better to walk in a shuffle because to actually walk in the wooden clogs risked wobbling, and this might mean spraining your ankle. A limp could slow you down and give an Aufseherin a reason to beat you.

The world was full of dark blue shadow as they passed beneath an avenue of lime trees. Although thousands of women were moving towards the Appellplatz, no one spoke. Occasionally, very occasionally, there were snatches of whispered Polish or French. Svea looked at Julienne, who was not much younger than herself, but yet she seemed more childlike. As she adjusted her striped cap, she fumbled with something in her pocket and Svea slapped her elbow. It was forbidden to have your hands in your pockets. "Stop," she hissed.

"Quickly, quickly!" an Aufseherin yelled from the front. She had a high voice and spoke with a southern accent. From Bavaria, Svea thought, keeping her eye on Julienne. Thoughts of Bavaria filled her mind and she allowed herself to imagine a dazzling table weighted down with food. There was noodle soup, pig knuckle with dumplings, schmaltz on grainy bread, mutton stew, white sausage, and spaetzle. It was such traditional food from that part of the Reich. She licked her dry lips. There was the iron taste of her own blood and, immediately, she started to daub her pinky against her lips. She worked a fresh bead of red onto her upper lip. Her mother once told her that was called the Cupid's Bow. Hopefully she hadn't overdone it, she thought, sucking her pinky.

"Line up, you bitches!" another voice shouted. It was a Blockova, a female prisoner who had the power to punish. A Blockova ruled each barrack and, in return for keeping order, she was given extra food, clean clothes, and cigarettes. "Hands by your sides. Shut your mouths. Eyes forward!"

A whip cracked somewhere in the rear. Svea glanced at Julienne and then looked over to her friends, Hannah and Maria. Their bare legs seemed so suddenly naked, so unprotected. The hair on her legs sizzled with goose pimples and her fingertips were numb. When she was a child, she believed that May was a warm month, but this wasn't the case in the early morning air. It was crisp. Freezing.

When they arrived in the Appellplatz, which was the size of a football pitch, there was the sound of shuffling and a skittering of pebbles as each block formed up into tidy rows. They straightened their spines and stared ahead at the kitchen block. The sky was—my God, Svea found her breath catching in her throat—it was beautiful. Grapefruit pink and streaks of cantaloupe. There was warming peach and tangerine and lemon. The yolk of the sun was just beginning to rise and it dragged shadows across the cindered square. She breathed in and enjoyed the bellows of her lungs expanding, withering. Expanding, withering.

A few Polish women next to her murmured the Hail Mary. "*Zdrowaś Maryjo, łaski pełna…*"

As Svea stood at attention, her arms tight at her sides, she wondered how they could possibly have faith in a God that allowed Ravensbrück to exist. For all of their worship and praise, this camp—every molecule of it—was allowed to come into existence and metastasize like cancer. God doesn't care about us, she thought. God doesn't care about good and evil. Her eyes narrowed in anger. Maybe it was a waste of time to care about God? If anything, an all-powerful God ought to be in prison for allowing this crime to happen.

She looked at the shadowy bulk of the camp prison, known as the Bunker, and her eyes focused on barred windows. Anyone taken in there didn't come out alive. Or maybe they were taken elsewhere after they had been marched into the Bunker? She held onto this hopeful belief but it faded when she glanced at the chimney beyond the camp wall. Dark smoke rumbled up into the sky. One of the guards once shouted at roll call, "See that? See that smoke? That's the only way out of here. Through the chimney."

"*Zdrowaś Maryjo, łaski pełna...*" the women continued to mutter. "*Pan z wami.*"

Svea wanted to laugh. If Mary was alive today, she would find herself sewing socks in this place. A Jewess. She would have been tossed in here years ago, and her son would have been ripped away from her and sent to another camp. He would have been made into ashes long ago. There would be no Easter. There would be no rising. There would only be ashes.

Svea felt her knees buckle. Her stomach grumbled and she closed her eyes to imagine that glorious table of food again. It was a banquet of fat and calories. There were grapes and hard-boiled eggs and thick slices of meat. There were also pitchers of water. Huge chunks of ice bobbed on the surface. Beads of cool water blistered the glass.

She shook the thought away and tried not to lick her lips. It was dangerous to think of meals gone by. Just wait, she told herself. After they were counted, they would each get a cup of cabbage soup. And then? Then they would be marched to the sock factory for eleven hours of nonstop work.

A Blockova shouted numbers and Svea waited to hear her new name. To her friends she was Svea Fischer but to the female guards she was 18311. Numbers shot into the air like fireworks and, all the while, a large iron clock on the Administration building glared down on everyone, the enormous minute hand barely moving.

Roll call was boring, yes, but it was also dangerous. Aufseherin often pulled prisoners out of line to beat them with riding crops or truncheons. Last week, a guard had ordered a prisoner to take off her glasses. Then the guard began hitting the woman in the face with an uncoiled whip. The prisoner's nose was broken and a long gash ran from her temple to her lip. When the woman was handed back her glasses—carefully, Svea noticed—they sat lopsided on her face. The wound didn't heal properly, there was an infection with a lot of pus, and the woman was taken away. Where to, Svea couldn't say.

Her eyes flicked to the chimney. Sometimes, when the wind was right, you could feel fine dust in the air. It brushed against your face and crawled down into your throat. Yes, she nodded to herself, she was in the very nucleus of Nazism now. She was in the middle of the dark heart of it all. That chimney was more of symbol for National Socialism than the swastika ever could be.

Lice nibbled in her armpits and, although she badly wanted to scratch, she didn't dare move. Little translucent bodies jittered in the seams of her dress. It felt like having a bad sunburn. Or maybe having bleach poured on your skin? It was a constant low burning, a constant biting, it was always there, like hunger. How strange, she thought. She was thin, but the lice were fat.

When her name was called, it almost surprised her.

"18311."

She raised her hand and shouted, "*Jawohl!*"

How many of her mornings had begun in Ravensbrück now? It had been at least three years, and because of her low number she was considered a camp veteran. It wasn't always this way. Sometimes her first day seemed like it had happened only a few hours ago. She had been loaded into a cattle car with a hundred other women and they were sent north from Berlin. When they arrived at Fürstenberg they were ordered down from the cattle car—it hurt to jump out after standing for so long—and they had to march. Svea had clutched her pink sweater close to her neck and searched for the single suitcase that she was allowed to bring, but it was nowhere to be seen. A female guard with dirty blonde hair raised a riding crop and brought it down hard onto her back.

"Move!" she had shouted.

It was the first time Svea had been hit. The sting of it wasn't nearly as bad as the surprise of being attacked by a stranger. She stumbled along in shock that a woman could be so violent and, as they marched down a road, she wondered why she was in shock. Why did she think that a woman couldn't be as cruel and vicious as a man?

They formed two lines and had no idea where they were going. The village of Fürstenberg was so pretty, so photogenic, and it was so profoundly odd to walk past neat little houses with flowerpots. Gardenias were in boxes and the postman was busy delivering mail. Children stopped playing to watch them march past. Their shoes scuffed against the asphalt as they moved beneath beech trees that must have been planted two hundred years ago. Sunlight flittered down and no one seemed at all bothered that two long columns of women were tromping down the street. Most of the adults turned away. Not all of the men did, though. Svea was used to being looked at and, as she grew up, she began to notice how men stared at her when she crossed the street or how they eyed her at the beach. Her changing body involved pain and too much blood. The boys, meanwhile, learned that they had a weapon. Sometimes men passed her on the street and said things that dragged like a weight on her for the rest of the day. *Hey honey, great tits. I'm going to follow you home and fuck you.* To be a woman was to be observed, she came to realize. It unnerved her, and it could be scary. But on that day in Fürstenberg, as she walked down that street on a bright sunny morning, this type of staring was different— it was more terrifying. She was both temptress, and enemy.

After two kilometers, they finally arrived at the camp. The walls were impossibly high and fortified with barbed wire. Once they passed through the main gate they were ordered to strip naked. Svea hesitated. But when the Aufseherin started to hit and punch and kick, the clothes began to drop on the cindery ground.

"No rings. No wristwatches. No bracelets or necklaces. No earrings," a guard shouted, orbiting them with a black dog. It snapped and growled. It wasn't muzzled and its teeth were yellow. The guard held the leash lazily with one hand. It would be so easy for her to let go. Svea imagined the angry dog leaping for her thigh.

"Hand over your jewelry!"

A cluster of SS administrators appeared and they leaned against the wall, smoking cigarettes and pipes. They laughed and pointed as she took off her dress, her stockings, her blouse, her underwear. She unclipped her bra and let it dangle in her right hand before she let it fall. Now she was completely naked. She covered herself with one hand and used her arm to hide her breasts. The dog continued to patrol. The men continued to leer and their eyes raked across her body. She had only been naked in front of her doctor.

Soon they were all naked. Clothes were scattered everywhere and the women began to press against each other for protection and warmth.

"Arms at your sides!"

Svea shivered in the September air and looked at the maple trees beyond the electrified fence. Leaves were torn away from the safety of their branches and they floated helplessly on a river of air.

They were then ordered into a nearby building for a cold shower, which was followed by delousing with some type of burning powder. It made her eyes sting. They were ordered to line up and spread their legs. A vaginal examination was done to make sure they weren't hiding any valuables. They stood against a cold wall and, to Svea's horror, she realized the same plastic glove was going to be used on all of them. Some of the women were on their period and the glove was quickly stained red. When it was her turn, she spread her legs and blinked back tears. It was the first time a woman had put her fingers inside of her, and Svea winced at the prodding and jabbing. The SS had followed them into the showers and, now, they watched the vaginal searches. They smoked casually and pointed at thin women with large breasts. The men nodded as if they were assessing cattle. Svea looked at her feet.

When the examinations were finished—and when the plastic glove was finally peeled off and dropped into a metal bin—Svea and the others were taken to another room where her pubic hair was shaved, roughly and quickly. The electric razor nicked her labia. And then, in a state of shock, she was forced to sit on a wooden bench and have her long beautiful hair cut off. As it fluttered down in twisting curls, her throat tightened with tears. Who was she without her hair?

Finally, at last, the new prisoners were given striped dresses that had a collar. They were told to grab a pair of underwear, an apron, a bandana, and wooden clogs. "Get dressed," a female guard said. She touched her truncheon. "Do it quickly now."

Svea didn't know anyone around her and she had absolutely no idea what was coming next. When she slid the dress over her head and wiggled into it she noticed a number on her left shoulder. 18311. To her deep astonishment, she began to laugh. It was all so absurd that she couldn't help herself. It was a release, to laugh. The other women around her began to shush her.

"Be quiet," one of them hissed.

"Shut up."

But she couldn't stop laughing. She looked ridiculous in a striped dress and wooden clogs. They all did. And her head was as bald as an egg. To laugh helped her strangle the rising terror in her chest. It felt something like protection to laugh.

Someone punched her arm. "Quiet!"

An Aufseherin with a pretty face and perfectly coiffed black hair came over with her dog. She scanned the crowd for whoever was laughing and let her dog off its leash. The animal bounded over silently to the woman next to Svea and tore into her shin. When the woman fell to the ground in yowls of pain, the dog attacked her face. It ripped open her cheek and tore off the tip of her nose. Shrieks of horror came from the woman as she curled into a ball. The black dog hooked onto an arm and began to tug.

"Halt," the female guard said calmly, and the animal let go. The prisoner wept in pain and begged for someone to help her.

"Do you see what happens?" the guard asked the crowd without raising her voice. "Do you see what happens when you laugh?" The guard went over and fussed with her dog. She played with its ears and reached into her pocket for a bit of salami. "Good, Mitzi," she cooed. Then she leashed the animal and straightened up. "You and you," she said, pointing to two nearby prisoners. "Pick that up and take it away."

As two prisoners reached down for the wounded woman, one of the new arrivals took of her cap and began to touch her shaved head. She trembled and wept as she cupped her skull. She began to scream—full lunged screeching. And then, in a moment that Svea would see in her mind's eye for months to come, this new prisoner ran directly for the electrified fence. She threw herself against it and there was a terrible crackling sound. The woman twitched like a fish caught in a net. She continued screaming until she was still.

This was Svea's introduction to Ravensbrück.

She was numb. She couldn't speak. She felt like a dying star. She stumbled through the hours and did whatever she was told. And that first night, when she wanted to cry herself to sleep, the tears would not come. A prisoner named Katya crawled into the bunk and wrapped Svea in her arms. She brought her close.

"Listen," she whispered. "If you cannot survive a week in this place, you will not survive at all."

That was three years ago, Svea thought. Three long years. And Katya was now—

She didn't want to complete the thought. She took a deep breath and concentrated on the here and now, on this living second. She filled up her lungs and let her mind drift towards the goodness of cabbage soup.

"18729."

Julienne raised her hand and shouted, "*Jawohl.*"

Hearing her friend's voice made Svea smile. She was like Katya for Julienne. She was campwise. She was a mother figure and teacher to a new prisoner. It felt good to know that she was needed.

"18743."

"*Jawohl.*"

"19003."

"*Jawohl.*"

Each number brought them closer to food. Cabbage soup and a chunk of bread waited on the horizon of the future. All she had to do was be patient.

An Aufseherin strolled through the ranks and hit women for having messy uniforms. The guard wore leather gloves and sometimes grabbed at faces to study a complexion. It was for this reason that Svea had daubed blood onto her cheeks and her lips. It was this guard—this nameless unknown guard—that worried Svea the most during morning roll call. A few women had been dragged out of the square and never seen again, all because they looked weak.

Svea kept her eyes on the kitchen block and watched smoke billow from a stubby chimney. A door opened and a huge 600-liter pot of soup was trundled out by four prisoners. *Don't spill it*, she almost said as the prisoners moved it towards a wooden pallet.

A cuckoo called from beyond the wall and she scanned the tree line. It was strange to think of life beyond the camp. "Life beyond the camp," she murmured to herself. It made her consider the many reasons you could find yourself behind the barbed wire of Ravensbrück. There were political prisoners and resistance fighters and prostitutes. There was even one woman—Svea stared at the soup pot and tried to remember her name—this woman—Sylvia?—she was dropped off at the gates simply because her husband no longer wanted to be married. He drove up and dropped her off as if she were a coat he no longer wanted in his closet.

The cuckoo sounded again. Another large pot of soup was carried out from the kitchen and she winced when she saw a wave slosh over the side.

Everyone wore a blue-striped dress with a triangle—a winkel—on the upper left sleeve to mark their crime against the Reich. Criminals wore green. Political prisoners had red. Deviant women, alcoholics, the homeless, violators of German race laws, women who refused to get married, prostitutes—anyone who was deemed asocial by the Nazi party—they all wore black. Jehovah's Witnesses got lavender. Gypsies were brown. Jews were yellow.

Svea glanced at her own triangle. It was black. So much time had passed, however, that it was now more of a shadowy grey. She could have had a yellow winkel though because she was a quarter Jewish. Her grandmother, who had passed away when Svea was only a child, had been Jewish. When Hitler came to power in 1933, Svea's parents told her to hide this branch of the family tree and she did, especially when the Jews of Berlin were rounded up and taken to the East. She told no one about this secret: not her friends, not her dancing partners, not her employer, not her boyfriend, and certainly not anyone in camp. Not even Julienne knew about her Jewish blood. By stitching her mouth shut and saying nothing, she had perhaps saved her own life. It wasn't that long ago that all of the Jewish women of Ravensbrück were rounded up and sent to Poland. No one heard anything about them again. As far as the Nazis were concerned, it was a way of making Ravensbrück free of Jews, but it didn't last long. Within four weeks, new Jewish prisoners were in camp.

But what made someone Jewish? Was it blood? If so, then what about conversion? What about marrying a Jew? She knew this much: the Nazis didn't like mixed blood and that's exactly what she was, a *Mischlinge*. How much longer could she keep this secret hidden? "The Jew smells." That's what the Nazis said in their newspapers. But they hadn't sniffed her out.

"Not yet anyway," she whispered to the morning.

No doubt a file existed on her somewhere in the Administration building, and no doubt it labeled her as an asocial because she didn't embrace Nazi ideology. It had all started with music. She loved American songs and listened to broadcasts of the BBC playing Benny Goodman, Duke Ellington, Glenn Miller, and Count Basie. There was something about swing that made her feel alive and carefree. The thumping drums and soaring trumpets got her spinning in her apartment, and it wasn't long before she was finding underground dancehalls where she could try new moves with cute boys. The Lindy Hop. The Saint Louis Shag. Boogie Woogie. She let her long blonde hair float as they jumped to "Sing, Sing, Sing (With a Swing)". Worry melted away as she shimmied across the dancefloor, spinning and wheeling.

The Nazis had outlawed such music—it was too degenerate—too Negro—but she kept going to dances instead of hikes in the woods with the League of German Maidens. She turned her back on Hitler's vision for Germany and embraced music from wide-open America. The place seemed impossibly big and vibrant and absolutely bursting with ideas, and she wondered what it might be like to see the lights of New York or step into the Cotton Club where great musicians played right before your eyes. Harlem seemed like a huge engine of art. She looked at American culture, especially black culture, and saw not danger, but possibility. Her grandmother once said that in life you can choose to be curious or you can choose to be suspicious.

"Choose to be curious," her grandmother had said. "Life's more interesting when you're curious."

Svea found herself leaning into swing and jazz as a way to cope with the brown shirts marching through the streets of Berlin. They carried brass knuckles and punched anyone that didn't salute. They sang anthems as they moved in lockstep while she—in her flat—let her feet whirl to whatever freedom was coming from the record player. She didn't stop, not even when buses with darkened windows pulled up to buildings, and not even when people started disappearing.

When the Gestapo searched her flat and found a stack of illegal records, they snapped them in half and she was ordered to sign up for a new job. The economy needed her and if she didn't find suitable work in a Nazi approved office or factory—well then, something would be done to correct her behavior.

"Stop being a swing kid," the thin man from the Gestapo said while stepping over black shards of snapped records. His eyes were as cold as mountain air. He stood in the doorway and added, "Don't let America corrupt you." He held up a finger in warning. "Register for work. Or work will be found for you."

"But," she started to say.

"This isn't a game, Miss Fischer. Your neighbors are watching and listening. There are eyes in this building, yes? You understand me? You can either join the future or be crushed by it."

She stared down at her black triangle, her winkel, and once again considered that it looked like a snapped bit of a record. After what happened to Peter, she began to think, it was only a matter of time before they came for her too. Peter, she thought. Where was...?

She turned from the past and stared into the clear morning air. Five huge soup pots were now lined up and she shifted her weight in anticipation of marching for the warm vegetably broth. The wind picked up, fluttering the hems of everyone's dresses. She stood on unmoving feet. There was never music in Ravensbrück. When was the last time she had danced?

On the far end of the roll call square came a shrill cry. There was the sound of someone getting hit. Svea looked ahead and pretended to hear nothing. Look away, she thought. Look away like your neighbors did when the Gestapo came for you.

A siren pierced the air and then came a sharp female voice. "Fall out!" It was an Aufseherin and she held a riding crop. Behind her, office lights were clicking on in the Administration building and a truck could be heard somewhere beyond the camp walls. The sky was a deep salmon-pink and the sun was above the horizon. Svea closed her eyes and felt warmth on her cheeks.

When it came time for her block to step forward for soup, she placed her hands in the pockets of her dress. It was such a normal thing to do, so casual, it was a sign of being at ease with your surroundings, but she immediately pulled her fists out and let them dangle at her sides. It was forbidden to walk with hands in your pockets—who knew what you might be hiding? It was also forbidden to keep anything in your pockets, which begged the question: why have pockets on their dresses in the first place?

She nudged Julienne and motioned for her to step forward. "You first," she whispered.

Only a few more meters to go and she would hold out a dented metal mug for cabbage soup. She could smell it now. Svea listened to the clanging of a ladle hitting the inside of the enormous pot. All around her, women scratched their armpits, their scalps, their buttocks, their shoulder blades. There was a pong of body odor. She stood there, waiting.

And then something strange happened. The Aufseherins that had been strolling through their ranks—hitting here, hitting there—all hurried to the front. Svea wasn't sure why they half-ran, but it was worrying. Anything outside the borders of routine was something to fear. She watched the Aufseherin hurry to the main gate to greet the Commandant. Tall and lean, his eyes were closely set together and he wore a leather trenchcoat. His SS cap sat neatly on his head, and the silver threads of his lapels were bright against the black fabric. Although this was a camp for women, the Nazis had decided that it should be run by men. Svea didn't know his name— he was simply known as the Commandant—and as he strolled into the roll call square, the Aufseherin crowded around him like schoolgirls. He smoked a cigarette and pointed at something at the far end of camp. The sock factory perhaps? Svea turned to look.

She wondered what this could possibly mean. Instead of sewing, were they going to build a barrack or dig a drainage ditch? Although the sock factory was loud and dangerous, at least it kept her indoors. That was something, especially during winter. She studied this man who could order her death at any moment and noticed several new faces among the Aufseherin. She hadn't seen them before. New recruits? One of them had bright red lipstick, which was surprising because most of the Aufseherin didn't wear any makeup at all. This new guard had long blond hair and it had to be said that she was attractive, especially when she smiled. She was the image of the perfect Aryan woman, and she was so striking that she could easily be in one of Goebbels's movies. The Commandant said something to this new guard and there was laughter. He touched her arm and pointed to the back of camp. He took a deep inhale on his cigarette and blew smoke from the side of his mouth.

Svea looked at the new guard's long hair, which was perfectly pinned in a loop and caught beneath her cap. This made Svea touch the back of her scalp. She felt bristles. To look beautiful again—what a pretty thought. Everything about Ravensbrück was designed to make her feel muddy and small. Useless.

Julienne stepped away from the soup pot, already drinking in the broth, and Svea stepped up with her mug in both hands. The cabbage soup was greyish green. It looked like boiled poison ivy. The ladle was brought to her dented mug and then the only meal she would have until nightfall was splashed in. Warm drops spattered her thumb.

She followed Julienne and, together, they drank. It tasted like leaf rot but she didn't care. It was more important to get calories into her stomach. When she was finished, she licked the inside of the mug clean. She used her finger to skim the bottom.

"Where's the bread?" Julienne asked, also licking her mug.

"No idea."

Others were looking around too, but no one dared to ask the Blockovas if they were getting bread. And to ask an Aufseherin such a question? That would get your fifteen lashes. The bread they *did* get over the last few weeks had a powdery taste, like sawdust. Svea wondered about this. It was true that Berlin was getting bombed by the Americans more or less routinely—she could see their planes cutting white trails high above—so maybe flour was scarce? If regular Germans were rationing bread that meant prisoners would get nothing. Maybe this is why they didn't have bread?

She looked up and noticed the new guards were eyeing their ranks suspiciously. These fresh Aufseherin stood with their arms crossed, as if protecting themselves, and this made Svea feel like an animal that couldn't be trusted. In particular, the new guard with red lipstick wasn't smiling at all now. She looked—Svea searched for the right word—she looked nervous. It was odd to see a guard trying to hide her fear and this made Svea feel powerful. Good, she thought. You be scared for once.

A Blockova yelled for them to head out for their work details. "Same ones you had yesterday," she added, cupping her hands around her mouth like a megaphone.

"Quickly!" another Blockova snapped.

Her barrack moved for the sock factory at the back of camp. The sky was pale and a few lone clouds scudded on the horizon. As they walked down the cinder path, their wooden clogs sounded like a threshing machine.

Julienne bumped into her—hard—and reached for her hand. "I have a little surprise for you," she said happily. She leaned in. "You have been so good to me, Svea. Thank you."

"Surprise? What kind of surprise?"

"Oh, it is something I made for you," she whispered in her French accent. She let go of Svea's hand and fell into marching. Julienne glanced over and offered one last comment. "You look pretty today."

Svea knew it was a lie, but she was grateful to hear it anyway.

CHAPTER THREE
Harm Itself

Anna watched the prisoners march away in sloppy formation and she studied the empty soup pots. The faint smell of cabbage was in the air, but what was really overpowering, what really made her wrinkle her nose in disgust, was the smell of the prisoners. *That* would take some getting used to. And the lice. She worried about getting too close to a prisoner and having the little beasties leap onto her grey uniform.

She crossed her arms over her chest and took a deep breath. She thought this made her look defensive and standoffish, so she placed her fists on her hips—this made her feel more powerful—and she turned to the other guards to see what they were doing. They were standing with their arms at their sides, and she hurriedly did the same.

"As I was saying," the Commandant smiled. "Welcome to Ravensbrück. I'll let *Oberaufseherin* Binz take over from here. Frau Binz? If you would."

Anna glanced at his leather trenchcoat and wondered if it was hard to keep clean. No, she had to conclude. He probably ordered servants to buff and oil it every night. She looked around. They all had servants now. This whole camp would do whatever they wished.

"It was nice meeting all of you," the Commandant said, touching the brim of his cap. "It's good to have so many pretty faces around us." He turned on his heel and moved quickly for the Administration building. He snapped his fingers at an SS guard who was leaving the canteen and asked for a flask of coffee to be delivered to his office. And then, with his black leather trenchcoat floating behind him, he walked through the iron gates.

"Attention," *Oberaufseherin* Binz said in a smooth voice. It made Anna's spine stiffen. She pushed out her chest and stared at the horizon. Others were still slouching.

"Come to...attention!" Binz yelled, letting her voice rise with each word. Her tone was hard and her eyes flicked over them.

Anna heard a bird calling from somewhere beyond camp. Trees rustled in a low wind. The sound of a typewriter came from an open window. A truck backfired—or perhaps it was a pistol?

She stood ramrod straight. Here she was in an ordered row with other young women who were creating a new future. A new society was taking shape in Europe and it was like watching granite being chipped away from a solid block of stone. In order for a statue to appear, a chisel had to be used. Anything that was unnecessary and useless had to be struck off, and after these flaws were removed, only then could the statue be seen in all its pure brilliance. Violence could create beauty. She was a chisel in service to the state and, in time, yes in time, after enough hammer blows, something beautiful would arise.

"You are standing," Binz said pacing before them, "inside the only concentration camp for women in the Third Reich."

There was a pause as she looked around.

"In here we have communists, prostitutes, the work shy, the immoral, those who undermine the war, those who defy race laws, and political pests." There was a moment of hesitation before she added, "The most important thing to know? They are all criminals."

Binz stood with her hands cupped behind her back. The wind picked up, flapping her culotte-style skirt.

"I want you to remember that this isn't a playground. Our camp is the front line of the war at home. While our men are fighting the Soviets, it's our job, in this place, to let the criminals know *their* place. And while you aren't soldiers in the sense that you can carry a rifle, you are guardians of morality. You need to be models of National Socialism."

She uncupped her hands and adjusted her collar. Slowly, with both hands, she titled the cap left, right, straight.

"You've been training in Berlin for the last several weeks. In classrooms, you've studied different modes of punishment and you've been told to harden yourself against pity. You've had good training," Binz said, leveling a finger at them. "But training is over. You're neck deep in the real thing now."

Anna felt an itch on her nose. She dared not move and, for a moment, she allowed herself to imagine being in the roll call square as a prisoner. They must have similar moments when they wanted to scratch their bodies, especially with all that lice, but—but no.

No, she told herself firmly. She was nothing like them. Absolutely not. They were criminals and it was her job to keep them from polluting everything beyond the barbed wire. She took a deep breath and willed the itch to stop. After a moment, it faded. A small victory, she smiled. Mind over matter. The Führer was right. Her generation really was as hard as Krupp's steel.

Binz stood with her back to the factories. Without turning around, she pointed at what was behind her. "In a few minutes each of you will be assigned a factory to patrol. You will look for signs of sabotage. You will monitor for slow work. You will punish those who deserve it. And above all…above *all*…you will remember not to have personal conversations with the trash. They are the enemy. Treat them as such."

She took out a cigarette from a slim silver case. She tapped it once, twice, three times, and fitted it between her lips. In a smooth fluid motion, she pulled out a lighter and flicked the thumbwheel. A flame jerked to attention. She puffed. There was a red cherry glow, an exhale, and she flicked ash onto the ground.

"Prisoners cannot use your names and they should always address you as 'Madame Overseer'. Anything other than that gets them a box on the ears." She took in smoke again. "The *minimum* should be a box on the ears. We cannot let these creatures feel like they are our equals. Remind them they are not. Remind them what you can do."

In the coming days, Anna would learn a great deal about what they could do. She would watch Binz enter factories and swivel her head, hunting for the unruly and weak. She moved as though she were gliding and Anna noticed that a sphere of silence fogged around her wherever she went. No one spoke when Binz entered a room. Everything hushed and the room was charged with alarm. Such power, Anna thought. Such fear. In the coming days Anna would watch *Oberaufseherin* Binz slap and kick and whip. She would see her shove bony women to the ground and slam her boot down onto legs and necks. It was a strange new kind of power—to do whatever you wanted—and Anna was lured by the idea that the forbidden was now possible. The world had suddenly shifted from "you must not" to "you may". In the coming days she would hear rumors that Binz once knocked a prisoner to the ground who wasn't working quickly enough.

Apparently, *Oberaufseherin* Binz then lifted the woman's pickaxe and brought it down into the woman's back. She did this again and again until the woman was a bloody corpse. Binz then cleaned her boots on the prisoner's skirt and strolled away as if nothing had happened. *Had this happened though? Was this true?*

A wooden cart appeared around the corner of a barrack, pulled by a team of prisoners. It crunched over the cindery ground as prisoners pushed at the back and pulled from the front. The cart juddered for the main gate. It carried a huge pile of bodies. They were stacked in a sloppy pyramid and Anna found herself staring at an arm hanging over the side. A foot jiggled. One of the dead stared at the sky, open-mouthed.

"Most of you," Binz said. "Pay attention. Look at me. Ignore that cart and look at me. Listen up...listen! Five of you will go to the sock factory. That includes," she pulled out a sheet of paper and studied it. "Stein, Lugebel, Hentschel, Rentz, and Hartmann. The rest of you will report to my second-in-command and you'll search for contraband in the barracks like food, radios, books, homemade jewelry, and anything else suspicious."

As the cart neared the entrance gate, two SS guards with machine guns opened it. The bodies passed through. Anna wasn't sure where they were going but, glancing at the tall chimney behind her, she guessed what was going to happen next.

"If you're uncertain what to do, it's best to start hitting. Look to the Blockovas if you need help organizing things and have them do the shouting and bossing around. It's *your* job to be in control. Be silent and let your truncheons do the talking. Remember that fear is a tool."

She began to pace again, and this magnetized their attention. She was barrel-chested and built like a Valkyrie, Anna thought.

"None of you have a pistol because such things are in the realm of men...only men can kill with a gun. But you *do* have clubs and truncheons and your imaginations. Boots can be weapons, too. And remember, we're responsible for roll call, work details and—" there was a deliberate pause "—punishment. Beginning today, I want you to think of yourselves as hunters. You are harm itself."

Anna allowed herself to study her new colleagues, her new friends. They were all between eighteen and twenty-five, they were all unmarried, and from what she could tell they had all been in the League of German Maidens. It was only right that the boys of the Hitler Youth went off to fight while they, the girls, stayed behind to protect the kitchen and the nursery. What use was new living space in Russia if the fabric of home got frayed? Most of them had been shop girls, hairdressers, tram car drivers, and beer hall waitresses before they volunteered to be Aufseherin in the concentration camps. Anna liked how they dressed the same, how they stood at attention with flinty confidence, and she especially liked how they thought the same way. It made her smile. Yes, she thought, this is as it should be.

Binz looked at her wristwatch and half-turned to the factories. There was the muffled sound of hundreds of sewing machines hard at work. Grainy coalsmoke lifted from stubby chimneys at the back of camp. A generator hummed.

"Welcome to Ravensbrück, ladies. It's time to put your training to work."

CHAPTER FOUR

The Sock Factory

The sewing machines clacked and whirled so loudly that it was hard to speak. Svea's calloused fingers fed brown fabric into the throat plate and the needle flew up and down at blurring speed. She ignored the pain in her lower back and hips. Her fingers moved without thinking as she clipped the thread, reversed the fabric, and made sure the slack regulator was set properly. She fed the sock in once again and watched the pressure foot hop up and down as if it were dancing. Dancing, she thought dreamily. The thought skittered away as she finished the sock, reached for its partner, and rolled them into a ball the size of her fist. She dropped the finished product into a large wicker basket next to her sewing machine and worried that she wasn't working fast enough. If an Aufseherin or a Blockova came over they'd count her quota and she only had—what?—forty-five socks done? The quota for this time of morning was sixty.

Himmler had decided that female prisoners should do female work. As the leader of the SS, and as one of the highest-ranking Nazis in the Third Reich, he believed that men should build and that women should be homemakers. A woman's place was in the kitchen, near the washing tub, and she should only concern herself with matters of home. This meant cooking and sewing and raising children to look up at the swastika with stern pride. Even though Svea was subhuman, and even though she had been taken out of civilization, she was still forced to contribute to Nazi victory. And that meant sewing socks for the army.

She sighed. At least they were consistent, she had to give the Nazis that, she thought, dropping another pair into the wicker basket. The SS didn't allow women into their ranks, and although it was easy to consider the Aufseherin as female guards in an elite order, they were not, in fact, part of the SS. They weren't allowed to wear the runic lightning bolts on their collars, nor were they allowed to have the Death's Head on their caps. In spite of all of this though, they were masters of murder.

Her stomach grumbled. She couldn't hear it, but she could feel it calling out for food. The machines around her were given as many strips of brown fabric as they could eat, but she got nothing. Svea glanced around. At least one hundred women were hunched over sewing machines as if they were desks at school and they were all moving their fingers around a jabbing needle. It was a type of ballet, this movement of hand and sock. She reached for another length of thick fabric and set the needle nibbling. Her line veered away from the toe and she had to stop; she reached for the balance wheel and reversed what she had done. She snapped the thread free and looked around to see if anyone had noticed. Not a guard or Blockova was in sight so she adjusted the upper tension bar in order to throw stitches off the heel and toe. It was sloppy work and she would be accused of sabotage because the sock would wear out faster now. A big toe would poke through the fabric more quickly. She liked the idea of an SS officer, somewhere in frozen Russia, with cold blistered feet inside his boot. And this would happen because she had failed to stitch the sock properly. It made her smile.

As the wheel and bobbin continued to move, her stomach grumbled again. There was a clacking in her lower gut and she needed to use the toilet. She sat up and squeezed her asshole tighter. Using the toilet was forbidden and she worried she might soil herself. Maybe she was coming down with dysentery? She took several calming breaths and looked at her friends. Were they feeling this too? Was it the soup?

She knew how the body worked and she knew what was happening in the churning darkness beneath her skin. Before the war started she had been a student at Humboldt University. She loved walking past the dome of the cathedral and strolling over the River Spree. Sometimes she would pause on the bridge and watch the rippling water play with sunlight or sometimes she would watch swans move away from puttering motorboats. She liked to imagine her heart rocking gently in her ribcage and she sometimes closed her eyes to map the electrical charges of her nervous system. Her body worked so smoothly, so quietly, and it was a marvel that her internal organs required no conscious thoughts from her in order to keep her alive.

When she extended her fingers, she watched her tendons rise and the blue of her veins shift over a knuckle ever so subtly. And when a tram clanged its bell, she thought of the petite speaker system in her ear—the stapes, the tiniest bone in the whole body, tapped out sound waves which her brain somehow, astonishingly, turned into electrical pulse and "heard". What was sound, she wondered. Her brain was hearing the tapping of a tiny bone, and not the actual bell of the tram. How could she tell what a tram really sounded like? Svea enjoyed standing on the bridge and letting the big world come into her senses. She liked how her body received information and told her, reassuringly and effortlessly, that she was alive.

Alive, she thought, as she pulled fabric into the sewing machine. Thanks to her biology lessons, she knew that her body was starving. She knew about dizziness, and blood in her urine, and how her limbs felt as heavy as bags of sand. She knew why her intestine made popping noises and why her menstrual cycle had stopped. It had been over a year since her last period. The body was clever that way. It knew what to do in an energy crisis, and that meant shutting down the womb in order to focus on the stomach.

"…cooking today?" Julienne shouted.

Svea turned and raised an eyebrow. *What?* she asked, without saying the word.

"What are you cooking today?" Julienne asked again.

In order to pass the time, and when it was safe to talk, they sometimes pretended to cook. One of them would walk through a recipe and mention which ingredients they were using. They would talk about placing batter into a cake mold and sliding it into an oven. They would talk about flicking a chunk of butter into a cast iron skillet along with thick slabs of bacon and then watching it sizzle and bubble. They would talk about baking rye bread. Sometimes at night, if they could find paper, they would write down recipes and share them. To read a recipe was no different than reading a book. Moving from one step to another in the creation of food was like turning a page and seeing a new world reveal itself in imagination. Food lived in the head, and sometimes—Svea closed her eyes at the thought—oh yes, sometimes she could almost *taste* what she was reading. In the barracks of Ravensbrück, women shared recipes and they made presents for each other out of whatever they could find. Paperclips. Thimbles. Fabric. Buttons. It was an act of friendship to give, and it was only through giving that Svea felt like bits of her old self were still alive.

Svea looked around for a guard or Blockova. "I'm making fruit salad," she said, slowing the run of her sewing machine. She let the needle come to a stop as she talked about peeling oranges and licking sticky juice from her fingers. She brought out a large imaginary bowl and filled it with blueberries, strawberries, and raspberries. She zested orange rind on the top and reached for some brown sugar.

"Can you taste it?" she asked, offering up the invisible bowl.

"Oh yes," Julienne sighed. "Delicious."

"And you?" she asked, letting the needle come back to life again. "What are you cooking?"

"Chocolate torte."

"Oh, my goodness. It's been *years* since I had that!"

"I need to whip hazelnut butter though," Julienne said cutting a length of thread with her teeth.

Sunlight flittered down from the ceiling windows as Julienne talked about whisking butter and adding in freshly ground hazelnuts.

The woman next to Svea stopped sewing and dared to stretch. She put both arms high above her head and let out a yawn. It was such a stunning act of bravery that several women looked around for guards who would bring down an inevitable beating. But there was no one.

The pretty woman who yawned, Lorelei, was a former prostitute with a black winkel. "I'm cooking roast mutton," she said dropping a pair of socks into her basket. "I'll give you the recipe tonight if you like. You can make it in your head then."

Svea imagined going to her favorite butcher's on Oranienburgerstrasse and she saw herself bringing back a heavy package. Roast mutton in wax paper. She would unwrap it on the kitchen table and add garlic and thyme. Did the recipe call for that?

"Is it your recipe?" she asked Lorelei.

There was a shake of a head. "No."

Perhaps the woman who had written it down was dead now? Such things happened in Ravensbrück. Recipes were often stuffed into walls and whenever they were found no one knew who had placed them there. These ghostly prisoners who had been taken away and shot—they lived on through ingredients. An entire cookbook could be made from the kitchens of the dead.

"Enough!" came a voice behind them.

Svea didn't turn around. She knew it was Zofia Laskowski, who had been brought to Ravensbrück six months ago because she was in the Polish resistance. Blunt faced and wiry, she had a voice like gunfire and she spoke German with a heavy accent. It wasn't entirely clear what she had done to be arrested—perhaps she had blown up rail tracks—but apparently she was in charge of an underground movement in Kraków. Some people said she commanded ten women. Others said fifty.

"Enough useless dreaming," Zofia added. "Start sewing our professional socks."

This was code for letting threads slip at the heel and toe. It was Zofia who came up with the idea of sabotaging their work and making German soldiers miserable at the front.

"Be professional with your sewing," she added while reaching for more fabric.

The machines clattered and hummed in the long hall. A waterfall of oily noise bounced off the walls. There was no more talk of recipes or gifts.

"Think of the Ten Commandments," Zofia shouted. "What is number one?"

It was understood they shouldn't say these commandments, these rules of camp life, out loud. That would be foolish and it would surely bring a truncheon down onto their backs. Svea reached for a new spool of red thread and murmured, as if in prayer.

Never forget you're fighting a battle.

"What is Commandment Two?" Zofia asked in both German and Polish.

Serve the community altruistically.

The sewing machines sounded like trains over tracks. Socks were tossed into wicker baskets and one prisoner scurried away to get another bolt of fabric. When she returned, two others helped her unroll it on a wide metal table. They began to cut out strips.

"Three?"

Act in a considered way.

A Blockova strolled into their section and leaned against the wall. She cocked a leg beneath her buttock and crossed her arms. When Svea saw this, she stared down at the throat plate of her machine and let her fingers move on muscle memory. She felt herself drifting out of her own body. Flow—that's what they called it when the dancing went really well. You were able to do all of these complicated moves but you weren't *aware* that you were doing them. Your body just moved and jived and sashayed. Musicians told her they felt this way, too. The trumpet, one man said, seemed to play itself when he was in flow.

A high voice lifted from several machines down.

"And what it is four?"

Whoever spoke was brave because the Blockova pushed off from the wall and studied the hall.

Before spreading news, establish if it's true.

Another voice lifted. It was French.

"Cinq?"

Don't do more work than necessary.

A nasally voice came from behind. Svea recognized it as coming from a newer prisoner. Slight, quiet, from Russia.

"Шесть?"

Obey orders of a comrade in an emergency.

The Blockova began to pace and her eyes were furious. "What are you dirty pieces doing?" she shouted. "What is this all about? No talking!"

Svea waited for someone to say "seven" but there was only the rattle-snap of oiled parts moving up and down. The word twitched in her throat, and she took in a lungful of air to say it. Someone had to be brave. Someone had to say it. Her tongue moved to the top of her mouth to make an *S*. But instead of shouting out the number, she looked at the Blockova and breathed out. It shamed her that she wasn't brave enough to do something that would lift the spirts of those around her. Before being thrown into camp, she imagined herself as fearless and always choosing the right path even if it was the hardest hike. And yet here she was—cowed into silence. She licked her lips and took in another breath. One word, she told herself. It's one word. Shout it out and the Blockova won't know it's you.

"Seven!" a voice next to her shouted. It was Julienne.

"Who said that?" the Blockova roared. "Who the hell is talking when they should be sewing?"

She held up her fist and paced through the rows of women. She hit one of them, hard, on the ear, and the woman's dirty cap tumbled onto the concrete floor.

"What are you doing?" the Blockova bellowed. "Sabotage will be severely punished. You will be beaten like a carpet. Do you understand me?"

Svea caught Julienne's eye and winked. And in that moment, they seemed to say the words together in their heads.

Join the fight against corruption and bartering.

The shouting must have attracted the Aufseherin in another part of the factory because a cluster of them came marching in. Their crisp grey dresses swished, their heavy boots thumped. They held their truncheons and whips at the ready. There were six of them. It was too dangerous to say "eight" now, Svea considered. Whoever dared to stand out would surely be thrashed and taken to the Bunker for further softening up.

She watched her thin fingers dance and skip around a flashing needle. It would be so easy to draw blood.

Blood, she thought. The Ten Commandments had been brought down from Mount Sinai by Moses. A Jew not unlike her. He defied those who enslaved him and led his people across a desert to a new life. Yes, she considered. Words can be like compass points. Eight, she thought.

Be clean in yourself and your surroundings.

The guards were fanning out now and walking through rows of sewing machines. They were looking for a reason to hit and kick. Just yesterday, a Dutch woman was busy at work but an Aufseherin came up behind her and smashed the woman's head into the spiky bits of the sewing machine. The woman's nose was broken. She lost a tooth. And there was so much blood.

Nine, Svea thought.

Mind your health.

She allowed herself to glance up—briefly—and saw the new guard with blonde hair and dimples a few paces away. She was a nice shape. Even the uniform couldn't hide that. But then again, it was easy to have a figure when you were allowed to have butter.

Svea dropped a pair of professional socks into her basket. Ten.

Educate yourself and practice self-criticism.

"Why are numbers being shouted in here?" an Aufseherin asked, sniffing the air for an answer. "Why are you counting? Is it some kind of code?" The woman directed this last question at the Blockova, who came running over and stood at crisp attention. She clicked her wooden clogs together and offered a smart salute. Although she was a prisoner like anyone else, her uniform had been recently laundered. Starch had been used on her collar and her green winkel looked brand new. The Blockova's fingernails were free of dirt and she had long tresses of black hair spilling from her cap. How did she keep the lice off her?

"Well?" the Aufseherin asked again. "Who spoke?"

The Blockova with a green winkel shrugged a shoulder and immediately realized that such informality could be deadly, so she straightened herself again and placed both arms smartly at her sides. She barked, "I regret to inform Madam Overseer that I do not know who spoke."

The guard raised her truncheon and used it as a pointer. "Maybe you should find out."

The Blockova wheeled around and ordered everyone to stop their work. "Halt! Stop. I have some questions for you dirty pieces."

The Aufseherin was surprised. "Absolutely not. Don't stop working."

In a clean and fluid motion, as if she were walking across a room to slap a heavy curtain closed, one of the other Aufseherin approached the Blockova and hit her on the forehead with a truncheon. The woman dropped like a sack of wheat. Her cap rolled away and her black hair splashed over her face.

When Svea saw this, she hunched into her machine and ignored the pinwheeling fear inside her chest. Her heart beat wildly and her tongue seemed to shrivel. She tried to make spit by sucking on her front teeth, but there was nothing. She glanced at the Blockova. It looked like she was sleeping, except for the dark blood.

The sewing machines picked up speed and Svea watched her fingers continue to dance around the throat plate and the needle.

The Aufseherin all clustered around the Blockova and one of them—the new one with lipstick—used her boot to wiggle the body. "Is she dead?"

"No," another said. "It's still breathing. See?"

"Get up!"

But the woman on the tiled floor didn't move. Wisps of her hair fluttered from the breeze created by the whirling sewing machines.

From around the corner, a fearsome figure appeared. It was *Oberaufseherin* Binz. She was a tank of a woman and, when Svea saw this, she had to suppress a wish to run away. Every muscle in her body was a loaded spring. She had seen Binz talking normally one moment and then stomping on a prisoner's spine the next. She had seen *Oberaufseherin* Binz hit someone with so much force that they were immediately struck dead. One minute the prisoner was standing at attention and then, in a terrible arcing of a truncheon, she was on the ground, ready for the oven.

Svea glanced at the unconscious Blockova and couldn't help but think the woman was lucky. She might recover. Stay down, Svea wanted to whisper to the Blockova. She almost felt something like pity for this prisoner that had chosen clean clothes and extra helpings of food over her fellow prisoners.

"What's going on?" Binz asked calmly as she took off her leather gloves. Her voice was so soft that some of the Aufseherin didn't hear her at first. "I SAID…what's going on?"

Svea gently placed another pair of socks into her wicker basket. Usually she tossed them in, but what if she missed and the balled socks bounced over toward Binz? The most feared female guard in Ravensbrück was just a few meters away and Svea didn't want to make eye contact. Such a thing would be foolish. A death sentence. Instead, she looked at Binz's leather boots and saw blood. The black laces were slick with deep red. The toecap had bits of hair matted to it.

"Why is that thing on the floor?" Binz asked.

The furiously moving parts around them made it hard to hear. Svea felt herself shrink and when she reached for another strip of fabric she noticed that her hands were trembling.

The Aufseherin straightened their backs and came to attention. One of them said, "She couldn't answer my question. This was the result."

Binz scratched her ear and seemed to consider this carefully.

"There was concern of sabotage," another guard offered. It was the pretty one with dimples, Svea noticed.

"Well…" Binz smiled. "What are you ladies going to do about this?"

One of the fresh recruits immediately turned on her heel and stepped towards Lorelei's machine. She raised her truncheon and brought it down with shocking force onto the table. Lorelei flinched, and in that twinkling of fear the guard seemed to grow bigger. The guard prodded Lorelei out of her chair with her truncheon. She bent low to investigate the stitches.

"What is this? You've done it all wrong."

Lorelei didn't look up.

"Look at these stitches. LOOK AT THEM!"

Lorelei balled up her hands and took a step back.

"Your job is to sew. Do it properly!" the new guard roared, and she brought the oak truncheon down onto Lorelei's shoulder. There was a shriek of pain as Lorelei steadied herself against a sewing machine. Svea kept working and made sure all of her stitches were perfect. Don't look at my socks, she thought. Don't look at my socks. Please don't look at my socks. If any of the Aufseherin looked in the wicker basket and found her dropped stitches there would be trouble. Stupid, stupid, stupid. If something happened to her, who would take care of—

She glanced at Julienne. What if Binz checked *her* work? How could they have been so stupid to think they could change the war by throwing a few stitches? A greasy feeling filled her up.

The new guard stepped closer to Lorelei. "What are you doing…" she glanced at the number on the striped uniform. "What are you doing, 18743?"

In a swift motion, one that Svea didn't see coming, the guard kicked Lorelei in the knee. There was horrible *crack* and Lorelei tumbled to the ground, howling in animal pain. Her mouth opened in a wide O and terror knifed the air. Svea wanted to go over and comfort her friend but safety, and shame, kept her bolted to her stool.

"Stop!" Binz thundered. She walked over to an empty metal bucket, turned it over, and stood on it. "Stop! All of you," she shouted in a cool calm voice. "Stop working."

The sewing machines slowed on their oiled gears.

"All of you, stand at attention and turn out your pockets." Her neck turned a shade of raspberry and her eyes narrowed. "Do not hide anything."

Silence fell like a heavy quilt over the factory floor. There was only the sound of stools being scraped across the concrete as everyone, including Lorelei, stood up. She balanced on one leg—a bruise was on the side of her knee—and a sudden breeze rattled the rafter windows. The sound of sewing machines in the adjacent hall could be heard tapping, pecking.

Guards fanned out between the ordered rows and one of the Aufseherin threw a wooden cart of thread against a wall. Spools bounced and tumbled like dice onto the floor. Another one kicked over a wicker basket of socks. The guard that had hit Lorelei—the one with wavy black hair that was pinned beneath her cap—turned to Svea. She stood less than a meter away. Svea didn't look at the guard. It was forbidden to do so.

"Turn out your pockets," the guard said.

Good, Svea thought. She wasn't hiding anything so this meant the guard would go torment someone else. Svea reached into her dress pockets and was shocked to feel something. A flash of worry sliced through her as she tried to think what it could be. She hadn't put anything in there, so what was it?

"Turn out your pockets," the guard said again, stepping closer.

Svea turned out her right pocket and, while she was doing this, she cupped whatever was in her left pocket and made a fist. Maybe should could toss it? Or hide it?

"And the left?" the guard said, staring. *Oberaufseherin* Binz strolled over, clearly interested in what was happening.

Svea started coughing and, in a quick motion of her hand, she lifted the tiny stringy thing that was in her left pocket and placed it in her mouth. She continued coughing and kept her hand over her mouth. The thing—whatever it was—felt like a string of plastic beads. She placed it under her tongue and slowed her coughing. She thought about telling the Aufseherin that she didn't feel well and that, maybe, she had tuberculosis. That would make them back away and it would keep them from hitting her, but it would also mean a trip to the Revier, the so-called camp hospital from which hardly anyone returned.

"Stop!" the guard yelled. "I saw what you did."

Binz stepped closer and said, almost tenderly, "Open your mouth, 18311."

There was nothing to do but obey, so Svea reached under her tongue and pulled out something she couldn't quite recognize. It was a loop of purple beads. It was—she stared at what rested in her palm—it was a bracelet. It was a homemade bracelet. But how did it get into her pocket? It wasn't hers. Jewelry of any kind was forbidden and no one wore jewelry in Ravensbrück, not even the guards. Who put this in her pocket?

"18311. What do you have there?"

Svea tried to speak but nothing came out. She let out a slow "Ahh..." in the hopes that other words of explanation would stitch themselves onto it. But there was nothing. "Ahh," she tried again.

And then she remembered how Julienne had bumped into her—hard—after they'd finished their morning soup. Her eyes widened. *I have a little surprise for you.* That's what Julienne had said as they were marching to the sock factory.

"Personal items are not allowed," Binz said snatching the bracelet. She held it between her finger and thumb as if it were an earthworm. "What *is* this thing?"

"I...I don't know," Svea said at last.

"It looks like a bracelet," the black-haired guard said.

Binz frowned. The other guards huddled close. They formed a sloppy circle around Svea's sewing machine. She looked at the wicker basket and thought about all of her dropped stitches.

Binz raised her voice. "You know about personal items. You know this, yes? This is illegal. It is forbidden." She ripped apart the bracelet with both hands and sent the purple beads bouncing onto the floor. Binz flicked the string at Svea. "A rule has been broken and a price will have to be paid."

Svea backed up and tripped over her stool. It clattered to the ground and, as she righted herself, she found herself staring at the unmoving Blockova. Purple plastic beads rested against her bare leg.

Binz unhooked her truncheon.

Svea had been hit before, but never by this furious engine of a woman. Binz could usually drop a prisoner to the ground with a single blow and then she would kick at spinal columns, hip bones, breasts, and jaws. Svea's nerves lit up in terror and her legs burned for her to run, but escape would mean—what exactly? She would be shot for sure. No, it was better to face this head on. She took a few deep breathes to calm herself. Was it better to tense her muscles when the blows came or should she go limp? She tried to remember her biology lessons at Humboldt University. To be loose, like a ragdoll, might be better. Her bones would break no matter what but if she were limp it might save her ligaments and tendons. Whatever happens, she told herself in the dark realization of what was coming, she must not fall to the ground. She *must not* do that. To make a ball of herself on the ground would expose her spine. A well-placed kick could paralyze her. It could crush her vertebrae. To stand was to live. She glanced at Lorelei, who was wobbling on one leg. Yes, to stand was to live.

Binz took a step back and re-attached her truncheon to her belt. She waved over the guard with blonde hair. "Hartmann," she snapped. "Punish this thing for the crime of having a personal item."

The new guard with dimples and bright blue eyes took a step forward.

"Use your weapon," Binz encouraged.

Svea made her arms limp. She stared ahead and looked at one of the white walls. Prisoners walked by carrying bolts of cloth. It would be over soon, she told herself.

The guard with young skin cleared her throat and pulled out her truncheon. There was a long pause before she wound up and hit Svea in the ribs. It hurt, but it wasn't hard. It felt like she had slipped on a dancefloor and landed on her side. There would be a bruise yes, of course, but nothing seemed to be broken. She took in several quick lungfuls of air and didn't feel any sharp stabs of pain.

"Madam Overseer, I'm sorry for breaking the rules," Svea said, hoping this might end things. She came to attention and tried to strangle the worry in her voice. "It won't happen again."

To her astonishment, the new guard took a step back and fidgeted. She seemed aware that everyone was looking at her and then, slowly, she replaced her truncheon into her belt loop. Svea noticed that the woman's hands were shaking.

In the next hall over was the sound of needles at work. Svea hoped the noise might remind the guards there were quotas to meet and socks to stitch. Men were getting trench foot on the Eastern Front. The word floated in her mind. Trench foot.

What happened next happened very fast.

"This is how it's done," the guard with wavy black hair half-shouted. In a smooth motion, as if she were drawing a sword, she rushed at Svea and brought the weapon down onto her head. The pain was blinding and the world went murky black. Blobs of color—reds, oranges, greens—floated before her and she felt her knees sliding beneath her. She reached for the sewing table and felt something crush her hand. It was the truncheon coming down on her knuckles. There was another blow to her side and this made her drop to one knee. It hurt to breathe now. It felt like a Roman candle had been ignited in her ribcage and with each huffing breath she worried about passing out. Dusk was poured onto the world and wispy blobs of color moved across the Aufseherin that towered over her. The truncheon hammered down again—this time on her shoulder—and even in her wooziness Svea knew this was a miss, a mistake. The woman had been aiming for her head again. Svea gasped and tried to stand, but she stumbled forward onto Lorelei's sewing table. There was a blow to her back and the factory began to tilt and slide.

"No! Personal! Items!" the guard yelled.

A voice came from somewhere behind Svea. It was familiar, and for a moment she wondered if she was dreaming. Maybe it was an auditory hallucination? Such things happened with head wounds.

"Stop!" came the voice again.

It was Julienne.

Svea turned and saw the guard do the same.

"Stop," Julienne said, more softly. "I gave it to her. She didn't know. It was a present."

There was a look of confusion on the Aufseherin's face. "What?"

"It was a present."

The guard looked at *Oberaufseherin* Binz for advice, but the barrel-chested woman just stood there with crossed arms. An airplane droned overhead and everyone looked up, wondering if it was the enemy. Svea waited for an air raid siren, which might change the situation. The guards and the prisoners followed the sound across the ceiling. A minute passed, and the engine dissolved into silence.

Binz cleared her throat to get the attention of her guards and then flicked her chin towards Julienne. The black-haired guard paced over and began beating her, mercilessly. Svea wanted to look away but it seemed that the more courageous thing, the right thing, was staring evil straight in the face. She clamped her lips shut and watched Julienne get hit in the belly—this brought her to the floor—and the guard began to kick. The woman in a field grey uniform said nothing as she brought thunderous pain down onto Julienne. There were grunts, and kicks, and yips of stifled screams. After what seemed like several minutes, although it couldn't have lasted more than fifteen seconds, the guard stepped back, panting hard. Her grey cap, which had been so neatly pinned to her hair a few moments ago, was at an angle. Long strands of hair spilled over her face like a veil. She used the back of her hand to wipe spittle from her mouth and then, with satisfaction, she slid her truncheon home and flapped dust from her skirt. She used both hands to comb wayward strands of hair beneath her cap. She adjusted the straps of her bra.

Svea wanted to run over to Julienne. The poor thing had her hands balled up in obvious pain.

"There will be silence on this factory floor from now on. Do you understand? No more coded words. No more numbers." Binz snapped her fingers for work continue. "And if I *do* hear numbers being said on this floor, *your* numbers will be sent up the chimney. Are we clear? Do you understand? Yes? Get back to work."

She turned on a booted heel and her grey culotte-style skirt bloomed in her wake. Without looking, Binz pointed at the unmoving Blockova and said, "Get that thing off my floor."

The remaining Aufseherin followed after her into another section of the sock factory, and Svea heard the purring whirring machines move faster.

"What is the quota here?" Binz asked, her receding voice drowned out by moving iron and thread.

Svea hurried over to Julienne. "You must get up, my darling," she begged. "Please."

Talk of the bracelet could wait for later. Right now, she had to get Julienne sitting on the stool and, with both arms, she lifted. Although Julienne was light and her body had once floated gracefully as a ballet dancer in Paris, she was floppy now and surprisingly heavy. Svea struggled to lift her. Zofia came over and, together, they got Julienne seated in front of her sewing machine. They wiped away blood and tapped her cheeks to bring her back to consciousness.

"Julienne?"

Svea examined her friend's head and worried about a concussion. There was a long laceration just above her ear, and bandages would be needed to stop the flow of blood. Maybe some stitches too, but with so many needles and thread in the sock factory that wouldn't be a problem. It wasn't the worst beating she had seen. It had clearly been done by a beginner who was new to the ways of brutality.

"I'm sorry," Julienne finally said, her eyes fluttering open. "What have I done? What happened?"

Svea kissed her forehead. "You're fine. Work, and we'll take care of you this evening."

Zofia looked around for any Blockovas or Aufseherin. When she didn't see any, she took off her cap and plucked out a sugar cube that was hidden in a secret pocket. She placed it in Julienne's bleeding mouth.

"Suck that," she said. "He is not much, but he will help with the energy," she offered in broken German. "Work," Zofia said to the rest of the hall. "Remember to sew professionally."

Stools were rumbled back into place and the machines became slippery with noise. The smell of oil lifted.

Svea patted her friend on the arm and went back to her own machine. She watched her fingers feed brown fabric into the throat plate. She watched the needle fly up and down, piercing everything beneath it.

CHAPTER FIVE

The Lives of Inferior Things

She had always wanted to be a nurse.

The idea of taking care of bodies was appealing and, even now, Anna sometimes imagined smiling over a ward of patients and helping the worthy to recover. With a tray of syringes, she would move from bed to bed and remove toxins from bodies. With her crisp white uniform, she would help a doctor snip out what should not be there. She pictured herself passing a scalpel and watching him slice out tumors and polyps. And then, a few days after surgery, patients would rise whole and clean, and she would move to other beds where unwell bodies waited for her.

Anna nodded at this. Oh sure, she thought, she was wearing a field grey uniform instead of a white one but, in a way, she was like a nurse. After all, she was removing tumors from the diseased body of society and making what needed to be healthy, healthy. That's why Ravensbrück existed—to remove foreign and unwanted objects. She liked the idea of being a new type of nurse, and she let the thought swirl in her mind. Yes, she told herself. What she was doing was respectable. Necessary, even.

It had been a strange first day, she thought, taking off her heavy black boots and placing them beneath the radiator. Her new socks were damp from sweat and she placed them carefully over the radiator, just so. It felt good to wiggle her toes. Her truncheon was on the desk next to her lipstick.

She had to admit that she wasn't prepared for the sock factory—all of those unwashed bodies and mucky uniforms—and the noise was like standing inside a steam engine. She had to shout just so the other Aufseherin could hear her. A few times, she even had to make hand signals.

She undid the bobby pins that kept her cap secured to her hair and she placed them next to her truncheon. She let her long hair tumble down over her neck. When she first entered the sock factory she had to suppress an urge to say "excuse me" whenever she bumped into a prisoner. Shame filled her up when she thought of the weak beating she gave to that one prisoner—the one with an illegal bracelet. She only hit the woman once. In the ribs. It wasn't even that hard. It certainly wasn't like what happened to that Blockova. Now *that* was a beating. That's how it was supposed to be done.

Why had she failed?

Her new friend, Ruth, walked into her room and flopped in a wooden chair.

"I'm exhausted," she said extending her legs. She still had her boots on but she had unbuttoned her uniform. She wasn't wearing her cap, and her black hair splashed down around her neck.

Anna said nothing as she cracked open her window. She worried that her socks might stink on the radiator. A soft breeze fluttered the drapes and she spritzed the air with perfume. From downstairs there was music and occasional bursts of laughter.

"Come and join us," Ruth said, nodding to the floor below. "There's cake."

Anna touched her hair and wondered about the likelihood of picking up lice. Maybe she should get a bob? Was that kind of haircut allowed or was it too modern, too jazzy? She imagined herself looking like an American floozy and suddenly didn't like the idea of cutting off her hair. Ever since she was a girl she had long hair. Sometimes in a single braid, sometimes in twin pigtails, but it had always been long.

"Sounds fun," she said, replacing the bottle of perfume. "Especially if there's cake."

Ruth smiled. "It's supposed to arrive soon. It's coming out of the ovens in the canteen."

"Are…are the *prisoners* baking it?" She didn't like the idea of dirty fingernails whipping batter or making buttercream frosting.

"Of course they're baking it!" Ruth laughed. There was a pause as she picked fluff off her uniform. "Some of them were professional cooks before they came here. Highly trained. Why not use their skills to our benefit? They get clean uniforms and they have to shower every day."

How could she be so confident? How was it that Ruth was at home in this place so quickly while she was floundering and trying to act like she knew what she was doing? It was surprising how Ruth transformed into this new being—a fury—when she attacked that prisoner. It was such a cheap thing too, the bracelet. Little pips of plastic that had been strung together. And when Ruth saw this in the prisoner's hand an internal switch seemed to have been flicked and she became something else, something wild.

Anna looked at her, now at ease with her legs spread out and her arms dangling at her sides. She hated how that prisoner had made her look clumsy and weak in front of her friends, not to mention Binz. Tomorrow she would search out that prisoner for special treatment. Her eyes narrowed. Yes. Tomorrow. 18311. There would be a fresh chance to prove herself.

"You were amazing today," she told Ruth.

"Was I?"

Anna leaned against her wardrobe. "Absolutely. You remembered our training, and I'm sure that prisoner will remember you."

There was a snigger as Ruth rubbed her knees. "It was…it was almost fun, wasn't it?"

"Fun?"

"The power. I mean, if I did that in Berlin I'd be sent to jail. But in this camp, it's expected." She stopped rubbing her knees and sat back. "It's strange. In this prison, I've never felt so free."

All her life, Anna had been told that violence was wrong—her mother had said it, her father too, even though he hit when he was drunk—so maybe it was a question of shedding her old skin? Don't overthink it, she thought, strangling the idea. Perhaps it's like leaping into a pool. Once you launch yourself off the dock, it was about falling. All it took was a running jump, and then instinct took over.

"By the way," she asked Ruth. "When did you learn to sew?" She wanted to change the radio channel in her head and learn how Ruth had thrown herself at that prisoner so effortlessly.

"When did I learn to sew?" There was a look of confusion. "Never. Why do you ask?"

"But you told that prisoner…you said she was dropping stitches and committing sabotage."

Ruth waved her hand. She played with a long strand of her hair and combed her fingers through it. "I don't know the first thing about sewing. Look, I don't give a cow's ass if she was doing it right or wrong. It was about letting her know who's in charge." She stopped combing her hair. "Do *you* know anything about sewing?"

"Not really."

Ruth pulled out her truncheon. The wood had recently been oiled. "Knowing the work doesn't matter. It's about reminding these pieces of garbage that they're only allowed to live if we say so."

Anna wasn't sure what to make of this so, after a long pause, she moved for the open door. "How about that cake?" She clicked off her desk lamp. "Shall we?"

The two of them pushed each other playfully towards a rectangle of light that spilled from the hallway and they laughed at a game of seeing who could leave the room first. They kept pulling each other back into the dark. After several attempts, Ruth managed to push her way out first and, together, they ran downstairs and burst into the common room, giggling. The other guards looked at them with a mixture of smiles and frowns. Anna wasn't sure this was proper behavior when prisoners weren't around so she straightened her dress.

The room had creamy white walls and there was a fire in a stone hearth. The overhead light was off and someone had lit candles. The kitchen was to her right and she heard dishes being washed. A toilet flushed down the hall. Someone was listening to the Berlin Rundfunk Orchestra and Anna found herself wishing that she knew more about music. There were a lot of violins. A cuckoo clock was ticking on a wall.

Cake and coffee were on a table near the fireplace and when one of the guards—Erna—saw them she patted an empty seat. "Join us," she said.

Anna walked over in bare feet and sat down. She curled her legs beneath herself and reached for a slab of chocolate cake. She scraped frosting with her finger and took a few licks. It was delicious. Pure sugar. Real cocoa. For the last few years she had been used to rationing so it was a surprise to find such rare ingredients in camp. And they had been mixed into a cake that was just sitting there for anyone to take.

Ruth reached for a slice and, when she went to take a bite, frosting smudged her nose. She chewed away, not noticing. One of the guards—Hilda—pointed to her nose. "You've got some..." she started to say.

PATRICK HICKS

Ruth wiped her nose. "Better?"

"Yes."

"What's that?" Anna asked, covering her mouth as she spoke. She used her tongue to suck bits of cake from her molars. "The music, I mean."

"Oh that?" Erna said, brightening. She wore slippers and was already in pajamas. "It's Strauss. Beautiful, isn't it?"

"Wagner. Mozart. Bach. Brahms. Handel. Beethoven," Hilda added. "There is no classical music without us Germans."

Anna looked at Hilda with surprise. How did she know such things? It made her look at the cluster of women huddled around the fireplace and she realized she didn't know them very well. Glowing chunks of coal spit and popped. Fiery shadows flickered across their faces. Anna readjusted her legs and flapped crumbs from her culottes.

"The SS for example," Hilda continued, "many of them know classical music. I've met officers who play the violin and cello. They can sing. Men of good standing, you know? Training. Breeding. Culture."

Music waltzed around the room and, in the coming weeks, Anna would get used to this evening ritual. Sometimes wine or brandy was poured into ceramic mugs and they would sit in a circle, talking about their long day at work. In the coming weeks, Anna would learn that her friend, Ruth Stein, had strong feelings that beauty was about having a good diet and being athletic. She saw no need for lipstick or eyeshadow because she felt that such things were created by Jews to weaken women and hide their natural features. She felt the same way about fingernail polish. She had a spray of freckles across her nose and she said this was makeup enough for her. In the coming weeks, Ruth would hold a large glass of wine and talk about how she had no patience for women who dyed their hair. It was inauthentic. Fake. A lie. Anna would watch Ruth walk around camp with a spring in her step and she would whisper one morning during roll call that Ravensbrück was the first place where she felt valued. In the coming weeks, Anna would watch Ruth embrace ferocious brutality. She would kill a prisoner by kicking her in the head and, that night, to unwind, she would go to Fürstenberg to watch a movie that took place on a Bavarian farm. It showed an aproned woman doing her best to keep the fields whole and the chickens safe while her husband

52

was fighting at the front. This woman had to shoot foxes and she leveled the gun with steadiness. When Ruth returned to camp that night, she shrugged at her first killing. "Pests need to be kept down," she explained.

In the coming weeks, Anna would also learn that Hilda Lugebiel was proud of her "child-bearing hips" and that she hoped to meet a good man before Christmas. She wanted at least seven children because a pregnant belly was a clear sign that you were serving Germany. From the port city of Kiel, near Denmark, she often talked about missing the sea. She loved to swim and she often wrote letters home to her mother. Whenever the Americans bombed the submarine pens at Kiel, she tried to call and make sure her mother and sisters were all right. She came from a large family and worried about them being in the bombsite of some Yankee plane. What if a 500-pounder missed its target and whistled down the chimney of her childhood home? She loved music because her father played the violin. He taught her the classics and, often, while she walked around camp, she whistled. In the coming weeks, Anna would watch Hilda gather prisoners and teach them to sing. As they dug ditches or hammered clapboards onto new barracks, she would order them to break into song. "You are my personal radio," she would shout. In the coming weeks, Anna would watch Hilda greet prisoners by yelling, "Ahoy!" It was their cue to begin singing popular Nazi songs. And if they didn't, she would reach for her truncheon.

In the coming weeks, Anna would also watch her fellow new recruit, Erna Hentschel, become so vicious that the prisoners would call her The Beast. She had no time for suffragettes and, during one of their evenings around the fireplace, she would say that she appreciated the Nazi movement because it had righted the natural order of things. "Hitler has liberated us from the tyranny of women's emancipation." She believed in tradition and thought it was only acceptable for women to take jobs in the factories when the men were at the front. She wondered, frequently, what it would be like to carry a gun. Women, she had been told by her father, would be clumsy with firearms. He was a decorated veteran of the Great War and she talked about him often. Erna would sometimes ask the other Aufseherin if they ever wondered what it would be like to be a man, to have possibilities open before you, to carry a gun. She liked the power that came with bringing out her truncheon and she liked how it made her feel. Fear, she would say in the coming weeks, was useful. "It's good to be feared. You know where you stand when people are afraid of you. Imagine how much you'd be feared with a gun?" She would later say that it must be how men felt all the time, and after drinking several glasses of pinot noir she would add, "Maybe that's why men are violent? To be feared. Why can't a woman be violent?"

In the coming weeks, Anna would learn that Lotte Rentz had an extensive perfume collection and that she used a new one each week. She had strong feelings that no one should touch the prisoners because of their lice. "You don't want to touch them, skin on skin," she would say, making a sour face. "It's better to use your truncheon." Her father had been a fruit vendor in Potsdam before the war and if she said too much or laughed too much while he was trying to relax with a newspaper, he would cane her. She had been bullied in school (she mentioned this quietly one night) and she used to run away from fights. Now she marched into the sock factory and feared no one. She talked about helping her father run his fruit stand and how he had become an early supporter of Nazism. He hung a banner on his stand and whenever a brown shirt passed he would offer an apple. As a child, she loved the sureness of the world around her. Right and wrong were clearly spelled out. This was driven home one day when her father took her on a field trip to a mental hospital. He paid a few Reichsmarks so they could watch patients in their cells—the craziness of them, the dribbling, the vacant stares. It was like visiting a zoo, she thought, and it reminded her of the importance of racial health. It only made sense for the sick to be locked away so they couldn't contaminate the herd. And when her father showed her the job posting for Ravensbrück, it was an easy decision to apply. Of course she would join. It wasn't unlike that mental hospital. In the coming weeks, Anna would watch Lotte hit prisoners in the stomach and literally walk over them without saying a word.

The radio down the hall was turned off, and as the fire continued to crackle and spark, Anna looked from face to face. None of them had been in school beyond the age of fifteen and they had all been in the League of German Maidens. They came from poor backgrounds where they didn't know where their next meal was coming from—Lotte was the only exception because unsold fruit was always on her table. As fiery shadows flickered across their faces, and as a strong wind began to buffet the dark windows of the chalet, it felt good to be indoors. She realized she had become lost in a world of her own thoughts and shook her head to awaken herself. The conversation slowly came into focus. Rain tapped on the windows.

"...Berlin will be the capital of Europe when this mess is all over."

"Of course it will."

"In a strange way, those American bombs are helping because they're demolishing the old world. Once we win, we can rebuild Berlin as we like."

They laughed at this and Anna joined them—not because it was funny but because she didn't want to appear as if she had drifted away from what they had been talking about.

"What about you?" Lotte asked, reaching over and slapping Hilda's thigh. "What're you doing after the war?"

"Hang up this uniform and marry a good SS man, of course. I want to be a mother and have lots of kids. You know the old saying: children, kitchen, church."

Lotte played with her left earlobe and pretended to turn an earring that wasn't there. She nodded her chin to Ruth. "And you?"

"Easy," Ruth said, sitting up with excitement. "With all the land we're clearing in the East—Poland, Belarus, Ukraine—there will be a call for settlers. I'd like to go East and start a new life on new German land. It's exciting, isn't it? It'll be our own American story. Instead of taming the Wild West, we'll be taming the Wild East. I'd like to set up a farm, get married, have some kids, plant some trees. Grow wheat and grow fat." Ruth played with her long black hair and combed it with her fingers once again. "Imagine all that empty land just for the taking."

Erna nodded. "The Americans cleared their land of Indians. Now it's our turn to do the same."

Lotte clapped her hands to get everyone's attention. "Wait, wait... what about...shh, quiet! What about you, Anna? What do you want to do after the war?"

The question surprised her because she hadn't given it much thought. "*After* the war?"

"Yes. The war can't last forever."

Anna stared into the dull red coals. "I think...I think I'd like to marry a handsome man. Children, of course, but I'd also like to..." She paused and wasn't sure if she should say it.

"Yes?" Ruth asked, cracking her knuckles.

"I'd like to become a nurse. I like the idea of caring for people."

This sent a ripple of laughter through the front room.

"A nurse?" Ruth asked with an incredulous look. "Have you seen where you work? In Ravensbrück we *send* people to the nurse."

There was another ripple of laughter, and this made Anna cross her arms. She stared at a plank of wooden floor and let her eyes linger on a nail head. The chuckling continued.

"Well, I suppose you're soft enough to be a nurse," Ruth said with cruel eyes. "I mean, in the sock factory you hardly beat that prisoner at all." She swatted the air lightly with a pretend truncheon and when she spoke her voice was ladylike and posh. "Take that, you filthy swine or I shall have to tap you once again."

The room roared with laughter. Anna glowered at the floor until her vision blurred. In her mind's eye, she was back in the sock factory and that prisoner was standing before her. This time there would be no hesitation or mercy for 18311. Yes, she thought. She would find this number, this winkel, this trinket, this useless eater, and she would make her pay. The shame in her chest started to dissolve at the thought. Tomorrow would be a new day. When she looked up, her face was hard and flinty.

"Oh, come on," Ruth said, rolling her eyes. "I'm *kidding*!" There was a moment of silence before she added, cruelly, "Or maybe not. Is our little nurse up for the job?"

Anna looked at her bare feet and made a motion to stand up. It was time for bed. But at that moment the front door opened. Binz came in and stomped her boots on a woven mat—once, twice, three times—then she took off her overcoat and gave it a shake. The smell of fresh rain came into the room and, behind her, lightning splintered across the sky. A low rumble of thunder followed. The *Oberaufseherin* shut the door and placed her coat on a peg. She turned and stood before them. "Good," she said. "You're still awake."

Rain prattled harder and the two front windows began to streak with water. Binz motioned for them to remain sitting. "Good job today, girls. It's one thing to train in the parks of Berlin but it's quite another to step into the real thing. For those of you who felt a bit... let's say *uneasy*...it takes a week to get used to this place. Don't be too hard on yourself."

Anna felt everyone's eyes upon her, but ignored this feeling and kept looking at Binz. Her senior officer went over to the fireplace and reached for the poker. She gave the dying coals a few jabs and this created sparks. There was a hissing as she stirred the coals. The wind picked up outside and the flue made a deep bassoon of sound.

While prodding the coals, Binz added, "If you do what is expected here, new worlds can open up for you. Who knows? Maybe you'll be promoted. In fact," she said turning around, "many of my girls have moved on to grander things. Just a few months ago, my own Irma—a very reliable guard—was sent from here to a much bigger camp." Binz continued to hold the steel poker. She tapped it against her boot. "It's called Auschwitz. It's ten times larger than this place. More efficient, too."

Anna lifted her eyebrows. Ten times larger?

Oberaufseherin Binz placed the steel poker next to the fireplace and adjusted the belt of her dress. She let out a long exhale and glanced at her wristwatch. "But anyway, tomorrow's a new day. And remember," she said holding up a finger, "the lives of inferior things don't matter. Not to us. Not here. Mercy is not allowed to pass through the gates of Ravensbrück, understand?" She held her hands close to the fire. "Any questions?"

Anna opened her mouth to ask about the Blockova in the sock factory—what happened to her?—but she decided it was a foolish question.

"Good," Binz said, walking back to the front door. "Anna...? Ruth...?" she said sliding on her coat. "Meet me in front of the Administration building tomorrow at 0600. You have a special assignment." The door opened and a gust of humid night air came rushing into the room. Rain came down in thin daggers. Binz offered one more piece of advice. "All of you, go to bed. Being an overseer can be exhausting. Good night, girls."

The door shut, quietly, and they sat looking at the spot where their senior officer had stood. The fire was going to sleep and this made inky shadows veil their faces. The cuckoo in the clock popped out of its little home and this made Anna jump. One of the weights shaped like a pinecone fell a few inches. The cuckoo called out into the darkness ten times and snapped back into its little chalet.

"Well," one of them said, standing up. "I guess it's time." The shape stretched and moved like a ghost for bed.

Anna got up, wordlessly, and padded upstairs on bare feet. She closed her door and didn't bother turning on the desk lamp. She unbuttoned her blouse and draped it over a chair. A quick movement of her fingers and the belt that kept her dress tight around her waist came loose. She shimmied her hips and let it fell to the floor. She unhooked her bra—it felt good to loosen herself—and she fumbled for a nightgown in a side dresser. A stab of lightning attacked the window as she put on her silk nightie and crawled into bed. The sheets were cold and it felt good to lay her head on a feather pillow. Her first day was nearly over.

Thunder grumbled across the sky and it sounded like—she opened her eyes at the thought—it sounded like the crematorium. It was a low roar moving across the sky, rumbling and mumbling. She rolled onto her side and bunched up the pillow just like she had done when she was child. Outside, the storm lashed the chalet.

There was a yawn, and she fell into a deep, undisturbed, blissful sleep.

CHAPTER SIX

After the Storm

Wind battered the barrack and rain drummed against the metal roof. Water leaked in from a window and lightning shocked the dark awake. Svea shivered in bed, hurting everywhere, and she kept her eyes closed. Pulses of color filled up her eyelids and, a moment later, a clap of thunder roiled overhead. The wind was so hard that she worried the whole barrack would crash down around them but, finally, the storm plodded towards the horizon. There would be leaves and branches everywhere in camp, and it would all have to be cleaned up in the morning. She was happy for the storm because it meant the Aufseherin probably wouldn't come crashing into their barrack for a little fun with night terror.

She winced. Her ribs and right shoulder and the bony front of her skull were swollen with pain. Perhaps something was broken? Her friends helped her get into a lower bunk and they made bandages of fabric for her head. Every now and then, one of them would place a cool hand on her cheek and ask how she was doing. "Fine," she would lie, asking for water. A cup of rainwater was pressed to her lips and she swallowed. Her tongue was as dry as steel wool.

Over the last few years, she had cared for others who had been beaten like this. She was the one who made dressings and splints, she was the one who daubed wounds, and she was the one who tried to tame pain. Now it was her turn. Svea pulled Julienne closer. The poor thing was in worse shape and they cuddled together, breathing softly, and they tried to stay warm. They had managed to stitch the long cut on Julienne's head shut with some thread from the factory. Normally, Svea would do the stitching, but because she had been hit on the knuckles with a truncheon, her right hand was stiff. Zofia helped Julienne stand during roll call, and it was Zofia who guided them back to the barrack.

As the storm tripped drunkenly to the horizon, Svea made soft cooing noises into Julienne's ear. No matter how often she told herself to stop thinking about the beating, her mind kept snagging on it like a nail. Images came in flashes. The truncheon. The boot. The blood.

"I'm sorry," Julienne whispered to the dark. "The bracelet was meant to make you happy."

Svea said nothing for a long moment and, when she spoke, her voice cracked from lack of use. "I know. Get some sleep."

It was something the women did for each other. They made necklaces, fabric dolls, scraps of poetry, drawings, embroidered handkerchiefs, and rosaries. They gave each other tiny heart-shaped boxes and leather bags and homemade birthday cards and miniature Tanakh. It was a way to feel human again—this offering of gifts—and they risked their lives for the simple pleasure of making someone else smile. These forbidden presents were hidden in straw mattresses or tucked into cracks in the wall. Creating art was not only a way to show someone you cared, but it also meant you still had something to give. Svea wondered if the men did such things in their camps. Did they make presents for each other? Did they offer little possessions? She frowned and shook her head. Probably not, she considered. But if they *didn't* do these things, how did they endure the camps without proof that their friends cared for them?

The rain had cooled the air and she continued to shiver. Or maybe it was shock? Would she still be in shock this many hours after the beating? She almost laughed out loud. When wasn't there a time to be in shock at Ravensbrück? The whole camp was wired with the electricity of terror.

"That Blockova is going to recover...just a broken rib," came a voice from the foot of her bunk.

A group of women were sitting in a circle delousing each other's uniforms. They had a candle on a wooden box and their faces flickered in the dark. The flame jerked as they pinched lice between their fingernails—they lined up the tiny bodies in ordered rows.

"She'll be back in the factory tomorrow. That's the rumor."

"Too bad."

Another voice chirped up. "I hope she's in pain. *Lots* of pain."

"Serves that bitch right," someone else said. "It made me happy to see her flattened on the floor."

"She beat you last month, yes?"

"Knocked out a tooth. Look at this," Maria said lifting her lip. There was a hole where an incisor should have been. "Cunt."

Svea looked at the circle of women and watched them continue to snap lice. It was like pinching bits of semi-boiled rice between your fingernails. Each woman lined up the dead creatures and then, when the circle decided it was time for bed, they would count the bodies to see who had won. Last week, Svea was declared "World Champion Lice Hunter." She scored 217 snapped white bodies in seven days. A barrack record.

Julienne twitched on the cusp of sleep. Good, Svea thought. She breathed in the smell of her friend's wet hair—there was the whiff of bandage and dried blood—and she considered the good women around her. Over the past few months, Julienne Besson had become something of a family member. Although Svea was only a few years older than Julienne, she felt like a mother to her. Julienne, for her part, seemed happy to have someone looking out for her. She was training as a ballet dancer when the Nazis invaded Paris, and she was only thirteen when her parents disappeared into the night. They had gone out to run an errand of some sort and they never returned. Julienne stayed up with the lights on, and whenever she heard steps in the stairwell outside their flat she stood up and expected the door to open. Two days passed like this and her parents still didn't come home. She ate food and waited. Another day passed. She danced around the living room and did pirouettes next to a tall mirror. She listened to the radio and decided that, maybe, they had been arrested. On the fourth day, a sharp knock came, and when she opened the door, two men stood outside. They were with the Gestapo. They said her parents had been detained. "Come with us," they said, motioning with their hands. She was taken to a prison cell and questioned about any ties her parents had with the French Resistance. She knew nothing—this was shocking information to her—and instead of being sent back to her flat or given into the care of her aunt, she was placed on a train and sent to Germany. A few days later, she was in a concentration camp for girls called Uckermark. She spoke no German and was forced to repair ripped clothes. As she worked, she cried and worried about her parents. Where were they? Were they still alive? Uckermark was full of teenage girls and they were forbidden to speak. Over time, she would learn that a larger camp was just over a wooded hill, and that when she turned eighteen she would be sent there. It was a type of graduation, she was told by the female guards. And when she turned eighteen, she was marched over that hill and pushed through the gates of Ravensbrück. In her first few hours, she met Svea. Julienne spoke German with a heavy French accent. The language came to her slowly and she said the names of the concentration camps with a puzzled look on her face. Uckermark. Ravensbrück. Dachau. Sachsenhausen. Buchenwald. They sounded like demon speech, she said. They sounded like an evil spell or an incantation.

"My parents are dead," she said a week ago. Svea tried to convince her otherwise—"Be hopeful and think about seeing them again"—but her young friend simply shook her head. "No. They are gone. I will not see them again in this life."

And now, Julienne was curled in her arms, breathing softly. Svea kissed the back of her friend's head. Her lips felt the bristle of short hair and she closed her eyes to imagine Julienne's parents, somewhere in Paris, asking about their daughter. Svea had seen so many women come through the gates and disappear. It was like a magic trick. One morning they were at roll call, and the next they were gone. Some had been killed in the factories, some had been taken to the Bunker, and some had just—vanished.

When she thought about this, she looked out from the bottom of her bunk and watched the women in the flickering candlelight continue to pick lice. Any one of them could be gone tomorrow. You had to live in the moment in Ravensbrück, she had once told Julienne. There is no past, no future. Hold onto the now.

Even though she had built a stone wall around her heart, she felt warmth for the women who had taken care of her. It was dangerous to get too attached to anyone, but it was also deadly to believe you could survive the camp alone. As she watched the circle of women murmuring and laughing, she smiled.

Over the past year, Svea had learned that Hannah Holm was sent to Ravensbrück because she was a communist. This wasn't true, though. Her husband wanted a divorce and she wouldn't give him one, so he went down to the police station and said she was a communist. An arrest followed and she was brought to Ravensbrück. Hannah had two young daughters and the last time she saw them was when she was cooking dinner. A knock came on the door, her husband rose to answer it, and she was placed in handcuffs. Her daughters yowled with grief and it was he—her husband, the man she had taken for better or worse—it was he who watched her get dragged away, and it was he who gently closed the door when she was taken from the apartment. She had been a teacher and she refused to hang Hitler's portrait in her classroom. She also refused to join the Nazi party in order to keep her job, and these things were held against her when she was interrogated. A few days later, she was sent to Ravensbrück. Sometimes, under the cover of night, Hannah taught classes in the barrack—history, literature, philosophy. She had a map of Europe hidden in the wall. She made it from clippings of *Völkischer Beobachter* and sometimes she would pull it out and point to places where the Americans and the British had attacked. She came alive as a teacher. Her whole personality changed when she stood in front of a cluster of women and shared knowledge. She could rattle off facts as if they were ingredients and she was especially kind to the new girls from Uckermark who suddenly found themselves in the adult world of Ravensbrück. "You remind me of my daughters," she sometimes said, covering her mouth with grief.

Over the past three years, Svea had changed her thoughts about prostitution. When she had a normal life, she looked down on women who worked the seedy streets of Berlin, and she sniffed at the idea of selling her body. But when she learned a few things about hunger, she found herself wondering if she would open her legs for a man and hold out her hand for payment. A simple transaction, she thought. After all, you can't eat ethics. The promise of a full belly would make anyone question what they thought was right and wrong. That was the insidious thing about Ravensbrück: it twisted your beliefs and made you wonder what was legal and illegal. At first, she'd been surprised at how easily Lorelei Wreschner called herself a prostitute. She tossed out the word as if she were saying that she was a teacher or librarian. There was no shame involved. And whenever Lorelei was asked about getting naked with strangers, she shrugged. Berlin was full of rich men who wanted a pretty face. They wanted certain things done that their wives would never do. One of these rich men, a regular, turned her in for being a "social deviant." He did this after he'd paid for an hour of pleasure. The next morning she was arrested and taken—not to jail—but to a hospital where she was sterilized. They bound her to a surgical table and injected her womb with a cocktail of chemicals. Afterwards, she was sent to Ravensbrück. Lorelei was brave, kind, and generous. Once, in an attempt to feed one of her friends, she was caught stealing potatoes from the camp kitchen and was badly beaten. Her pretty face was damaged; her nose, broken. "My whole body has been abused by men," she once said. "But the guards here are the first to beat me. Really beat me. I've been hit by men before, but not like anything that happens here."

In the last two years, Svea had also gotten to know Maria Zimmer. Good Maria. She and her husband printed anti-party newsletters and scattered them around Dresden. When the Gestapo finally caught up with them, they discovered that Maria had been hiding Jewish children in a secret room and getting them across the border into Czechoslovakia. From there, a hidden network of men and women smuggled them to Switzerland. By the time she and her husband were caught in 1938, she had gotten ninety children out of Germany. She was tortured, forced to watch her husband get shot against a brick wall, and then she was sent to Ravensbrück. In fact, she was one of the first prisoners to arrive in camp. How she was still alive was a mystery to her, and she had one of the lowest prison numbers. Mother Maria, she was sometimes called.

Although Maria had been in Ravensbrück longer than anyone else, the clear leader of their barrack was Zofia Laskowski. She had been involved in the ZWZ, the Union of Armed Struggle that waged guerrilla war on the Nazis in Kraków. Although she had been arrested for sending coded messages, she quietly admitted to her fellow prisoners that she had also planted bombs, sabotaged rail tracks, and cut telephone lines. She walked with confidence and almost seemed at peace for finding herself in Ravensbrück. "Why should I be ashamed?" she once said. "Being here means I'm their enemy. This is a place for the righteous." Svea wasn't sure she agreed with that, but she did admire how this woman in her thirties took up arms to fight the occupation of her country. And now that she was imprisoned, she continued to do acts of sabotage whenever possible. She stole supplies, she dropped stitches, and she once managed to puncture a gas tank on a truck. She hated the Germans with a glowing fury. Her whole face changed when she talked about what they were doing to Poland. The Nazis, she said, conducted "Ghetto Tourism" in Kazimierz where they went to see how the Jews were suffering. One officer told her that Poland was lucky because it was finally being civilized. With a straight face he said, "Your country is a place of dirt, laziness, fleas, and scabies. Things will be much better now that we control it."

When Zofia's country was invaded in 1939, she didn't join the resistance at first. Like everyone else, she kept her head down and tried not to care that street signs in Polish were being taken down and German signs were being put up. She turned her head when Jews had to wear yellow stars. She didn't say anything when professors, journalists, and politicians started to disappear. What changed her mind was a walk on a gorgeous Sunday afternoon. She and her husband, Janusz, decided to get out into the countryside with the idea of having a picnic in a meadow. They wanted to blow the cobwebs out of their minds and breathe fresh clean air. They wanted to be in a place where no one knew them. But instead, they stumbled across something in the woods that made Zofia's insides feel slippery. A lump came to her throat and she couldn't stop staring at what they saw. It was a mass grave. The dirt was still fresh and, here and there, was a hand or finger poking up. Clothes were scattered about. There were two bags of lime chloride leaning against a tree and there were also—she took a few steps forward—there were brass shell casings. From high above, crows cawed. There was a smell too. Dirt and corpses. It crawled into her nose and she started to throw up. To her right were black rocks that, upon closer inspection, turned out to be shoes. Children's shoes. Cigarette butts were on the ground. She looked to her left and saw a scattering of a woman's clothes. Ripped dresses. Bras. Panties. She turned away and began to stumble backwards. How many souls were beneath the dirt? How many had been shot? When she and her husband returned to Kraków that night they held hands and promised they would do something. "It was like taking a wedding vow," Zofia said. "For better or worse, we were in it together." And now she was in

Ravensbrück. *What about your husband?* Svea had once asked. Zofia looked away and said just one word. "Dead."

The women continued to laugh quietly around the flickering candle. They whispered about cooking meals and taking long strolls through parklands.

"Okay…who has the most?" Zofia asked, pointing to the box.

They began counting their rows of dead lice. After a mumbling of numbers, Maria clapped her hands together. She had twenty-seven dead little bodies. There were smiles as they brushed the snapped white specks onto the floor. There would be more tomorrow. Lice were everywhere in camp—clothes, blankets, on window sills, in the straw mattresses—they were as inescapable as hunger.

"Time for bed," Zofia said, blowing out the candle.

The bunk shook as the women climbed it like a ladder. The bunks trembled again when they pushed into their sleeping spaces. They had been designed for one person, but it was common for four prisoners to be fitted against each other like herrings. If one person needed to roll over, they all had to roll over.

From the next bunk over, someone started to cough. Rain continued to patter the roof and, in the distance, there was the low rumble of thunder moving towards Poland. Just as Svea was beginning to find sleep, there was muttering from the other side of the barrack. Her eyes fluttered open as she tried to figure out who was speaking. It was a man's voice. She lifted her head and felt a depth charge of worry inside her ribcage. Why was a man in the barrack?

After a moment she realized it was a radio. A prisoner from Lübeck had hidden one beneath the floorboards and she must have taken it out to listen to the BBC. Svea couldn't understand English so she let the foreign words wash over her. English sounded like birdsong, and although she tried to understand the lyrics to the songs she loved to hear, they often didn't make sense. Flat Foot Floogie with a floy floy. Stompin' at the Savoy. Minnie the Moocher. It was the music she loved. The language? Not so much.

There was a flash of lightning and the man's voice turned to static. When darkness returned to the barrack again, his voice returned to normal. Another flash. More static.

The prisoner from Lübeck—Eva?—was that her name?—didn't

bring the radio out every night because it was too valuable and too dangerous. It was smart to bring it out tonight because the rain would keep the Aufseherin away. She could listen to it with the knowledge that she probably wouldn't be caught.

The British voice continued speaking and Svea recognized a few words. *Sicily. Patton. Rome.* She lifted her head and whispered into the dark, "What's he saying?"

"Shh!" Zofia shushed from the bunk above.

After another minute, the man finished speaking and this was followed by the opening notes of a Glenn Miller song. Svea nearly begged for the music to stay on, but the trumpets were shut off and silence filled the night. The song, however, continued in Svea's mind and she found herself smiling. It was good to hear notes from her old life and, for a moment, she was dancing in Clärchens Ballhaus again. The whirl of dresses. The thump of drums. Cigarettes and champagne. Peter. He smiled and held out his hand.

Her face curdled—she didn't want to think about what had happened—and she focused her attention on Julienne's weight. She was resting on her left arm. Her fingers sparkled with pins and needles.

A voice spoke into the dark. It was Eva. "The BBC is saying the Allies have invaded Sicily and that General Patton has captured Palermo. The Americans have also bombed Rome for the first time." The happiness in her voice was like a clear bell. "The war is coming closer to Germany!"

She then said the same words in Polish, and then in Russian. Excited whispering moved up and down the barrack and there was something almost like hope in the air.

"I hope you're feeling better," Lorelei said to Svea from the bunk above.

"Thanks."

"There are worse things than a beating."

It was true of course. There *were* worse things than a beating. Dog attacks. The sound of pistol shots near the crematorium. The camp prison. Medical experiments.

She had seen a cluster of Polish women taken to the camp hospital a few months ago and something was done to their legs. A long cut had been made in their calf and bacteria had been placed into their muscles. When the wound healed, doctors sent them back to work. They hobbled around camp and called themselves "rabbits" because they had to shuffle and hop. Rumors started that staphylococci had been injected into their tissue. But why? No one knew.

A few women started coughing and this made Svea wonder if they had typhus. Lice could easily carry that. A problem for tomorrow, though. Better to rest and think later.

As the storm softened into silence, crickets began to sing. Svea heard the sound of kissing and moaning—little pleasures in the shadows. She had once been repulsed by the idea of women sleeping with women, but now—? Here? Love was a gift, and a precious one at that, especially in a place like Ravensbrück. Any one of them could be fed into the flames tomorrow.

She felt the itchiness of the straw beneath her body and concentrated on Julienne's lungs, how her chest moved up and down. She hugged her friend and started to fall into a deep, undisturbed sleep.

Outside, black smoke lifted from the crematorium. It floated up into the sky and followed after the storm. The electrified fence continued to hum and spark.

CHAPTER SEVEN
A Woman's Place

Ravensbrück did not fall from the sky. It was planned. It was built. It was managed. The only all-female concentration camp in the Third Reich was so large and complex that no single person—whether they were a prisoner or a guard—could possibly know it all. By the end of the war it sprawled deep into the woods, but it all began one day with a simple architectural drawing on a draftsman desk. It started with a ruler, a T-square, and a pencil.

In November 1938, boundary markers were staked out next to Lake Schwedt, an idyllic body of water ringed by spruce, pine, and oak trees. The nearby church bells of Fürstenberg echoed across the water and it was common to see storks soaring across the sky. Soon, a massive courtyard was built by prisoners and this was surrounded by a rising wall of concrete. An enormous iron gate was fitted onto hinges. Lime trees were planted to create the Lagerstrasse—the wide avenue that cut through the camp—and this would become the main thoroughfare which funneled the women to work. Hammers and crosscut saws were brought out to create barracks. Electrified fencing was fitted into place and a generator hummed to life. Architects stood around, smoking. They consulted blueprints and pointed at what still needed to rise up from imagination. Trucks loaded down with bricks and iron kept on coming. Roads were graded smooth by prisoners, stone stairways were fitted into hills, and homes for the SS were constructed. A large plaza was laid out before the Administration building and a flagpole was sunk into the soil. A Nazi flag was tied onto snap hooks and it was slowly raised. It fluttered and flapped in the crisp wind.

Ravensbrück officially opened in 1939—the same year the war started—and when the Soviets finally liberated the camp on April 30, 1945, it had grown to monstrous size. It had expanded far beyond its original blueprint and it had become a center of gravity for a number of subcamps. Rail lines were laid out in the woods. Huge wooden warehouses with wide platforms were assembled near the tracks and goods were stacked high. These were things that had either been stolen from the prisoners or they were products the prisoners had been forced to make—things like socks, blankets, electrical components, shirts, fuses, mats, and servomotors. During its ruthless years of operation, some 132,000 women passed through the gates of Ravensbrück. At least a third of them perished.

Those parts of camp that belonged to the SS and the Aufseherin were made functional and attractive. There was an art deco gas station near the Administration building along with a row of fine garages that kept a fleet of Mercedes safe during thunderstorms. As for the Administration building itself, it had a large foyer with a huge painted swastika and eagle on the wall. Beyond that were two wide wooden staircases; they rose to mid-floor and then merged to become one set of stairs that lifted up to the second floor. A stained-glass window was on the landing and, when the sun hit it just right, pools of color shimmered on the oak parquet floor. The upstairs corridor was long and clean. Flags stood at attention and plaques were on the walls. The Commandant's office was in the corner of the upper floor and his desk was positioned so that he sat with the windows at his back. There was the sound of typewriters and the occasional flare of a telephone ringing. The wooden floors had wool carpets scattered about and there was the frequent smell of cigarettes, brandy, and aftershave. Boots clicked quickly off the wood floor—silenced now and then by carpets—only to click off wood again. There was a small room for tea and biscuits, as well as a larger room for dinners that required fine china and silverware.

It wasn't just the working spaces of Ravensbrück that had an air of wealth and gentility to them because the men who ran the camp also had luxury at home. The SS had family houses built on a low hill near the Administration building. Stone stairways climbed up to these mountain chalets and, in each of them, was a wide fireplace, handsomely carved wooden ceilings, a kitchen, a dining area, and a bathroom with a toilet. A set of stairs curved up to the second floor, which had three bedrooms. A balcony was off the master bedroom and there were ceiling fans. Wives and children lived here and made their way into town for shopping and school. At night, as they climbed into their beds, an orange glow came from the chimney of the crematorium. There was the constant smell of burning kielbasa and grapefruit in the air. No one needed to ask what was being put into the ovens.

As for the Aufseherin, they had barracks that could hardly be called "barracks" at all. They looked like something out of a mountain scene in Switzerland—white walls, carved wood, and pretty flower boxes. There was a front porch with seats to enjoy a view of the lake and, inside, there was a cozy front room. Down the hall was a kitchen and individual bedrooms. Each room had a fitted cupboard, a wash basin, and a radiator. Newspapers like *Völkischer Beobachter* and *Das Schwarze Korps* were delivered each morning along with the milk. A mirror was next to the front door so that the Aufseherin could check to see if their coifed hair was properly arranged under their caps.

Construction at Ravensbrück was relentless. Ever since the first boundary marker was hammered into the sandy ground, there was a need for more buildings, more roads, more housing, more rail tracks, and more barracks. Just a few years after opening, Ravensbrück had factories full of sewing machines, it had villas, gardens, kitchens, huge laundry facilities, kennels, storage depots, a shoe repair shop, a furniture repair shop, a painters' shed, and a water treatment plant. It had potato cellars, a mat weaving factory, a thread spinning workshop, huge hutches full of Angora rabbits, a telephone exchange, an electrical substation, and a furrier shop that made winter hats out of Angora wool. It had warehouses next to a rail line, gasoline tanks, a massive sand pit, a coal bunker, chicken coops, and medical facilities that almost certainly killed more women than it cured. There was also an SS canteen that served gourmet food, a two-story prison known as the Bunker for those women who required special punishment, and there was a crematorium that had three coal-fired ovens. At least one gas chamber was at Ravensbrück and the guards called it the "New Laundry". Built in early 1945, it was given its euphemistic name, of course, to hide its lethal function. This secret concrete room could hold 150 women and, according to camp survivors, it was dynamited by the SS on April 23, 1945 in order to pretend that it had never been built in the first place. There are rumors that several rail cars were hidden in the woods near Ravensbrück and that they were used as mobile gas chambers. While this is certainly within the realm of possibility, especially near the end of the war when the population in the camp soared, there is no definitive proof beyond the adamant testimony of survivors. This, however, is the nature of mobile gas chambers. They are meant to be moved and, in that moving, the reality of their existence is taken with them—they disappear into fog, dragging facts with them.

After only a few years, Ravensbrück was so big that it began to gather subcamps around it, not unlike how a planet begins to collect moons. Soon the subcamp of Uckermark was created on the southeast perimeter and teenage girls were forced into it where they had to sew and stitch. If they spoke, they were beaten, and when they turned eighteen they were usually sent up the sandy path to the main camp. To the south was a subcamp run by the Siemens Corporation. It was here that women were forced to build electronic components for secret wonder weapons that might change the course of the war. As with other camps like Auschwitz, Buchenwald, and Sachsenhausen, the SS at Ravensbrück rented out their prisoners to corporations for a fee. When it was suggested that the Siemens Corporation could build a factory to their specifications outside of the main camp, and that they could have labor at an unspeakably cheap rate, it wasn't long before high technology came to Ravensbrück. These facilities were kept sanitary in order to protect the electronic parts that had to be built. Prisoners assigned to the Siemens Camp felt as if they had entered a different world because they were rarely beaten as long as they kept up with daily quotas. Here, they were reasonably well fed. Here, they got their own bed and a blanket. Here, they worked long hours in clean clothes and, although the work was fast-paced, the Siemens Corporation had a vested interest in taking better care of their prisoners. All these women had to do was put electronic parts together quickly and efficiently. It was precision work. They built servomotors that were then transported to the secret underground concentration camp of Dora-Mittelbau where prisoners there fitted them into V-2 rockets. The women who built these rocket parts had little idea what they were creating, but it hardly mattered because these bits of technology—whatever they were—gave them a better life. Perhaps not surprisingly, when word got out about the Siemens Camp, those in the sock factory and mat weaving factory began to look upon it with envy. To build rocket parts was to find yourself in the aristocracy of the camp. To build weapons of death meant that you might live.

Best of all, if you were in the Siemens Camp it meant that you were mostly beyond the reach of the Aufseherin. Mostly.

Because Germany was supposed to win the war and make a colony of the Soviet Union, the realities of Ravensbrück were never supposed to appear in history books. After victory, the camp was meant to be repurposed, buried, forgotten. But the past often has an unexpected future. We know that Ravensbrück was a training ground for violence and that over 4,000 Aufseherin passed through its gates and went on to terrorize other camps, including Stutthof, Majdanek, Vaivara, Mauthausen, Bergen-Belsen, and Auschwitz. Ravensbrück was a type of finishing school of brutality. When the time was right, female guards would pack their suitcases, hug their friends goodbye, and get onto a train that would take them elsewhere in the Reich.

The women who wore the dark grey uniform of the Aufseherin had little use for school and most of them had dropped out early. They believed in the bold future that Hitler had mapped for Germany and they signed up knowing they would be working in a concentration camp. Most of these young women were nervous and fidgety at first, but when they were given truncheons, and when they were allowed to beat others, they quickly warmed to violence. Many of them grew to like it, especially the power. Yet the idea of women enjoying violence is taboo in most societies. We like to assume that violence is a male trait and that any woman who embraces savagery has somehow crossed a border. Women who act with fury and spill blood are often seen as entering a land that does not belong to them, that they have somehow trespassed onto foreign soil and entered territory that is instinctively alien to them. And because of this, violent women seem far more monstrous than men who commit the very same crimes. We want to imagine that women are nurturing, caring, and motherly. We want to believe that bloodshed does not come naturally to women, and we do not want to imagine our mothers, daughters, or wives as being agents of destruction. And yet, all across the world, mythology is full of women who are at home in the dark landscape of butchery. The Furies. Medusa. Circe. The Sirens. Amazons. Banshees. Soucouyants. Manananggals. Kumiho. Succubus. Lamia. Our stories say much about our fears.

While the Aufseherin may have controlled the barracks and factories of Ravensbrück, they existed in a society that saw their gender as a limitation. The Third Reich was a thoroughly patriarchal nation and it was believed that women should stay home in order to raise children. And yet, during the war, women were allowed into male spaces that would normally be shut off to them. They were both women, and not women. They did their hair and they used perfume. They were also given heavy boots and truncheons. Notably, they wore a culotte-style skirt, which is both a dress and also a type of trousers, depending upon how one moves. When standing around and chatting, a culotte looks like a dress, but when marching across a factory floor, it looks more like baggy pants. Put another way, a culotte is sometimes a skirt and sometimes wide-flared trousers. These uniformed women in culottes were at peace with what they were doing in the concentration camps because it was legal and acceptable. The state, after all, had hired them to commit acts of violence. At Ravensbrück, killing became normal, beating became normal, sexual abuse and prostitution and infanticide—they all became normal. What was once forbidden was now permitted, so long as you had a grey uniform. And of course, although Ravensbrück was a place for women, it is good to remember that it was run by men. The freedom to commit violence like a man did not mean that women were trusted with governing themselves. That power rested with the men in the Administration building.

As for the prisoners, they also wore a uniform and it stripped them of not only their femininity, but also their humanity. In the natural order of things, the Nazis viewed prisoners as being less worthy of care than horses or dogs. They were useless eaters. Sub-humans. Vermin. The women of Ravensbrück were forced to work, and this usually happened in four different ways. First, they could be assigned to the SS-owned textile factories inside the camp where they were forced to sew and weave. Second, they might have to fix buildings, dig ditches, smooth out bumpy roads, tend a farm, collect garbage or climb down into toilet pits with buckets. Third, they might be listed as one of the "Availables" and they had to do whatever odd jobs were asked of them. Fourth, if they were very lucky, they might be assigned to the Siemens Camp or the Administration building.

For those prisoners who found themselves cleaning the Administration building or carrying trays of biscuits, they were given clean uniforms and they were ordered to bathe with soap. The SS didn't want the distraction of body odor and they certainly didn't want to worry about catching lice. To work in the Administration building was to have a little sphere of protection from the barbarity of the larger camp, and this occurred at its very core where all major decisions were made.

It is easy to imagine one of these prisoners finishing up a long day of serving coffee and emptying ashtrays in the Administration building. As she walks back to her special barrack, as she turns on the taps of a bathtub and, as hot water gushes in, she takes off her uniform. The world falls away as she steps into the steamy tub and reaches for a bar of lemon soap. She lathers her underarms, her face, her breasts. She lets her dark chocolate hair get wet. She scrubs the filth of the camp from her skin. She lays back for a moment, closes her eyes, and considers all that she has seen.

But no amount of soap can clean her of Ravensbrück.

It will always be there. It will never leave her eyes.

CHAPTER EIGHT
Little Nurse

As they waited in front of the Administration building, Anna played with a button on her uniform and looked around the plaza. The storm had certainly made a mess. Sticks and twigs were scattered around the oval, dead worms were drying out, and puddles were everywhere. Clouds glowered overhead and the air was fresh, new. Every now and then, puffs of tarry black smoke drifted by. The flag of her nation clanked atop its pole—it rippled out, then fell. From inside the camp she could hear numbers being called out.

She stopped playing with her button and looked across the lake at the town of Fürstenberg. A steeple poked the air and there was the dull chitterchattering of a train. A whistle came and this made her look at her wristwatch. Binz told them to be at the Administration building at 0600. That was five minutes ago. She looked around and saw that Ruth was staring at her.

"What?"

"How's Little Nurse doing this morning?"

"Don't call me that."

"Why not?" Ruth said as she touched her chest in mock surprise. "You don't like it?"

"You know I don't."

Ruth smiled, but the smile didn't reach her eyes. "Why's that?"

"I just—" Anna paused, took in a sharp breath and decided to change course. "Did you sleep well? With the storm and all?"

"Like the dead," Ruth said without blinking or looking away. "The beds are comfortable and the sheets are nice but don't change the subject. I asked you a question: why not?"

"Why not what?"

"Oh for God's sake, don't play stupid. What's wrong with calling you Little Nurse?"

Anna searched for Binz's form near their chalets. Surely she wasn't going to be late? It was already five minutes after and this wasn't setting a good example.

Ruth tried again. "I *said*, why's that?"

"Stop it."

"Why, Little Nursey Nurse?"

Anger flared inside Anna's ribcage. "Because I don't like to be teased," she said sharply, perhaps too sharply. She held up both hands in apology. "I didn't mean it that way. It's just that my father used to—"

"Stop," Ruth said. "You think there's room for hurt feelings and weakness in this place?"

Anna played with the top button of her uniform again.

"Stand up for yourself. You can't be weak...*not here*. Here you tell others how you want to be treated. You don't like being teased?" Ruth asked, rolling her eyes. When she looked back, the mischievous smile returned. "So Little Nurse, who doesn't like to be teased and has a glass heart, what are you going to do about it?"

Anna looked away and wasn't sure. She touched the side of her cheek and felt the ghostly sting of her father's hand. She took in a breath to say something, she felt her voice box begin to tighten on a vowel, but her lips stayed shut. She smiled to make herself more welcoming, more likeable.

A black Mercedes appeared and, as it slowly rolled past them, the gravel beneath the tires crunched. The chrome headlights were buffed to a high shine and, in the back seat, was the Commandant. He was reading a file. As the sleek black machine moved past her, Anna watched her reflection in the window. Her face was distorted, stretched. The car turned lazily and moved away, dragging the sound of the engine away with it.

She didn't look at Ruth. Instead she scanned the front porches of the chalets. Maybe Binz didn't sleep where they did? Maybe she had a house of her own? The camp was big after all. There were whole parts of it she had yet to explore. Her eyes flicked to the grainy black smoke tumbling upwards into the sky. They weren't allowed in that place, for example. Fine, she thought. Maybe she didn't want to see bodies being fed into the flames. She watched the smoke curl and dissolve. It drifted out to the lake.

"Little Nurse. Maybe the others should start calling you that?"

"Don't," Anna said, wheeling around.

"Or what?" Ruth asked, nodding to Anna's truncheon. "What're you going to do?"

Anna thought about making a sudden move and bringing out her weapon—just to scare Ruth—but it seemed childish. It seemed like something they might do in the League of German Maidens when Frau Pfeiffer wasn't watching. She had seen men taunting, teasing, and rough housing in beer halls, but their name calling didn't seem to be about abuse. Oddly, if men liked each other, saying such things brought them closer together. Mocking was a way to show affection. Her eyes focused on Ruth. There was a stony grin and cold eyes. That didn't seem to be what was happening here. Ruth wasn't making fun of her as a friendly joke.

"Are you going to be strong?" Ruth asked. After a long moment, there was a thawing. "What I want to know is simply this: do you have what it takes? To be with us?"

The front door of the Administration building opened and a prisoner came out carrying a silver tray with a coffee pot and several china cups. She used her rump to keep the wooden door open and, when she saw the two Aufseherin, she paused. Anna could tell the prisoner knew she should salute but she couldn't without dropping the silver tray.

"Madam Overseers," she said smartly. "Good morning."

They watched her, wordlessly, and Anna considered putting this woman—this thing—in its rightful place. Maybe she should trip her as she walked past? She looked at Ruth.

But then she saw that this prisoner had a spotless uniform and she didn't have a cap. Her dark chocolate hair fell down in lush curls and she had a pretty face. She wore lipstick and her fingernails were clean. Anna watched this curious prisoner move away from the door with a heavy tray and glide down the front steps. She looked at the ground and moved towards the SS villas. A lemony smell trailed behind her.

Anna didn't know what to think of this. She looked at the second floor of the building and began to nod in lifting realization. So, some prisoners had it better off than others, she thought. A good thing she didn't trip her and send the coffee flying. What would the men say?

The prisoner hurried across the plaza and began to climb a stone staircase up to an SS villa. Wood smoke came from a chimney and a young boy was on the patio playing with a toy airplane. He moved back and forth, strafing the world.

Binz appeared. She held open the wooden door of the Administration building and looked at her watch. "I told you 0600."

"But Frau Binz, we're here," Ruth said coming to attention.

"Not out *there*," Binz said flapping her hand. "In here. What good are you out there? My God, you're late for our meeting. Hurry up, girls."

Anna felt her skirt swish around her knees as she hopped up the stairs. Ruth was a step in front of her, and she pushed her aside so that she could enter first.

The foyer was a large rectangle and two sets of heavy doors were on the other end. Between the doors was a painting of a huge eagle gripping a swastika. The floor was tiled and two cigarette stands were near the doors, along with a coat rack. A framed photo of Hitler was on one of the walls.

"Come on," Binz said, motioning with her right hand. "Hurry."

They moved through one of the doors and Anna found herself staring at a wide wooden staircase. It rose to half-a-story before it curved to the center and continued to the next floor. Light came through a stained-glass window and this cast colorful shadows on the carpeted landing. Two enormous plants—she didn't know what they were but the leaves were the size of her hands—were on either side of the stairway. Binz began to climb and Ruth followed. Anna wondered how often she might find herself in this building. Was it rare to come here or would this become part of her daily work?

They reached the landing and turned to the right where they climbed another set of stairs to the second floor. Binz turned and spoke without stopping, "Remember, you are womenfolk of the Reich. Follow orders. Do as you're told."

"Do you know what this is about?" Ruth asked.

Binz shook her head. She reached the top stair and pointed to the right. "This way."

Their boots were loud on the parquet flooring, and as they moved down the wide hallway a prisoner came out of an office with a mop. She stood at attention as they passed. Again, this prisoner had a crisp, clean uniform. They came to an office and Binz held up a hand for them to wait. She opened the door and went in. Anna and Ruth looked at each other awkwardly. Flags were stationed like sentries in the corridor and, behind closed doors, typewriters thwacked out sentences.

Binz called for them. "You may enter."

Although Anna let Ruth go first, she crossed into the office with purpose. An SS officer—a high ranking one—stood behind a desk. He looked familiar. Yes, she had met him after roll call yesterday and he was kind enough to point out where the sock factory was located. He motioned to the small men's camp near it and used his arms to explain why the walls were so high. "A men's camp inside a women's camp?" she had asked. It was strange to learn and he explained that several hundred men were kept at Ravensbrück for work that women weren't strong enough to do. Pouring concrete. Lifting walls. Laying rail tracks.

She marched over to the SS officer's desk and raised her right arm. "Heil Hitler."

Ruth must not have thought to do this because a half-second later she also snapped her heels together. "Heil Hitler."

"Don't they look smart?" Binz beamed. There was a pause before, "Girls, this is *Schutzhaftlagerführer* Keller, assistant to the Commandant."

"At ease," he said, adjusting the cuffs of his uniform. "I think we can dispense with formality, don't you Frau Binz?"

"Of course, yes."

Anna continued to stand at attention because she knew that it thrust out her chest. His attention wouldn't be on her face and she could use this opportunity to scan the office. She let her eyes dart here and there. A silver chandelier hung from the ceiling and there were heavy maroon drapes tied back to reveal a large window. He had not two—but three—radiators bolted to the wall. A large potted plant was next to his desk and a hat rack was in the corner. There was an umbrella stand next to it made out of what looked like an elephant's leg. Peacock feathers sprouted out, along with several collapsed umbrellas.

He came around from the back of his desk and bowed at the waist. "Welcome. It's good to have fresh faces here." He cocked his head, and his eyes lingered on her chest. "Yes, yes, welcome," he said, extending his hand. He had a firm grip.

Schutzhaftlagerführer Keller turned to Ruth and did the same. Anna could smell his cologne and she noticed that he had nicked himself while shaving. The crust on his chin looked fresh.

"Frau Binz," he said opening his arms and gesturing for the door. "If you don't mind, I'd like to talk to Frau Hartmann and Frau Stein alone."

She seemed surprised. "I…as their immediate superior, I thought…well, I thought I'd be staying."

He waved his fingertips to the door. "I think not. Adieu."

Binz nodded and spun on her heel. She left, and Anna listened to her boots moving down the hallway. Soon, there was only the sound of typewriters.

Keller moved to his office door and closed it, slowly. The latch clicked.

"So," he said, reaching into his breast pocket. "No doubt you're wondering why I've called you here." He pulled out a cigarette from a brass case and lit it. As he did so, he squinted to keep smoke from his eye. When a cherry red glow appeared, he puffed a few times and walked back to his desk. He leaned against it and crossed his legs at the ankles.

"Oh, my goodness, at ease!" he laughed. "I won't bite."

Anna relaxed and wasn't sure what to do with her arms. Should she cross them over her chest? Should she cup her hands behind her back? Maybe she should place her palms over her bellybutton like a shop girl waiting to take an order?

"It's always nice to have new faces," he said tapping ash into a coffee cup. "Keeps things interesting, yes? That's one good thing about this camp. There are many ways to advance, many ways indeed. "There's always something that needs done and there are no shortages in getting ahead, if you show willingness."

Anna looked at the peacock feathers in the elephant leg umbrella stand and wondered where he had gotten such a hideous thing. A safari, perhaps? A flea market?

"Which brings me to you," he said pointing his cigarette at both Anna and Ruth. "You're new to this place and I think it's best to make veterans of you quickly. Toss you into the deep end, yes? Like I tell my men, not everyone is suited for this special kind of work and it's good to find out who is best—" he studied the ceiling for the right word, "—best *matched* for camp life. Yes?"

He took another drag and blew smoke up to the chandelier. It swirled among the silver arms.

"And so, here is my question for you," the assistant to the Commandant said. He crossed his arms and flicked ash onto the floor.

"We need volunteers."

Ruth took a step forward. "I'll do it."

Keller let out the bark of laughter. "No, no, my dear. You don't want to volunteer for this type of work, believe me. You will however be *getting* volunteers."

Anna furrowed her eyebrows. Keller must have seen her confusion and continued on.

"Our troops at the front, who are bravely fighting the Soviets *et cetra*," he said, pointing at a map of Europe on the other side of his office. "See there? The fighting is ferocious and I'm confident we will win."

"Of course we will," Ruth said.

He ignored her. "Our men are getting stung by bullets and this is causing horrible wounds. Simply awful. Berlin is trying to figure out how to—" He paused and shook his head. "You don't need the details. War, after all, is the sphere of men. No, the reason I've asked you to come here on this bright morning is to ask a simple question."

Anna was still looking at the elephant leg when she got the feeling that he was speaking to her.

"Yes, *you*," he said pointing his cigarette directly at Anna.

"Me?"

"Yes, you, Fraulein Hartmann! Our records say you want to be a nurse when the war is over. Is that correct? Do you want to work in the medical field?"

Little Nurse. Should she deny this was the future she wanted? Was this some kind of test? Should say that she had no interest in healing people? Maybe Ruth and the others had told him something.

"Well…?" Keller asked, opening an arm. "Is it true?"

"Yes," she said without hesitation. "I want to be a nurse when the war is over." Her eyes did not slide over to Ruth when she said this.

"Good. A woman of conviction. I like it. Now listen, I want you to do something for me. Roll call is happening right now," he nodded towards the Appellplatz, "And I want you to find a volunteer. I want you to bring her to the Bunker. Take her to cell 14."

Anna squinted. "Find a volunteer?"

"Any prisoner you like. And I want *you*," he said turning to Ruth, "I want you to help her out. It's best to do these things in pairs," he said bobbling his head. "To make it easier."

Anna wondered why he was telling them this and not Binz. Surely this was something she could have done herself.

"Excellent," he said, standing up and moving around to the back of his desk.

Anna straightened and felt her uniform jacket tighten against her chest. "I won't let you down, *Schutzhaftlagerführer*."

"I won't either," Ruth added.

"Good. And now," he pointed at Ruth, "You may leave us." He flicked his fingertips towards the door the same way he had done with Binz. "Close it behind you, please."

Anna felt the floorboards move ever so slightly beneath her as Ruth moved away. There was a soft groan of hinges and the click of a lock. She was alone with him.

"You are an attractive woman, Fraulein Hartmann," he said, picking a fleck of tobacco from his tongue.

"Thank you?"

"Nineteen?"

"Yes."

"Boyfriend?"

She wanted to lie. "Um...no."

"Some man is going to be very lucky," he smiled. He glanced down at his wedding ring and took another drag. Smoke fell from his nostrils and he cleared his throat. "It's hard being away from family, wouldn't you agree?"

She thought of her father and shrugged. "We're all working for a better Germany."

"True. Very true. And on that note...yes, on that *note*...after you've selected a prisoner for volunteer work, Fraulein Hartman, I want you to run an errand for me in Fürstenberg. Can you do that? It will be a nice break in the day for you. You'll need a wooden cart and a few prisoners to push it." He came around the front of his desk and reached into the inside of his uniform pocket. He held a folded piece of paper between his thumb and forefinger. "Go to this address. Tell them I sent you. They will know what to do."

Was this the reason she had been kept behind? This errand? She reached for the folded note and, as she did so, he didn't release it. He held on to it.

"You're doing this errand by yourself. Understand?"

"But I think *Oberaufseherin* Binz is expecting me to patrol the sock factory."

He shook his head. "Tell her I gave you a special assignment." He let go of the note and took a final drag on his cigarette. The cherry tip burned close to his fingers. He exhaled through his nose and turned to the glass ashtray. With a quick movement, he snubbed it beneath his thumb.

Outside was the lone voice of a Blockova, shouting. A work patrol was on the march.

"I hope I'll see more of you," he said. "If you need anything, don't be a stranger." He moved to kiss her on both cheeks, and she let him. His breath was scented with coffee. As a shop girl in Berlin she was used to such things.

She turned to leave and tucked the note into her pocket. She opened the frosted office door swiftly and, when she saw Ruth standing in the hallway, a cold smile formed on her lips. She walked ahead and thudded down the wooden stairs with purpose, her gaze was straight and her steps were sure. This is what power felt like, she thought. Her right hand went to her truncheon.

"Wait," Ruth said. "What did he say? What does he want us to do?"

But she was already stepping into the sunshine and turning for the iron gate. She knew exactly which prisoner she was going to find.

CHAPTER NINE

Punishment

Goose pimples prickled her calves and she shivered in the cold breeze. Even though it was spring, the mornings still felt like winter. She never realized May could feel like this at sunrise until she had to stand in melting shadows. Soon, she told herself, soon the Appellplatz would get warmer. Without moving her head, she watched Blockovas hurry through their ranks, glowering as they looked for infractions. Dogs barked behind her. When she was a child she loved dogs but in Ravensbrück they were a source of fear and humiliation. Fear because they could tear your body a part at any moment, and humiliation because one of the Aufseherin had trained her animal to urinate on the legs of prisoners. This had happened to Svea on a few occasions and she just had to stand there and take it. The warm wet on her shin and ankle soon turned cold.

Cold, she thought, feeling the breeze on her cheek.

Sticks and leaves were everywhere. No doubt a work detail would be made from the Availables and they would have to walk the ground in a single line, picking up all that had fallen during the storm. It would be a terrible job. Back breaking. Imagine crouching down and living with the risk of being kicked at any moment. Whoever was chosen for clean up—and God she hoped it wasn't her—would become a ripe target for a boot. It was humiliating to be kicked. At least with a truncheon there was a sense of fighting. But a kick? Whenever that happened, she felt like a muddy animal.

Svea let her eyes readjust on the woman standing in front of her. She was a skeleton with thin arms. Her elbows were bony knots and her skin was papery grey. The poor woman had dysentery. Svea could see it. Brown watery stains ran down both of her legs. There was no question of using the toilet during roll call. If she wandered off to clean herself, she would be beaten. The woman probably had cramps, Svea considered, but if she did have a tightening in her guts, she hid it well. Svea looked at the watery bloody shit on the woman's right ankle. If one of the guards saw what had happened, she would be taken away to the Revier or maybe shot. Good, Svea thought without shame. Let her be a magnet of attention.

She stared at a fresh line of reddish-brown trickling down the woman's leg. It made her think of that time when Peter was knocking on the bathroom door and she was in the bathtub and there was so much blood and—

She shook her head. No. Don't think about that. What good was the past now?

The breeze fluttered her dress. Her number had been called ages ago so she only had to stand and wait. It was almost like being alone. Before Ravensbrück, she didn't realize that privacy was a luxury. Only the Nazis were allowed to close a door, click a lock snugly into place, and slump into a chair where they could be alone. Ah, to enter a kingdom of privacy. To not be watched.

She glanced at Julienne.

The bruises on her face weren't nearly as bad as they could have been, and Svea studied the discolored welts on her friend's shoulders. She thought of the needle and thread that had been used to stich Julienne together. Would it hold? What if it bloomed open?

From the corner of the Appellplatz, there was the pistol crack of a whip. Svea looked over and saw a cluster of women using the roller. It was a huge concrete cylinder that was used to smooth the cinders of the yard. It weighed as much as an automobile and it took five women to get the iron frame moving. If you stopped the forward momentum, it was absolute hell getting it to crush the ground again. And of course the Aufseherin whipped and kicked, which made it all the harder to keep a steady pace. Svea closed her eyes and heard the roller slowly crunching over wet pebbles. A Blockova shouted to keep up rhythm.

"1, 2, 3…ROLL!" A pause. "1, 2, 3…ROLL!"

Svea doubted the women would see tomorrow. She looked at their threadlike bodies trying to pull and push the metal frame. Puddles were everywhere and this would make it even harder to get the thing moving. Their hands would be slippery. They all wore a yellow star; they were all Jews. Everyone suffered at Ravensbrück but a yellow winkel made things so much worse. She watched them strain against the weight. One of the women had a black eye.

"1, 2, 3...ROLL!"

She wanted to look away from this punishment, this pointless hurt, and pretend that it wasn't happening. After all, she told herself, if she didn't see it, she couldn't remember it. And yet, by worrying about remembering it, that meant some tiny part of her still hoped to survive. Why else would she care about what she remembered of Ravensbrück? Memories were for survivors, and there was no way she was going to survive this place.

Was it better to ignore the evil swirling around her and protect herself from ugly memories or was it better to stare everything in the face and become a witness? Yesterday, when she was being beaten in the sock factory, did she want someone to remember what had happened and pass it down through the decades? Did she want someone to retain what had been done to her? Part of her said yes. But would she feel this way if an SS officer placed a pistol against the back of her head and pulled the trigger? Would she want *that* to be talked about after the war? She wasn't sure. One thing was certain: when death came for her, it would happen fast, so fast that she probably wouldn't stop to think about whether or not there was an audience to her destruction.

As the Jewish women grunted against the concrete roller, numbers continued to be shouted out into the chilly air.

"16741."

"*Jawoh.*"

19023."

"*Jawohl.*"

There was the smell of earthworms. How would they taste?

An old wooden cart moved towards the front gate. It had huge wheels and it was stacked with the naked dead. Mouths and eyes were wide open. Wrists and ankles. Toes. Breasts. Heads. Arms and legs juddered as the cart was pushed by a team of prisoners. Sitting on top of this puzzle of limbs was a lone prisoner—she munched on a baguette and stared out at camp. She chewed slowly and was completely indifferent to the dead beneath her. She tore off a chunk of baguette and ate it. Now and then she told the others to push to the left or right.

Two Aufseherin appeared near the kitchen block. They scanned the crowd, looking for someone, and Svea immediately recognized them as the new recruits from yesterday. Her stomach dropped. She coughed three times—it was their signal—to get Julienne's attention. When her friend looked over, Svea raised her eyebrows and nodded to the front as if to say, *up there. Look.*

A prisoner with the concrete roller started shrieking in animal pain. It was a shattering of panic. She screeched and yelled out a single word, over and over again. "No!" It was sparkling and raw with terror. "No, no, no, no! Oh my God, NO!"

A type of squealing stabbed the air as the woman wept with horror. She took in a lungful of air and let out a wild roar of horror. It was a sound no human should make.

At first, the pretty blonde Aufseherin didn't glance over at the noise—she was too busy searching for someone in the Appellplatz—but as the screaming continued the woman in a grey uniform looked over at the roller. She seemed annoyed by the distraction.

≈

Anna looked for the source of the screeching. At first, she wasn't sure what was before her eyes. She blinked and considered it. What were the prisoners huddled around? It slowly came together in her mind the more that she stared: it was an enormous concrete roller on a crude metal frame and the prisoners were trying to—they were trying to push it. At last she realized it was something like a monstrous lawn roller. Except here, it was used to smooth gravel and cinder. One of the prisoners was on her knees and she was screaming at the sky. Lotte Rentz stood over her, holding her truncheon, and she looked surprised. Her cap had tumbled onto the wet ground and her neatly coifed hair was a snaggled braid of black that fell down the side of her face.

The prisoner continued to wail and scream. Her right forearm was bent at an unnatural angle and a stubby bit of bone was sticking out. There wasn't much blood, but the woman kept screaming and screaming. It was a death sentence. Her arm wouldn't be put into a splint, there would be no bed rest with clean sheets, and there certainly wouldn't be weekly visits to a doctor to make sure the bones were setting properly. No, Anna realized, her broken arm—along with the rest of her—would be made into ash by lunchtime.

"Someone help! I don't want to burn. HELP ME!"

The cart full of dead bodies came to a stop and the whole camp was focused on this lone woman, kneeling on the ground. She rocked back and forth and begged God for help. Why wasn't Lotte hitting the woman to shut her up? Why wasn't she kicking her in the stomach to stop the noise? Lotte just stood there, frozen.

And then, in a moment of startlingly swiftness, the door to the camp prison opened and an SS officer hurried out. He surveyed the Appellplatz and quick-marched over to the sobbing woman. He studied her arm, pushed Lotte aside, and unholstered his pistol. He leveled it at the prisoner's head and took aim. There was an echoing crack and, immediately, the screaming stopped. The prisoner slumped to the side as blood spurted out. She sank to the cindery ground. The SS officer used the toe of his boot to make sure she was dead. Satisfied, he replaced his pistol and snapped his fingers at the cart of the dead.

"You there. Clean this up," he shouted while walking back to the camp prison. He moved swiftly and, after he entered the stone building, he shut the door. The silence that followed felt both heavy and fragile.

Anna stared at Lotte and was almost glad this had happened. Everyone would talk about this tonight around the fireplace, she was sure of it, and the focus would no longer be on her hesitation in the sock factory. They would talk instead about this hesitation. She glanced at Binz, who was already moving towards the mess. She scowled and ordered Lotte to pick up her cap and fix her hair.

The numbers started up again.

"18340."

"*Jawoh.*"

19003."

"*Jawohl.*"

The cart moved in front of her and the nakedness of the dead embarrassed her so much that she glanced away. But in looking away, she felt shame that maybe she wasn't strong enough for Ravensbrück.

The thought made Anna lift her eyes and stare into the faces of the dead. They looked cold and rubbery. How could that prisoner eat a baguette on top of corpses like that? Savages. Savages one and all. No wonder they were here.

She turned her attention to the rows of prisoners before her. Her eyes flicked from face to face. One was needed for volunteer work in cell block 14 and she would need several prisoners to push that cart into Fürstenberg. Who to choose?

"Who?" she said aloud.

"What was that?" Ruth asked. "Who what? You still haven't told me what *Schutzhaftlagerführer* Keller asked us to do."

Anna smiled. The solution was obvious now. She thought about the ratty bracelet from yesterday—the one found in a pocket—and she realized how she could punish the prisoner that had caused her so much shame. When she left the Administration building she was originally going to pick the one with a black winkel to become the volunteer, but she had a better idea now.

"Much better," she said, moving into the prisoners.

It was the first time she had done this alone and she wasn't scared. Instead, it felt like she was floating on power. The smell of their bodies and the dirt on their faces made her nose crinkle. She eased her way down a straight column and, as she moved, she liked the worry in the eyes of the prisoners. She took out her truncheon and let it touch forearms as if she were carrying a stick and letting it brush against a wooden fence. She kept her head on a swivel. The two prisoners had to be here somewhere.

"What is it?" Ruth asked, trailing behind like a kid sister.

Anna glided on the knowledge that she was in control.

Yes, she nodded, she wouldn't bring the prisoner that had *received* the bracelet to cell block 14—she would take the *giver* of the bracelet to prison. Make the French girl the volunteer. That would cause 18311, the one who had filled her up with shame, all the more pain. She'd be able to punish that prisoner far more by hurting the French girl. And if she made 18311 push the wooden cart into Fürstenberg, she could make her life more miserable. If she did this, it would make for a good story around the fireplace.

Instead of looking for a familiar face—they all looked the same with their short hair and dirty cheeks—she scanned the winkels for an F. After strutting briskly down one column and orbiting back up another, she grunted in frustration. There were too many of them. She cupped her hands around her mouth and shouted.

"Raise your hand if you're French!" She hurried to the front and yelled again. "Raise your hand if you're French!"

Thirty hands lifted and she knew there had to be more. "*Français!* Hand up if you're *Français!*"

The hands doubled and she began to half-run through the prisoners searching their faces. Ruth panted behind like an obedient puppy. Binz watched them with curiosity.

And then, towards the back, she saw the little bracelet giver. Even with bruises and a wide cut across her eyebrow, she was pretty. Anna marched up and slapped her across the face. The pretty French girl recoiled, and when she righted herself, Anna slapped her again. Rosy patches bloomed on the prisoner's cheeks. Anna realized in that moment, in a way that she hadn't quite before, that she could do anything she wished to the body standing in front of her. She took out her truncheon. Could she break the girl's arm?

Anna stared into the girl's terrified blue eyes. No doubt she once floated into coffeehouses and knew that men watched her. Her beauty would have been a hypnotizing power. But no longer.

"Our Little Nurse…" Ruth said in a mixture of admiration and surprise. "Can you please tell me the plan?"

Binz arrived, out of breath, and Anna could smell her perfume. Lilies and lemon. *Oberaufseherin* Binz said nothing at first. Finally, she cleared her throat and asked, "What's going on, girls?"

Anna didn't turn around. She kept staring at the French girl. Anna liked the mystery of it all because no one knew what she might do next—not the girl, not Ruth, not Binz.

A voice from a nearby prisoner came to her. "Madam Overseer? This French girl can't speak German very well. I can take her place for a job, if you like."

Anna turned and sized up the prisoner that dared to speak. It was—Anna smiled at the ease of it all—it was the receiver of the bracelet, the one who had stuffed it into her mouth in an effort to hide it. 18311.

"Did I speak to you?" she asked, looking at the prisoner's number. "I don't remember asking you a question." She tightened her knuckles around her truncheon.

"No, Madam Overseer," the trinket said, coming to attention. She took off her cap and added, "I was hoping to help."

It seemed like the whole camp was leaning in to see what would happen next. Anna felt like she was on stage and she let seconds tick by knowing that she was the center of attention. Clouds rolled overhead and a bursting breeze made the lime trees on the parade ground shake. Leaves skittered over the sodden ground. Anna stared at the creature before her and considered that if she waited much longer it might appear like she had frozen up like Lotte. Suddenly, she wheeled her truncheon overhead and brought it down hard on 18311's head. The prisoner dropped.

And then, very calmly, Anna stated, "Don't speak."

The prisoner stumbled to her feet and winced.

Anna used her truncheon as a pointer. "You," she said to the French girl. "Come with me."

"What's going on?" Binz finally asked.

Anna half-turned and explained, "I have orders." She heard Keller's voice in her head. *Choose a few prisoners for your errand.* She knew the French girl was going to the Bunker for volunteer work, but she didn't know what was written in the note. She wasn't sure if she was allowed to read the note or if she was expected to simply deliver it to the address written onto it.

"What orders?" Binz asked.

"I'm on special assignment," Anna explained. "*Schutzhaftlagerführer* Keller ordered me."

The note in her dress pocket seemed to burn now. It was given to her in private and surely that meant Binz and Ruth shouldn't know about it. *You're doing this errand by yourself. Understand?* That's what he had said. He trusted her and that trust made her feel special. She decided in that moment that whatever was in the note, it wasn't for her. The secret words were for whoever lived at the address.

"What kind of special assignment?" Binz asked.

"Yes," Ruth said with false chirpiness in her voice. "What are we doing?"

"I'm not patrolling the sock factory today," Anna said, making eye contact with her superior. "Keller asked me to do something for him. I am to do it alone."

Binz scrunched up her eyebrows and her mouth became a thin slash. "Oh."

Anna pointed at 18311 and spoke to Ruth. "Take this one to the main gate. Take that one with you as well...and that one," she said pointing to prisoners as if picking cuts of beef. "I'll meet you at the main gate in ten minutes. I have to deal with this one first."

She turned to the French girl, who was quaking with fear.

"Move," she said, jabbing the girl in the ribs. As she nudged her towards the Bunker, they marched between rows of prisoners, and when they were at the front of the roll call square they walked past the cart of dead bodies. Anna watched a team of thin and ragged prisoners lift the woman with a broken arm—they tossed her remains into the back. A hole the size of a pfennig was in her skull. Her eyes were open. An oily line of blood traced down the side of her face.

Anna focused on the ground. Her boots crunched over cinder and sticks. She considered how the sun was beginning to warm the world. The clouds were clearing.

When they reached the prison door, she opened it, and prodded the French girl into the darkness.

CHAPTER TEN

The Beautiful Town by the Lake

She burned to run. Her whole body tingled for her to *do* something for Julienne, to run, to move, to shout, but there was nothing she could do. It was like sinking into quicksand. Before Ravensbrück, she had frequent nightmares of men in black coats coming for her, and no matter how hard she tried to run she just couldn't move her feet. She, a dancer, couldn't make her legs take a few simple steps. She was frozen. Paralyzed. And as these men in black leather coats got closer, she watched her arms slowly paddle the air. They came closer and she could do nothing. She couldn't even scream.

That helpless feeling was with her now. Julienne was in the Bunker and there was no way to reach her. Svea knew all too well that women who were pulled into its shadow were rarely seen again. There were rumors of torture and beatings. Hangings. Firing squads.

She plodded behind the wooden cart and examined the chains on her wrists. Her skin was already rubbed raw and it was only a matter of time before blood would appear. With that came the worry of infection. Zofia and Lorelei were chained to the wooden cart with her. It was the size of a large dining room table and, thank goodness, it didn't weigh much. It certainly wasn't like the concrete roller. The three of them pushed the cart down a clean street lined with homes. Old oak trees lifted up and met in a canopy overhead. Sunlight dappled down and, every now and then, she heard the chittering of squirrels. A few cars were parked next to homes but, mostly, the street was quiet. Since gasoline was needed for the war, people walked or biked. A boy peddled past them making vrooming sounds like he was on a motorcycle. An older woman tending a flower garden stood up and stretched—she massaged her lower back. Svea wondered how often these people saw prisoners. Was it common to see women in striped dresses chained to a cart?

They were heading into Fürstenberg on some kind of errand, and it struck Svea that the last time she had walked down this road was when she was traveling in the other direction: towards the camp. Back then she had arrived by train and they were forced to march in two columns. And now she was in rags and heading the other way. How strange. Ever since that first day in Ravensbrück, she had dreamed of leaving and walking back to Fürstenberg. And now—oh irony—now that she was actually outside of the camp, she was frantic to get back inside. She wanted to run into the Bunker and throw open the doors.

The town was beautiful, she had to admit that. It was on Lake Schwedt and the homes were like something in a medieval painting. Flower boxes were on windowsills, wind chimes were next to front doors, and nearly every home had a swastika flag. They passed one house where a girl was doing cartwheels in the front yard and laughing. She rolled like an X in motion, over and over. One of the front windows popped opened and a woman appeared. She yelled at her daughter not to do cartwheels in her skirt. Svea noticed a fat man on the other side of the road, watching.

"Faster," the Aufseherin said without anger and without raising her voice. It was the way someone might command a horse.

Svea turned from the fat man and looked at the Aufseherin. Her last name was Hartmann. Svea had heard *Oberaufseherin* Binz call her that. A few minutes later, in a moment when they didn't think the prisoners were listening, someone else called her Anna. Such a pretty name for such an ugly soul.

"Faster."

As they picked up the pace, their wooden clogs clattered faster. Just like horses, Svea thought.

They came to a bend in the road and the handsome homes gave way to shops. The camp couldn't be more than a kilometer away, Svea thought, and when she looked over her shoulder she could see the crematorium. Oily black smoke lifted up like an exclamation point.

"I don't want any funny business," the guard said. "I expect you to say nothing when we get there." She pointed a finger at Zofia and said, "I'm making you the Blockova of this outing. If anything happens, if any of you try to escape, I will punish you—" she jabbed a finger into Zofia's shoulder "—I will make *you* pay. Understand?"

"Yes, Madam Overseer."

There was a nod of satisfaction. "Good."

Svea looked down and continued pushing the cart. She watched the wooden wheels, banded in rusting steel, roll over cobblestones. There was dried horseshit and leaves. She glanced back at the lake and saw a beach. The water was speckled with sunlight and, in the distance, the camp chimney spewed up the burnt exhaust of bodies.

They passed a white sign that was surrounded with marigolds and lilies.

𝔚illkommen in 𝔉ürstenberg
— 𝔍uden sind hier unerwünscht —

Svea glanced down at her hairy legs, her soiled clogs, and the swish of her fraying dress. *Jews are not welcome here.* She moved down the road and thought about her grandmother, and this in turn made her remember that she was a quarter Jewish. But which part of her body wasn't welcome in Fürstenberg? Her leg perhaps? Her right arm maybe? Svea let the idea amuse her for a moment until a more chilling thought took its place. When was the last time a Jew was in Fürstenberg? 1935? 1938? By now, they had probably all been driven out.

A train whistle pierced the air.

"March in unison!" Hartmann shouted. She kicked Lorelei in the shin. "Be orderly. Don't slouch."

This was done for the benefit of the people around them, Svea thought. Hartmann wanted to look good, look tough. She wanted to show the civilians that everything was under control.

No one paid any attention. Men walked by with newspapers tucked beneath their arms. A boy kicked a football against a brick wall. Women walked on high heels, their hair perfectly curled, and many of them had a smile of pearls around their necks. It made Svea feel dirty. The lice in the stitching of her clothes, her unwashed parts, the fuzziness of her teeth. She hadn't seen a toothbrush for years. And no doubt schmutz was on her face and her eyebrows needed tweezering. The luxury of taking care of your own body, she thought with a groan of envy—none of these people knew how lucky they were to bathe.

As they continued up the cobbled street, she looked out across the lake. Someone was in a rowboat, fishing. And beyond them, on the other shore, was the chimney. She heard the crack of a pistol being fired, and there were two more shots in quick succession. None of the people around her stopped to look at the camp on the other side of the water. There was a smell, too. How could they pretend it wasn't there? It was the sour stench of burnt flesh and bone. And yet, the people in this beautiful town carried on as if death wasn't hanging in their streets. How could they pretend that Ravensbrück didn't exist, just there, across the lake?

They passed a jewelry shop that had a large window with silver necklaces on display. Rings were lined up on velvet and several women stood there, pointing. Svea thought of the bracelet. That's what started this whole thing. A gift. A simple gift. And because of that, Julienne was now—

She couldn't let herself sink under the weight of such thoughts, at least not yet. When she was back in camp maybe there would be more news. For now, it was better to lock her worry in an iron box and not open it until she got back. To distract herself, Svea looked at the tidy streets and flowered baskets of Fürstenberg. In another time, she might have strolled around this touristy town and admired its little shops and delights—it would have been a wonderful daytrip from Berlin. With the war on, though, there couldn't be many tourists. Who has money to buy jewelry? How can these people have such chic clothes when all of Germany was rationing? And then it hit her. The camp. The shops benefitted from having Ravensbrück in their backyard. The butchers, the green grocers, the bakers, the fruit vendors. They all sold to the camp. Everyone around her was getting fat and rich off Ravensbrück. She was called a useless eater but, really, who was the bloodsucker, who was the parasite? Hatred flared in her eyes.

"Halt!" the Aufseherin yelled.

They stopped in front of a delicatessen. A large black and gold sign was over the door. HIMMEL MARKT. There was a large bay window and, almost like a framed piece of artwork, Svea could see all types of meats and cheeses and grapes and bottles of champagne. There were salami as large as her forearm and bottles of whiskey and huge wheels of smoked gouda on a bed of mint. Slabs of bacon had been organized to make a swastika. She stared at the food and blinked. It was like being in a dream. There was so much food and it was right there, right in front of her. As customers went in and out, a little brass bell ting-tinged. She focused on a pot of raspberry jam. And there was a tub of Bavarian honey. Baskets of apples. There was even a bowl full of oranges. She took a step forward like a sleepwalker. The chains woke her up, and she looked down at her bloodied wrists.

The Aufseherin, who might be the same age as she was, knocked on the glass and motioned for someone to come out. A fat man in an apron opened the door. The little brass bell jingled. He had mutton chops and wore a wool hat with a dingus feather on the side. As he wiped his hands, the young woman in a field grey uniform offered a salute. "Heil Hitler."

He returned the salute, sloppily. "You must be the new girl," he said.

The Aufseherin, Hartmann, reached into her pocket and pulled out a folded note. She passed it over. The fat man opened it slowly and nodded knowingly. "Ah yes, no problem," he said. "Payment is the usual?"

"I'm…I'm not sure."

"But of course, this is your first time," he laughed, and then touched her arm with a friendly twinkle in his eye. "*Schutzhaftlagerführer* Keller will send you back later today with a check. Do you know how to ride a bicycle?"

Hartmann raised an eyebrow at the question.

"The last girl, Irma, she biked here with the check."

"I don't know how to ride."

"A long walk for you then," he chuckled. "Let me get these things ready for you."

As the fat man in an apron opened the door—ting-tinging the bell—Svea looked around. It was surreal to be outside of the camp and it almost felt like Ravensbrück hadn't happened. She went to touch her hair—she often used to curl a strand around her forefinger absent-mindedly—but when she did it this time there was no hair to curl because it had all been cut. How strange, she considered, that an old habit came back now that she was out in public again.

Svea thought about her long curls and how she let them fly when she was dancing. She knew that men watched her. The bop of her hair, the shimmy of her hips, the twirls and side thrust of her hips. Before she became prisoner number 18311 she was used to walking around Berlin and having to be careful about making eye contact with men. Once, on a tram, she smiled at a man and he got off when she did and followed her for blocks. She couldn't be too friendly because men would assume certain things. When she grew into her adult body, she was careful about who she hugged, and where she walked, and if she needed to pick something off the ground she made sure to squat down so that it didn't look like she was showing off her rear end. She was self-conscious about eating ice cream cones in public. *And now?* Svea asked herself.

She looked at her reflection in the delicatessen window and started to laugh.

Hartmann spun around. "What are you doing?"

"I'm sorry," Svea said, pretending to cough.

The fat man came out with a box of tinned herring and he had two salami stuck under each arm. Hartmann pointed to the back of the wooden cart, and he loaded them in.

And now? Svea asked herself again. She brushed dirt from her dress and already knew the answer.

Her eyes fell on a poster of Hitler. He stood with crossed arms and looked off into the distance as if seeing a clear path to the future. It made her look around. What if she escaped? After all, if she got some new clothes and maybe some money she could catch a train. She looked around and tried to find laundry drying outside of a home or maybe a shop that sold dresses. If she could just get out of her uniform and steal something. She stared into this tantalizing future and wondered how she could make it happen. She would need to break the shackles first. She'd also need identification papers, but maybe she could get them on the black market? Oh, the food she would eat. And a real bed to sleep in. And a door that locked.

She sighed.

All of Germany was a concentration camp. She knew this, and it would be almost impossible to stay hidden. Worst of all, running away meant abandoning Julienne. She studied Hitler again and felt a sinking feeling in her stomach.

The fat man came out with a huge wicker basket of grapes. A young boy with blonde hair followed and placed a wheel of cheese into the cart. It was Gruyère. Julienne had said it was her favorite, so gooey and melty. One night, while they pretended to cook, she had mentioned the creaminess of this cheese and that she was making fondue. She stirred the air. They pretended to dip thick pieces of crusty bread into the pot and they ate air until they fell asleep.

"Madam Overseer," Svea said without thinking.

Hartmann glared. *What?* She asked without saying the word.

"I was…I was wondering if…could you tell me what's happened to my friend?" It seemed impossible that the words had stumbled from her lips, but it was too late now. She felt forced to add, "The French girl."

Anna turned and couldn't quite believe that this thing, this subhuman, was speaking to her. "If you ask me again, I will break your arm."

She stared at 18311 and placed her hand on her truncheon. It made her happy to see the rag worry. Good, Anna thought. For a moment she considered telling the prisoner what happened to her friend. Cell number 14 in the Bunker. A man in a doctor's white gown. His clipboard and a stethoscope. How he beckoned the prisoner to sit on the bed. Anna furrowed her eyebrows when she saw all of this in the Bunker. A comfy bed? What kind of volunteer work was this?

She looked at 18311 and enjoyed the power of knowing something that the prisoner did not. Anna thought about saying that her friend was receiving special treatment, but silence seemed like a better weapon. She said nothing, and turned away from 18311.

The fat man in a butcher's apron came out with a box of apples and placed them in the cart. He studied the pile for a moment. His finger moved over them and he plucked one out. He bent at the waist and offered it to Anna with a flourish. "For you, Fraulein," he smiled.

She took it and admired its redness, its plump. It had been a long time since she had bitten into an apple. A very long time. Everything was rationed. She polished it against her grey jacket and then, raising it to her lips, she crunched into it. She knew the prisoners were staring at her, watching with envy. She had been at the bottom of society her whole life and now she was at the top. "Delicious," she said with a full mouth. "So juicy. Thank you," she said covering her mouth.

The fat man stood with his fists on his hips. "There's quite a bit more," he said happily. He nodded to the prisoners and raised an eyebrow. "Perhaps one of them could help?"

Anna was surprised she hadn't thought of this earlier and immediately started nodding. "Yes, yes, of course," she said, pulling out a key. She went over to the Polish prisoner with large breasts and placed the apple on a wheel of cheese. She undid the iron handcuffs. "Do anything funny and I'll whip you until you pass out," she whispered. But even as the words came out, Anna wondered if she could do such a thing. Kicking and hitting were one thing, but to whip? That was more deliberate, more slow. The idea of hearing a shriek of pain with each flick of the leather whip made her queasy.

"This way," the man in a white apron said, snapping his fingers at the Polish prisoner.

Anna stood back and watched more wicker baskets come out. There were fat slices of bacon, a block of aged cheddar, a wheel of Jarlsburg, bottles of heavy cream, cornichons, knackwurst, blood sausage, three boxes of chocolate, a case of Dom Perignon, and a package of smoked tongue. As the delicacies kept coming, Anna felt her stomach grumble. Even before the war, she had never seen so much elegance. In shops, yes, of course, but nothing like this. If she took something, who would notice?

Anna bit into the apple again and watched the last of the boxes get snugged into the cart. Why hadn't she been given a truck for this? Why make the prisoners come into town? She shrugged at the thought and considered that maybe it was about rationing gasoline. After all, it was more precious than gold.

The fat man walked over and handed her a piece of paper. "For *Schutzhaftlagerführer* Keller," he said. "I'm Johann," he added, leaning in. "It was a pleasure meeting you Fraulein...? Fraulein...?"

"Hartmann," she smiled. "Maybe I'll see you again."

"Maybe for the next party, yes." He offered a little bow and walked back into his deli.

Anna handcuffed the Polish prisoner once again to the cart and stepped back. "Right, now move!" she shouted, and the cart began to roll.

She strolled behind them, crunching and munching the apple. It was a beautiful day, she thought looking at the grey lake, which was greased with sunlight. Trees murmured overhead in the wind. She finished the apple and dropped it into a nearby garbage bin. There was a soft clang as the core hit the empty bottom. She walked behind the cart and didn't mind how slowly the prisoners were going. It was nice. Pleasant. She thought of that quote by Goethe. "Nothing is worth more than this day." Indeed not, she thought. It was glorious to be alive.

She glanced at the town. Flower boxes were beneath clean windows and the hedges were neatly trimmed. The flag of her nation rippled gently in the breeze. Yes, it was a beautiful time to be alive and German.

CHAPTER ELEVEN

Teaching in Whispers

Svea looked out at the camp and studied the shadows. If you stared long enough, it was easy to convince yourself they were moving. Was that a guard pacing the ground or a trick of the eye?

She squinted and watched moths jitter in the lights. The barracks didn't have electricity but on nights with a full moon, and with the searchlights pointed just right, it often meant that panes of buttery light were cast onto the floor. And when this happened, it was possible to read. Svea was the lookout for any Aufseherin that might be patrolling, and if she saw a black form coming close to their door, she was supposed to cough five times. This would give Hannah enough time to hide her supplies and scramble into bed. Education in a fascist state was an act of rebellion and it nourished the hope that maybe, perhaps, against all odds, they might one day have a life beyond the barbed wire. Each week in her barrack, there were underground classes in Polish, chemistry, French, mathematics, English, ancient history, and German. Depending upon who had the right expertise, they took turns teaching. It was her friend Hannah who taught the most classes because she was a walking encyclopedia and she had also been a teacher back in "normal times," as she called it. She taught in a Gymnasium outside of Rostock, and when she refused to join the Party, she was arrested. The Reich couldn't have women teaching the next generation if they didn't fully embrace National Socialism. That was the official reason she was arrested, but her husband had wanted a divorce for a long time and she kept saying no. After he reported her, she was imprisoned. Svea wanted to ask if she regretted marrying her husband but she knew it was a ridiculous question. Who can change the past?

Svea turned from the window and watched Hannah's shadowy face hold up a map of Europe. She had been saving copies of *Volkischer Beobachter* that she had stolen from around camp. It was a Party newspaper and they had illustrations of how the war was going in Russia and North Africa. Sometimes they printed maps of the bombing raids on England. She took these illustrations, these drawings, and glued them together to make a jumbled map of Europe. There were missing bits—Greece wasn't there and neither was the Iberian peninsula—but she drew these empty bits in herself. She held up the map and taught in whispers. Svea turned to listen.

"Where is Romania? Come here and point."

There was a creaking on the wooden floor.

"Good. And where is Latvia?"

A shuffling, another creak, and a soft tap of a finger against paper.

"How about Albania?"

After several minutes, she rolled away the map and put it away.

"What is the capital of Norway?"

"Oslo."

"Czechoslovakia?"

"Prague."

"What's the capital of…let me see…Denmark?"

"Copenhagen."

Hannah asked these questions as if the countries were still independent and free, as if they were not under Nazi rule. It made Svea smile to think of Paris being free.

"What is the capital of Hungary?"

"I know, I know. Budapest."

"How about…Malta?"

"Valletta?"

Svea turned her attention back to the window and was content with the quiet night. None of the shadows were moving and, very happily, she hadn't seen a guard patrolling the square for over thirty minutes. There was little need for them to do so because the walls were so high and the main gate was so well fortified.

As she half-listened to the lesson she thought about how learning kept them all going. To give, that's what made life worth living. This afternoon, when she was forced to push the cart, it would have been so easy for any one of the citizens in town to offer up a crust of bread. But no, she had to push the cart—in shackles—

and stare at all of that food. It lay before her, taunting her, and she couldn't have any of it. She focused on a loose grape and willed it to roll towards her so that she might grab it and stuff it into her mouth before Hartmann could see.

The worst part about going to town wasn't what was done to her body. No, the worst part of the errand happened on the way back when she saw a woman pushing a mustard gold pram. The child was wrapped in white and the mother was cooing and giggling as she walked along. When Svea saw this, a stab of grief made her sob. She almost broke down completely and no longer cared if Hartmann beat her with a truncheon or kicked her in the stomach. She thought back to that horrible night when she was in the bathtub and there was so much blood and Peter knocked on the door to ask if she was okay. The cramping that night made her lean into her knees and yowl in pain. Their child. Gone. There was so much blood and she could see her daughter's closed eyes. She wasn't breathing and Svea screamed to Peter for help. The miscarriage happened so fast—there was a rush of pain and blood. It wasn't supposed to be like that. She was supposed to give birth in a clean hospital and bring their little girl home in a pram. But instead, they lost their first born and Peter was arrested two weeks later. He just vanished into the night. She never heard from again. Where was he? Was he even alive?

She thought of how he knocked on the door and how the Gestapo knocked on the door when they wanted him and now Julienne... Julienne was where, exactly? Behind a locked door. That's what the Third Reich was all about. Doors and secrets.

"How many *arrondissements* does Paris have?" Hannah asked into the moonlight.

"Twenty," came a whisper.

"Which is the most famous?"

"The eighth. Champs-Elysees."

Another voiced added, "Oh my goodness, think of the clean clothes you could buy. And the food."

"A follow up question." There was a pause before Hannah raised her voice to nearly full speech. "After the war, what city do you want to see?"

Names spilled into the dark.

"Rome."

"Barcelona."

"Vienna."

"London."

"Sarajevo."

"New York!"

The last city was said a bit too loudly, and everyone went silent. They froze in place and listened. Wind tapped against the windows. A rat scuttled under a triple-layer bunk. Hannah cleared her throat. She usually closed these whispered lessons with a saying—it must have been a line she used in Rostock before everything changed. "Remember," she said. "You can have everything you want, but you won't get it all at the same time."

After that there was the soft padding of bare feet on the floor, there was some murmured talk, and then there was the creaking of wooden bunks as exhausted bodies wriggled into each other. Svea stayed at the window and let her eyes linger on the dark shape of the Bunker. Julienne was in there, somewhere. Svea felt her throat tighten and her mind churned on the possibilities of what might be happening to Julienne. Was she being lashed with a whip that had been made from ox hide? There were rumors that such a thing existed. It was said that the leather was heavy, and durable, and cutting. Or was she chained to a wall? Was she being tortured with electricity? Or maybe she had already been turned into smoke?

Svea's eyes moved to the crematorium chimney, which was smearing black smoke across the moon. It was a demonic steam engine—dark clouds lifted up—all those bodies, she thought. All those loved ones. All those stories. Gone. Just like her baby girl.

Her eyes went back to the wooden door of the Bunker. The horrible cycle of possibilities began to flicker in the cinema house of her imagination once again: ox hide, chains, car battery, electrodes, cigarettes on skin, the exhale of human ash and smoke.

The thought of climbing into her bunk and not having Julienne next to her made her stand up. Her body demanded movement, for her to *do* something, so she paced the barrack. Their friendship—was that the right word?—had made life in the camp about something bigger than suffering. She had a reason to get out of bed every morning and take air into her lungs. Svea looked out the window for several long minutes.

She eventually walked over to Zofia, who was sitting on a stool near a drafty window. A milky sheet of moonlight spilled onto a notebook. The woman from Poland was writing down some numbers. She didn't look up.

"The answer is no," she said before Svea could open her mouth.

"But you don't know what I'm going to ask."

"I do," Zofia said, nodding towards the Bunker. "You are wanting information on that place."

Svea looked up at the rafters and closed her eyes. Everyone knew Zofia was like a telephone exchange when it came to camp gossip, and she really wanted to know what was happening—or what had already happened—to her friend.

"You must know something."

At this, Zofia looked up. Her stare was hard and yet, after a moment, it softened. "Make yourself useful. Read my dress."

Svea began to feel the seams of Zofia's dress for lice. When she found one, she tweezered it between her thumbnails. "What do you know?"

Zofia went back to writing, and after a long moment she shrugged a shoulder. "Your friend, she is solitary confinement. A doctor has visited her. I do not know how many times. That is all I know."

"A doctor? But why? She's not sick."

Zofia turned and for a moment it seemed like she was going to say something, but she changed her mind.

"Is she okay?" Svea asked. "They're not torturing her? Is she coming back? Can we get her out?" These were stupid questions, she knew this, but she had to ask. She needed to be calmed and she needed to talk about it. "Is she okay?" she whispered. "Tell me."

Zofia flapped her hand as if the words were a buzzing fly. "Stop."

Svea continued reading the seams of Zofia's dress. Her nails were wet with the guts of parasites. She wiped her fingers on her dress and kept going. Some of the women in the barrack were snoring.

"I am sorry for your friend," Zofia finally said, closing her notebook. She slid it between the wall and the bunk. "She is not our priority."

"But—"

"Shh! Enough, German woman."

Svea kept popping lice until, at last, Zofia turned around and motioned that they should switch places. Svea sat on the stool and looked out the window as she felt strong fingers move over her dress. There was popping and snapping. There was also quiet until Svea could hear a low rumbling, like thunder, on the horizon. It grew until she realized it was British airplanes flying towards Berlin. She saw faint scratches against the night sky. Vapor trails. They looked like icy claw marks dragging towards the capital. The engines of hundreds of bombers grumbled louder and louder. An air raid siren wailed from Fürstenberg. Svea knew the sleeping explosives in the bellies of those planes weren't for the village. No, they were moving for the factories and railyards and munition depots of Berlin. At the right moment, the bomb doors would crank open and those iron messengers of death would tumble down, down, down.

When quiet returned to camp, and when the air raid siren of Fürstenberg drifted back to sleep, Zofia patted Svea's head to say that she was done. She bent down to whisper in her ear. When she spoke, her breath was warm.

"I hear some news today. Worse things will soon happen to the entire camp. I have more to be thinking about than your friend."

"Worse things?"

"The next twenty-four hours will teach us much," Zofia said, her voice sliding into a whisper. "Now, sleep. If you want to be seeing your friend again, you must sleep. Save your energy."

Svea felt like she was dissolving into darkness. Worse things? Her heart began to beat faster and she wanted to ask more questions.

Zofia held up a finger in warning. "Eat your bread tomorrow. Do not save it for later. Eat your bread if we get some."

CHAPTER TWELVE
Wait and See

The sky was salmon pink and fluffed with white. The sun rose through a tufting of oaks and mourning doves called from the edge of camp. A train clattered on the horizon and, from a nearby window, Beethoven's Ninth Symphony butterflied through the air.

Anna stood at attention and kept her fingertips against her dress like she had been trained to do. Announcements were being read and although she tried to focus, her mind wandered to the expectations of the day. There would be time in the sock factory, a break for lunch, and then evening roll call. There was talk of the northern lights coming out before midnight and everyone wondered if this would keep the enemy from bombing Berlin. Maybe the electromagnetic currents would interfere with their radios?

Anna stood with her knees together and she thrust out her chest. Her belly was full of scrambled eggs and bacon. There had been raspberry jam and croissants, too. She ate it all and felt lucky to have such things when people in Berlin, Hamburg, Kiel, and Stuttgart were having their homes blasted into rubble. She closed her eyes and smelled Lotte's perfume—a new scent—one she hadn't encountered before—and she took a deep breath. It was a citrusy pepper. Spicy, but captivating.

Binz had them standing at attention in front of their villas and not near the motor pool where they usually gathered. They stood amid a cluster of trees and, around them, were the mountain chalets they called home. Everything was neat and tidy. There were no weeds, and debris from the storm had been satisfyingly gathered by a team of Availables and carted away. The windows were wide open and prisoners were polishing the glass.

Ruth cleared her throat and this made Anna glance over to see her, Hilda, and Erna. They had spent last night with bottles of wine. No one called her "Little Nurse" anymore. Not since she had been given special orders. There was admiration in their voices now, and when she spoke they leaned forward in their chairs.

"Can I join you next time?" Ruth had asked. "The shops in town are lovely."

Anna said nothing as she jiggled an empty wine glass and motioned that it needed to be topped up. Merlot was splashed in and she sat back, her bare feet tucked beneath her, and she took a long sip. She let it roll down her throat. "Delicious," she said, reaching for an apple tart. The fire spat as they asked about all of the food in the cart.

"What's it for?" Lotte had asked.

Anna smiled as if to say that she was keeping a secret, as if to say that she had been sworn to silence. But the truth was that she didn't know why she had been ordered to get the delicacies. Nor did she know who they were for. The mystery of not telling the truth was a way to stay in control, she thought, tipping back more wine and holding out her crystal glass for more.

"Hartmann!"

Anna blinked and realized that Binz had been calling her. "Yes, Madam?"

"Pay attention. This isn't a spa."

Anna offered up a salute because she wasn't sure what else to do. "Begging your pardon, *Oberaufseherin*."

"Well...off you go."

Anna looked around and felt a chill nibble up her spine. Where had she been asked to go? She searched the faces of the other women and hoped they might dart their eyes in the right direction.

Binz let out a frustrated groan and pointed at the Administration building. "He wants to see you again. Move."

With a skip, she scurried through the ordered rows of her peers. She placed a hand on her truncheon and jogged—the oak weapon at her side bounced up and down. With her left hand, she covered her breasts to keep them in place. When she was near the wide oval drive that stood before the Administration building she slowed to a quick-paced walk. The windows were open and a coal black Mercedes was waiting outside—its engine purred against the dawn.

Who was the *he* that Binz was referring to? It had to be Keller. Who else could it be? She didn't know any other *he* in the building so, as she took the steps quickly, and as she glided through the heavy wooden double-doors, she told herself she would go to his office first. If there was a mistake, she would set it right from there.

She moved through the foyer and passed by the large swastika that had an eagle perched atop it. She nearly bumped into the prisoner she saw yesterday—the pretty one with a spotless uniform and lush dark chocolate hair. She carried a large china plate full of cherry scones and she was so clean that she hardly looked like a rag at all. When this prisoner, this thing, didn't stop to acknowledge her, anger flared in Anna's chest. How dare she walk by as if she were an equal. Anna thought about kicking her in the ass—just to assert the natural order of things—but the thought of the plate shattering made her pause. No, this prisoner was protected, she reminded herself. The rag was both a thing, and not a thing. Best to let her go.

Anna placed a hand on the balustrade and climbed the stairs slowly so that she wouldn't be out of breath when she got to his office. At the landing, she paused before a large mirror and fixed her hair. She adjusted her collar and made sure her lipstick hadn't smudged. "There," she whispered. "Yes."

She climbed the remaining stairs and listened to typewriters clack. There was the occasional ding and slap of a roller being set back into place. Ceiling fans moved air through the hallway and a potted plant quivered in the breeze. She stood before his door and leaned in to listen. *SS-Schutzhaftlagerführer Keller* was stenciled on the frosted glass. She held up a knuckle and, just as she was about to rap the milky pane, a voice came from within.

"*Entrez s'il vous plaît.*"

She wasn't sure if that meant she should enter or not. Was it French?

"Come in," the voice said.

The door was heavier than she remembered and she had to push her hip against it. One of her bootlaces was untied and she wished that she had seen it earlier. It was too late now to bend down and fix it. She took a few cautious steps towards his desk and came to attention.

"Heil Hitler."

He held up a finger. He was on the phone. She hadn't noticed this—or heard him speaking—and she wondered if she should back away. She looked over her shoulder and thought about retreating into the hallway but he snapped his fingers. He cupped the phone and whispered, "Only a minute, my dear. Stay."

Keller lowered his gaze and grunted approval to whoever was on the phone. He took in a quick drag of smoke. "Yes, yes, of course—" There was a long pause. "I understand that but look, we need more coal if we're going to process everything in the next twenty-four hours. That's why I'm asking for an additional shipment."

The maroon drapes were still bunched neatly against the windows and the potted plants in the corner had shed a few fat leaves since yesterday. The elephant leg umbrella stand caught her attention once again and she stared at it, wondering if it was real. Where on Earth would you buy such a thing? The fanning peacock feathers were iridescent and they looked like unblinking eyes. She glanced at Keller and saw that he was looking at her chest. He continued to stare for several long seconds and, when he realized that she was watching him, he smiled and began to doodle on a notepad.

"Look, the simple truth is this: We. Need. More. Coal." He emphasized the last four words and took another drag on his cigarette. "It doesn't run itself, you know. It needs fuel."

The smoke threaded up and played in the slender arms of the silver chandelier. Although it was clearly designed to hold lightbulbs, there were none to be seen. Rationing, she reasoned.

"No, wood doesn't work. It needs to be coal."

Anna wasn't sure what to do with her hands. She cupped them behind her back, she let them dangle at her side, and she balled them up near her bellybutton. Keller rubbed his forehead and let out a slow exhale of frustration. As he looked down at his notepad, she wondered if she should tie her bootlace. She bent low and watched her fingers twist two loops into shape. She stood up, tall.

He began to play with the silver threads of his SS lapel. "I need two tons but I'll…no, hang on…I'll take what you can spare. Yes, thank you. Bring it this morning."

He dropped the phone into its cradle and stubbed out his cigarette. He seemed to have forgotten that she was there. Anna cleared her throat.

"Oh, yes," he said standing up. A wide smile appeared as he came around his ornate wooden desk. She offered a salute with a raised arm.

"Heil Hitler."

"Indeed," he said waving a hand. "Heil. It's good to be formal but it can be too much sometimes. We know who's in charge and there's no need to remind ourselves all the time." His smile stayed. "Relax, Fraulein Hartmann," he said shaking her hand.

His grip was strong. Her fingers were pressed tightly against each other and she waited for him to release her. Instead, he raised her hand up to his lips and kissed her knuckles.

"You wanted to see me?" she asked taking her hand back. She brushed specks of wetness against her dress and took a step back.

The main gate of camp clanged shut loudly and she looked over at the sudden noise. He didn't.

"Anna," he said. "May I call you Anna?"

She nodded and balled up her hands like a shop girl.

"Good. Yes, I wanted to see you." He reached for a mug of coffee and took two sips before saying, "Thank you for running that errand into Fürstenberg yesterday. It must have been a welcome break for you."

"I didn't know it was a break, sir. I was just following orders."

"We can do both sometimes, can't we? A break can sometimes also be an order. Can't it?"

"I'm not sure I follow."

He leaned against the front of his desk. "I appreciate your time, Anna. No doubt you're wondering why I needed So. Much. Food." Again, he emphasized the last few words.

A car pulled away from the front of the building. The black Mercedes, she thought. Her eyes went to the large window and she watched it round the oval drive and pass the Aufseherin, who were still standing at attention.

"What can I do for you?" she asked returning her attention to the office. "Do you have another errand?"

"What? No, no," he said, slowly moving around his desk. "I was wondering..." he seemed embarrassed by what he wanted to ask. An uncomfortable silence fogged the room.

"Yes?" she asked.

"I was wondering if...would you like to come to my villa this evening?"

Anna didn't know what to say. What did this mean? Could she go? Did she even want to go? What would Binz say? She cleared her throat and let the unasked questions in her head hang in the air.

Keller let out a bolt of laughter. "There will be many of us there, Anna. It's a party! It won't be just you and me." He chuckled and then, without dropping his gaze from her eyes, he backed up. He pointed out a window. "Do you see that villa there? The one on the left? That's mine. The party starts at seven this evening. Dress up. No uniform, you understand? You may bring a few friends, if you like. What do you say, hmm?"

"I…I'm not sure."

"I see good things ahead for you, Anna. Maybe you'd like to meet the others in charge? There are many possibilities for advancement in a camp like this and I'd like to help you. Maybe bring a friend with you who might also go far in a place like this? What do you say? Please say yes. Go on."

She imagined wearing a fine dress. She had one in her closet, along with a pair of red heels that she hadn't worn for months, and it would certainly be interesting going to an officer's party. It would be far more interesting than sitting around a fireplace and drinking wine.

"Yes," she nodded. "Why not?"

"Why not, indeed!" He clapped his hands together, once, dramatically. His bubbly smile turned serious. He returned to his desk and pushed paperwork around with his finger. "After what's going to happen this afternoon, we could all use a bit of fun tonight." A thought made him reach for a pad of paper and he scribbled a sentence. He sat in his chair and hunched over.

"What's going to happen this afternoon?" Anna asked.

He reached for a green folder and said nothing.

"What's going to happen, sir?"

He looked up and stared at her. And then, almost gently, he said, "You have much to learn about this place. Wait and see." There was a pause before he added, "Dismissed."

CHAPTER THIRTEEN

Those that Run, Live

Svea had been sitting in front of her sewing machine for so long that her lower back fizzed with pain. She ached to stand up, to stretch, to roll her hips back and forth and to get her ligaments and muscles moving, but she had to keep stitching and clipping. The needle jumped up and down as her fingers danced on the throat plate. Around her, sewing machines hummed out different rhythms and there was the smell of oily wool.

Someone else was at Julienne's sewing machine and Svea made a point to pretend this woman didn't exist. To acknowledge that a new prisoner had taken Julienne's place meant that her friend might not return. The woman had a yellow winkel with an R above it. She had piercing blue eyes and she must be funny because whenever another Russian talked with her they ended up laughing. Laughter, she shook her head. What could they find so funny? Svea shot her a stern look and resented how this Jewish woman was making herself at home on Julienne's stool.

She grabbed two finished socks and flip-scrunched them into a single ball. With a quick movement of her wrist, the pair was dropped into the wicker basket. She felt herself draining into dark thoughts and, without someone to care for, she felt like a demagnetized compass that didn't know where to point. At roll call she listened for Julienne's number in the ludicrous hope that maybe she was somewhere in the crowd, but after an hour her camp name wasn't called. She was still alive, Svea was sure of it, because she hadn't felt a shift in the universe. Surely, if her friend had been shot or injected with a lethal cocktail of poisons, surely she would have felt something. How could someone she cared about so much simply slip away?

After roll call, Svea drank her turnip soup and ate her bread just as Zofia had suggested. She came over to Svea as they marched to the sock factory and nudged her arm. "It is good you are caring for yourself."

That was hours ago. The soup had long ago leaked into her lower intestines and she needed the restroom, badly. To ask to relieve herself would mean a beating. She leaned forward and pinched her asshole tight. Maybe getting hit would be worth it? And then a more dangerous thought slithered into view. Was it even worth it to live? What if she just gave up? What if she just walked towards the fence and let the voltage take her?

Svea stood up.

It was almost liberating to move into her own destruction. At least she was in command of her own limbs, her own blood, her own tissue. She felt eyes upon her and she considered what to do next. Her bowels gurgled. Would it hurt touching the lightning bolts caged in the fence? All she needed to do was sprint out of the sock factory and reach out her arms. It would be so easy.

"Out!" an Aufseherin shouted from around the corner.

"Out, out!" came another voice. There was a crash and a cry of pain, as if someone had been thrown against a cart.

A fury of Aufseherin marched in and they began tipping over baskets of socks. A stool went flying over a sewing machine.

"OUT OUT OUT!" an Aufseherin shouted with such force that her face reddened. It was the one who forced them to sing. "Ahoy!" she shouted and everyone knew it was their cue to start singing the "*Horst Wessel Lied*," the Nazi anthem.

"Ahoy," she shouted. "Sing! You're my personal radio!"

The raging woman marched over to Svea and raised her truncheon. She motioned to hit but pulled back at the last minute and burst out laughing.

"Ahoy!" she screamed, her face crimson with rage, spittle on her lips.

The sewing machines were silent and everyone was running. The sound of wooden clogs against the concrete floor clattered and cracked.

"Sing!"

Svea jogged towards the exit and shout-sang. She felt herself bouncing inside her striped dress and cupped both of her breasts as she ran faster. The Nazi anthem lifted to the rafters as hundreds of women hurried for the wooden door.

> *Clear the streets for the brown battalions,*
> *clear the streets for the storm division.*
> *Millions look upon the swastika with hope,*
> *the day of freedom and bread is here!*

She sprinted past empty sewing machines and looms. Her feet were sweaty and she slipped a few times, nearly falling. What was happening? Was this the "worse thing" that Zofia had mentioned last night?

"Ahoy!" the voice yelled from behind.

When Svea burst through the rolling barn door of the factory entrance, she felt the sun on her face. Everyone was heading for the roll call square and she hurried along with women panting all around her.

"What's happening?"

"Where are we going?"

"Maybe it's a work detail."

Pebbles and sticks skittered around as Svea ran. She worried about twisting her ankle and this made her laugh out loud. A few minutes ago she was thinking about clutching the fence and now she was worried about rolling her ankle. She looked around, quickly, and took in all she could see. The Aufseherin were on the perimeter of the camp. The SS were there too, standing lazily with their hands in their pockets. A long table had been set up near the kitchen and several doctors in white coats stood there with clipboards. Three trucks idled with their back ends open, waiting.

"What's happening?" someone shouted in a terror.

The camp loudspeaker squawked. "Attention...attention. All prisoners report to the Appellplatz."

Svea ran until she reached the front of the camp. She slowed to a stop and formed up in an ordered row with the others. They hadn't been told to do this, but they knew it was expected. She held out both arms like wings and positioned herself evenly between the women on her right and left. Everyone was panting. Maria and Lorelei were only a few meters away and they looked at each other, shrugging their shoulders as if to say they didn't know what was about to happen. A selection maybe?

Svea swallowed once, twice, and felt the bellows of her lungs expand and shrink. She recalled a lecture from a biology class at Humboldt University. The professor was young, handsome, and had a neatly clipped beard. He pointed to a drawing of the lungs and said that we can only survive five minutes without fresh oxygen. "Imagine that," he said. "With each breath, we restart the clock. We breathe, we live. We're only immortal by a matter of minutes."

She wheezed and took in the gift of air. With each expanding of her chest, she reset the clock of her being. She glanced at the waiting trucks. Would she be here in the next thirty minutes? Cool delicious air filled her lungs. She inhaled. She exhaled. Her heart rocked inside her.

An uneasy quiet settled over the camp. A dog barked somewhere behind them. After several minutes, Binz stepped forward and surveyed the yard. The rest of the guards stood at slack attention behind her. The camp commandant, *SS-Sturmbannführer* Suhren, was near the gate smoking a cigarette. He leaned against the wall, taking in the scene. He had wide-set bulging eyes and he wasn't handsome, Svea thought. He had the body of a boxer.

Binz shouted for attention. "Listen! This is very simple. Those that run, live."

There was a crackling on the camp loudspeaker and then— softly—a flight of violins lifted into the air. Music, Svea thought. It had been months since she had heard music and, for a moment, she touched her throat in joy. It was Beethoven's Ninth. The notes rose as the women in front began to run. They formed a single line and ran around the perimeter of the camp. She watched this tide of women as she readied herself to do the same. The uniformed shapes in front of her began to fall away like a crumbling floor, and when it was her turn, she started to jog. The music lifted and swirled as she ran past the table of doctors, who were sitting down. They pointed at a slow woman and made notes. Flutes carried Svea along as she sprinted past the Bunker and looked at her reflection in a large puddle, her face was thin and she wondered how long this skeletal version of herself could keep on moving. She panted, she huffed, she gulped in air, and as she ran past the electrified fence she thought about reaching out with her right hand and letting her fingers graze the spikes. One pass, and it would be over. But she made a fist and kept on running. She worried about rolling her ankle on the cindery ground, and as she rounded the far corner of camp she jogged hard beneath lime trees thinking that, at least, Julienne wasn't here for the selection, surely that must be what this was all about. They would run until the weak dropped. Svea glanced back at the entrance of the camp and saw several older women struggle, a cluster of them were already standing near the trucks and when she saw this she knew that she must keep running if she wanted to draw breath into her lungs; she rounded another corner and felt Zofia at her side, they passed the sock factory, and the high walls, and she saw electrical poles on the other side of the camp wall; she thought of her muscles using oxygen and electricity and she felt her field of vision narrow as she passed the SS canteen and the main gate and the Commandant who was lighting a fresh cigarette, and as she lumbered past him on sore knees he sent a cloud of smoke into the air, he waved a burning match into the air and tossed it onto the ground. As she approached the table of doctors, she straightened up and ran faster, faster, she pumped her arms and held her head high. The first lap around the camp was over and she banked under the lime trees into the second lap.

While the women of Ravensbrück ran, the Aufseherin went into barracks and tossed illegal objects out the door. Books. A pillow. Extra shoes. Belts. Underwear. A loaf of bread was thrown like a javelin.

The new guard named Ruth stood near the sprinting women and yelled, "You'd like to stop and eat that, wouldn't you?"

Svea stared at the ground. Her legs were hairy and dirty and she tried to imagine herself running through the parks of Berlin. She was a girl again and her parents were waiting up ahead to buy her ice cream. She closed her eyes. Her lungs were on fire as she rounded the camp again, and as she passed the truck she glanced back at their barrack and saw a bench being thrown out. What if they found the radio? Or what if they found the map they used for teaching? Or the needle? Some of the female guards were coming towards them with riding crops.

"Faster!"

One of them—Hartmann—ran up and started whipping her legs.

"You're nothing but a stupid cow," the guard shrieked. She kicked a prisoner behind Svea and this sent her stumbling into the cinders.

Hartmann roared, "None of you matter!"

Beethoven's Ninth continued and Svea concentrated on the pounding heartbeat of drums. It sounded like she was being carried away and when she passed the sock factory she thought about running on a beach—the salt air playing with her long hair and the waves crashing against her legs instead of a whip.

"Useless eaters!" an Aufseherin yelled, lashing out with a riding crop. "You don't deserve bread!"

The SS leaned against the high walls of the camp and pointed at the show. One of them held a cup of coffee. The camp Commandant looked at his wristwatch and yawned.

Svea felt the weight of her feet and knew that she would be rounding the doctors again soon. How long could she run? She picked up the pace and told herself she could slow down at the other end of camp, but in front of the doctors she needed to sprint. Her number must not be written down. No, it cannot be written down.

The music was peaceful now—a whispering of notes—and she wished for something more energetic, something to get her blood dancing. Benny Goodman and "Sing, Sing, Sing (With a Swing)" always got her on the dance floor and, now that she passed the idling trucks full of women, she let that song play in her head. The ringing trumpets and rat-a-tatting snare, the thumping bass and trombones. Even though it felt like barbed wire was caught in her chest, she did not stop. Hartmann and the one called Ruth were whipping everyone now—striking here, striking there—they backhanded chests—they spun their riding crops and made yipping noises—they took aim at asses and faces. Svea ran towards them and closed her eyes against the future. Just run, she told herself. It will hurt less if you don't see it coming.

The sting on her forearm was a tongue of flame but she didn't yell out. She kept sprinting and she thought about that biology lesson, the one where the handsome lecturer talked about resetting the clock. If she kept on running, like a second hand lapping a clock face, she would earn the right to crawl into bed tonight.

The main gate was open and one of the trucks was driving through it with a heavy burden of women. The second truck was loaded now too—its tires weighted against the ground—and it hopped into first gear. It lurched and went through the gate. The third truck was idling, waiting, the mouth of its back gate open for souls.

The doctors were just ahead and Svea saw them eyeing her. She was breathing hard, there was a stitch in her side, and blood was leaking from her forearm. She passed beneath the camp loudspeaker as "Ode to Joy" flowered out. The SS men leaning against the wall perked up.

"Beautiful," he shouted.

A doctor turned to respond and he didn't notice Svea as she sprinted past. Blood dripped down the back of her hand, and as she ran by the kitchen and turned near the Bunker, she saw the SS singing along. One of them used his cigarette like a baton and pretended to conduct on orchestra.

> *All creatures drink of joy*
> *at nature's breasts.*
> *All the Just, all the Evil*
> *follow her trail of roses.*
> *Kisses she gave us and grapevines,*
> *a friend, proven in death.*

Svea looked back for her friends, but couldn't see anyone. Had they been taken away? Would she see Zofia and Maria again? Lorelei? Hannah? What if she was the only one left? As she passed her barrack she saw the map of Europe scrunched into a ball. The radio had been found and smashed on the ground. There would be beatings tonight. She knew this and, as she ran by the electrified fence, she wondered why she shouldn't grab it. Why not? Why not quit? Why live if her friends were taken away?

Even as this dark thought wormed through her mind, she looked at the women jogging in front of her. She stared at their shoulders, the determined run, and it felt like a steam engine pulled her on. Svea glanced back and saw a blank face breathing hard. She didn't know the woman—a green winkel from France—but the woman flashed her a look that said keep moving, keep going.

"Ode to Joy" danced around and the SS continued to sing.

> *Are you collapsing, millions?*
> *Do you sense the creator, world?*
> *Seek him above the starry canopy!*
> *Above stars must He dwell.*

As she returned to the front of camp, the last truck pulled away, the gate closed, and the music stopped. The only sound was hundreds of women, running and panting. Pebbles and stones skittered and danced.

"Attention," a voice on the loudspeaker said. "All prisoners to the Appellplatz."

Slowly, like a clock running down, the sprinting became sluggish until, at last, silence. Women clutched their knees and breathed deep.

Svea hunched over and felt her heart fluttering like a hummingbird inside her ribcage. Blood was on her arm and she looked at the wound. It wasn't deep. A bit of newspaper would make a bandage.

She did a little orbit around where she had stopped. She laughed at her good fortune. She had survived. She had survived the selection. She would live.

"Attention…all prisoners to the Appellplatz."

With leaden legs, she shuffled to her usual spot in the hopes of finding her friends.

"Faster!" Binz shouted. "Move it. We don't have all day."

The Aufseherin gathered behind her and they, too, seemed out of breath. The one called Hartmann gathered up her loose hair and tucked it beneath her cap.

Svea made a wing-span of her arms—still panting as she did so—and she looked for Zofia. Helen too. She couldn't see Lorelei or Maria. Maybe they had been taken away? Maybe they hadn't run quickly enough? And then she saw Zofia, who motioned for her to stop looking around and face the main gate.

Her legs were weak, but she was alive. She wanted to be happy but nothing like joy came to her. Her throat was dry, she felt woozy, dizzy, and she worried about fainting. More than anything, she wanted to sit down. Oh the irony, she thought. What she wouldn't give to be on her stool in the sock factory.

The Aufseherin gathered near the kitchen block and the camp gate opened once again. A column of new prisoners was brought in. They looked other-worldly. These women had normal dresses, and fine shoes, and their hats were pinned on their heads. As they were ordered to stand at attention, Svea watched them bumble into sloppy rows. A few of them looked around with detached curiosity as if this wasn't happening to them. One new prisoner had a mauve dress and a wide-brimmed cartwheel hat that drooped over half her face. She held a mug of coffee in one hand and a purse in the other. She glowed with innocence and acted like she was a tourist in this strange new place called Ravensbrück. The poor creature had no clue what waited for her in the next fifteen minutes.

What really caught Svea's attention wasn't the makeup or the dresses or their lack of bruises—it was their hair. So long and luxurious. One woman in a sundress had a thick braid that stretched all the way down her back.

"Fresh fish," someone whispered behind Svea.

"They'll cry themselves a river tonight."

Svea thought about her own entrance into camp, and the memories of that first day came in snatches. The undressing. The shaving of her pubic hair. The woman who ran into the electrified fence. The dog attack. Katya.

The new arrivals looked at the prisoners with unease. A few of them covered their mouths when they realized they were looking at their own futures. Give it a few days, a few weeks, and they too would be battered and ruined. One of the new women fainted. She crumpled to the ground and her sunny bright hat rolled away. No one went to help her.

The SS officers that had been leaning against the wall stepped forward and sized up the new arrivals. *That's* why they're here, Svea nodded in understanding. They had come for what was about to happen next.

Binz cupped her hands behind her back and turned to face the new arrivals.

"This is Ravensbrück," she finally said. "And there is only one way out of this camp."

Some of the new women looked at the main gate.

"No," Binz said, pointing in the opposite direction "The only way out is through the chimney."

Everyone looked at it and—how strange, Svea thought—the usual black smoke wasn't coming out. There was nothing. For some reason, bodies weren't being burned. And because of this, she was certain that the finely dressed women had no idea what Binz was talking about. How could they understand the coded language? What reality from their former lives could possibly prepare them for what they were seeing?

"Take off your clothes," Binz shouted.

There was laughter, and this made some of the Aufseherin step forward with their truncheons out.

"Take off your clothes," Binz yelled. "Leave them in a pile in front of you."

These women in sloppy rows, these women who didn't know how to stand at attention, these women who still held scraps of their old lives—they didn't move. One of them actually said, "No." This brought

123

two Aufseherin over who began beating her on the shoulders. When she dropped to the ground, they kicked at her chest. They aimed their boots at her face until she was unconscious. Maybe she was dead.

"Take off your clothes," Binz said again. "The world has changed for you. Take off your clothes."

Svea looked away. Her breathing had returned to normal and the sting in her forearm wasn't too bad. With a little fabric, she could make a bandage and all would be better by morning.

The loudspeaker rilled out feedback. A female voice—calm, as soft as perfume—echoed around the grounds. "Work details, return to your stations."

The women in striped uniforms fell out and dissolved towards different parts of the camp. The mat factory. The sock factory. Ditch digging. Svea hurried over to Zofia and wanted to ask about the missing from their barrack, but when she caught up to Zofia there was a lean look in her eye. She decided to tuck away the question for later. She would also ask about Julienne. Hadn't Zofia promised to help?

What happened next made all of them jump.

Svea thought something had fallen off the roof of the Administration building, but when she glanced back she heard it again—it sounded like a stick of dynamite going off. When it came again, and then a fourth time, and then a fifth time, she knew what she was happening. It was coming from near the crematorium. It was an echoing crack, followed by ten seconds of silence.

Crack.

Crack.

Crack.

She walked to the sock factory silently, they all did, and she didn't look back. The new prisoners would be naked now and they might realize what they were hearing. The smart ones might even comprehend they were literally stepping into shoes that had been filled by the life of another woman just fifteen minutes ago.

"Faster," Binz shouted.

The gunshots continued, rhythmic and terrible, and when Svea reached the entrance of the sock factory she glanced over her shoulder.

Black smoke was now threading up from the crematorium. It thickened. It plumed.

CHAPTER FIFTEEN
The Villa

It felt strange to walk down the paths of the Aufseherin village in a flowing red dress and high heels. Anna enjoyed the sound of her swishing stride and she knew her friends were watching with envy from their bedroom windows. None of them had been asked to the SS party and this made her linger in the front hallway to answer their questions and have them gush over her dress. Although she could have invited a few of them to join her, she liked the idea of keeping the event all to herself. Who knew what good things might happen?

The sky was bluish-black and the stars were just beginning to bud into light. As she passed the Aufseherin chalets, she heard music and laughter. There was a crash of plates into a sink and, to her left, laundry was drying on a line.

She walked towards the oval drive in front of the Administration building and saw an idling truck. It was large—huge wheels—and it had a canvas covered back end. The engine clicked and ticked while the driver sat behind the wheel, smoking. He was a civilian. As she got closer, she saw a huge pile of clothes in the back. They had been tossed in. Blouses, shoes, belts, A-line dresses with puffed shoulders, scarves, socks, bras, girdles, panties. She slowed and wondered, vaguely, what would happen to all of these items. Maybe they were being sent to Berlin for the homeless of the air raids? She shrugged and continued on.

When she passed the snout of the truck she heard a voice from the cab. "You make that dress look good."

She hoped he wouldn't say anything more or, worse, get out of the truck, but when it became clear she was heading for the SS villa, she felt this danger fade. Strange, she thought. When she wore her uniform she didn't worry about such things anymore, but now that she was in a long dress, the old fears came back. She touched her hair and smoothed a strand behind her left ear. It felt good to have it long again. Dusty blonde and wavy, she enjoyed how it felt on the back of her neck. Imagine having it cut off, she thought. That was the only time today she felt a pang of sympathy for the new dirty pieces. However, once they were shaved, and in their uniforms, and once they had their caps on their stubbly heads, everything was right again.

The SS villa was on a low hill that overlooked the Administration building and even though she was a hundred yards away she could already hear music. Each of the SS houses looked the same. They were mountain chalets which, she nodded with approval, kept up the beauty of the camp because they matched the Aufseherin homes. Sitting on a low hill, each one had a rock stairway leading up to it. Each one was creamy yellow and the windows had green shutters. Warm light glowed pleasantly within. The roof was ceramic tiles and a wide stone porch was outside the front door. As Anna moved closer, she saw several SS officers standing outside with glasses of wine. They smoked cigars and laughed.

She climbed the rock stairway and fought a sudden urge to turn around. What right did she have to be here? It seemed too high brow for a shopkeeper's daughter. She paused and looked back where she had come from.

"No," she told herself. The world was being rewritten and the old-fashioned ways of doing things were being tossed into a furnace. Maybe she was at the bottom growing up, but now that she was on the horizon of adulthood she could have whatever she wanted. She only needed to take it.

With this buoyant thought, she floated up the stairs and imagined herself as Kristina Söderbaum, that beautiful actress who appeared in many of the Reich's films. She had an hourglass figure, cascading golden hair, and her violet eyes were both innocent and worldly. When she entered a scene, everyone grew silent. They stared. She was a pure Aryan beauty.

When Anna reached the top, she smoothed her dress against her thighs and pretended the camp wasn't behind her. And yet, even as this pleasant thought started to nest in her head, the truck with clothes hopped into first gear—then second gear—and it complained up the road, its shocks bouncing, its headlamps feeling their way through the darkness. She smiled at the SS officers on the porch and opened the front door before they could say anything to stop her.

It was warm inside and she stood next to an open fireplace that crackled behind a metal gate. Wood that had been split with an axe was stacked neatly into a pyramid and she enjoyed the heat on her shins. She held out her hands and admired her painted fingernails.

It was cozy, she thought, looking around. The men wore their SS uniforms and she studied the silvery threads of their lapels. Many of them had the top few buttons of their jacket undone and their peaked caps with the Death's Head skull were on a hat rack—it was full, like a tree. A chair had been brought over and more caps were stacked on it. Women were in tight groups and they wore dresses and pearls. There was cheerfulness and laughter and classical music. Everyone held a cigarette or a pipe and, because of this, the windows were open. Anna found herself smiling.

The villa had a parquet floor and the windows were crowned with linen drapes that had been pinned back with silk bands. Antlers lined the walls and, beneath them, were silver beer steins from Bavaria. A framed photo of Hitler hung on a wall and, in the center of the room, was a chandelier with fine loops that supported unfrosted lightbulbs— the filaments flickered in thin bands of orange light. They looked like candles. The ceiling was beamed oak and it reminded her of something you might see in a medieval castle. A tapestry on the wall depicted a boar being hunted by a lord and, as she stepped closer, she saw that the hunter wore a tunic with a swastika.

Best of all—and it really was the best of all—there was a large oak table that had been shoved against one of the walls. It was a stage for all of the food she had gotten at Himmel Markt. There were plates of sliced salami, triangles of smoked gouda, sprigs of rosemary, cornichons and cashews and wedges of orange, open boxes of Belgian chocolates, and olives arranged in a perfect spiral. There were salvers of white sausages, knackwurst, caviar, and deviled eggs. In the middle was a pretzel tree. She wanted to reach for a plate and start eating, but when she looked around she saw that no one else held a plate of food. In fact, she reconsidered, nothing on the table had been disturbed yet—nothing had been taken—so she took a step back. Near the window was another table, and this one had bottles of whiskey, wine, apple schnapps, and five silver champagne buckets. Two bottles of Dom Perignon were uncorked. She went over and reached for a slender glass flute. The fizzing liquid sparkle-frothed as she poured it in.

"The French couldn't fight their way out of an empty room, but they know how to make champagne. You have to give them that."

She turned and saw an SS officer with a perfectly ironed uniform. His buttons were done up to the top, the silver threads of his rank insignia looked like they had been buffed, and his jodhpurs stuck out at precisely the right angle. His boots were shined. He wasn't exactly handsome—he had a long nose and only half of his mouth smiled—but there was a glow of confidence around him.

"Hans," he said, leaning forward.

"Anna," she said offering her hand. She expected him to kiss her knuckles like Keller had done, but instead he just shook her hand. He kept on shaking and allowed a full smile to fill his face.

"You look radiant," he said, releasing her. He placed his right hand over his heart and said the word again, "Radiant." He took a sip of champagne and used the crystal flute as a pointer, motioning around him. "It's good to have a party."

"Do they happen often?"

He bobbled his head at the thought. "Not lately. It's good to unwind though, especially after a difficult day like today. I understand you're new?"

She nodded and sipped at the same time.

He opened his mouth to say something but hesitated, as if he had second guessed himself. "In this ugly camp it's good to have beautiful things." He sized her up. "It is rare to see beauty in the camp system. I've been involved in this sort of thing since Dachau. Back in '33."

She didn't know what to say about this.

"Sometimes beauty *does* steal into the camps, though. Take this evening for instance. The Northern Lights are supposed to appear. Have you seen them?"

Anna shook her head. Her stomach growled and she was grateful for the loud conversation around her.

"They're enchanting," he said, taking a small step closer. "Absolutely mesmerizing. All of these ghostly colors shifting, twisting, and bending in greenish blue. I'm something of an amateur astronomer. In fact, I've got a telescope set up at the back of camp…away from the light pollution, you see."

She finished her flute of champagne and reached again for the chilled bottle of Dom Perignon. It was cold and slippery in her hand.

"The Aurora Borealis is like a gigantic moving oil painting in the sky. They're named for the Roman goddess of dawn, Aurora, and the Greek name of the north wind, Borealis. You get them when there is a disturbance in the magnetosphere, which is caused by solar winds. Ejecta from the sun, you see. Particles shooting out from our home star. They get ionized when they collide with our atmosphere and this causes them to emit fantastic shades of moving neon light. It starts with a mild glow near the horizon. Sometimes they look like patches of cloud or arcs that shimmer across the sky. Or maybe they look like rays that twist about? You should see them with me. Awe inspiring."

She filled her glass and yawned.

He took another step forward. "Did you know the Aurora Borealis make noise? It's true. They really do. It's like this crackling static that begins seventy meters above ground. It's caused by charged particles hitting the inversion layer. An amazing process. Astounding, really. Did you know it takes eight minutes for these solar particles to reach us from the sun, and when they hit our radiation belt the loss cone gets spent? In the magneto tail of the Earth, these particles sway around like they're waltzing."

She looked over his shoulder for someone she might know. Her eyes fell on a set of antlers that had been mounted to a wall and she wondered if Keller had shot the creature himself. Did he hunt in the woods surrounding Ravensbrück? Maybe he went with other powerful men from the camp? Her eyes refocused on the SS officer who stood in front of her. Was this man powerful?

"We're not the only planet in our solar system that gets Aurora Borealis. They can appear on Saturn and Jupiter. Even Venus. The goddess of love. Can you imagine what it might be like to see this phenomenon on another planet?"

Anna took a step back and touched her bare collar bone. "Forgive me, but I've forgotten your name."

"Hans."

"And what do you do, Hans? How do you know *Schutzhaftlagerführer* Keller?"

"I'm the SS liaison officer for the Siemens Camp. I keep Keller appraised of what's happening on the south end of camp."

"The Siemens Camp? I haven't been there yet."

"Nor will you. It's mostly off limits to Aufseherin. It's run by the Siemens Corporation—they build electrical components—and we let them use our prisoners. Can you believe that? They pay *us* for free labor. It's a wonderful situation because they also feed the prisoners, they house them, and they care for them." He laughed. "We do nothing but collect money."

Anna didn't know what to make of this.

"It's a totally different situation from the main camp," he explained. "The Siemens Camp is cleaner, it has better food, hardly any lice, and the work is easier. They're interested in getting electrical components made quickly and this means few beatings or selections."

"But how do they keep the prisoners in line?"

He took a sip of champagne and shrugged. "They know what the alternative is."

"So…if the prisoners don't need to be overseen, what exactly do you do there?"

He opened his arms as if admitting to a secret. "Very little. I make sure they have enough prisoners for their needs and I liaise with the Siemens Corporation on shared concerns like electrical demands and plumbing. Things that affect the main camp *and* this subcamp." He took a breath to keep talking but stopped when Keller approached them.

"Hans! Thanks for coming. I see you've met our new guard, Joanna." He smiled widely and motioned to the drinks table. "Have as much as your stomachs will hold. We've got cases of delicacies in the cellar and you never know what tomorrow will bring."

Anna thought about the failure at Stalingrad a few months ago. Maybe there would be a counterattack? There were also worries the Americans would attack Italy and push north. Their new general, Patton, seemed like an unstoppable plow.

The two men began talking about rail manifests—"Sorry," Hans said with the twinkle of an apology—and she let her mind wander. She thought of American GIs swarming into Germany. Surely that could never happen. It made her think about the gigantic failure of Stalingrad again. Hitler must have a plan. Yes, maybe he will be standing in the ruins of Moscow before Christmas? It wasn't outside the realm of possibility, she thought, draining her glass. After all, he conquered France in less than two months. Not even the Great War of 1914-1918 had accomplished that. She put her crystal flute down and reached for a Waterford tumbler. She unscrewed a bottle of Bushmills and let the amber glug-glug into her glass. She swirled it and smelled.

She imagined the frozen fields of Stalingrad. The iced-over boot prints and blood. The stiffened bodies. She swallowed and enjoyed the blazing heat as it moved down her voice box and into her stomach. A warm glow filled her.

She imagined kneeling behind a smashed brick wall and raising her rifle. Snow would melt beneath her kneecap as she squinted into the scope and took aim at a dark shape in a window. What would it be like to pull the trigger? To feel the recoil? To smell the flinty discharge and watch the figure drop?

Anna couldn't imagine herself using a machine gun, but a rifle? Yes, maybe. What would it be like to kill? Her eyebrows drew down at the thought. To take a life seemed very—she searched for the right word—it seemed very masculine. It would be so simple to kill with a gun. Just pull a trigger. It would be like turning off a light switch. It was a great responsibility, of course, to carry something like a pistol, which is why, she supposed, the Aufseherin weren't allowed firearms. Guns were for men. Everyone knew this. But what would it be like to take slow aim at a forehead and pull the trigger of a pistol? The crack, the pink spray, the body slumping, the widening pool of blood. The idea tumbled in her head like a stone being polished and she couldn't reconcile her understanding of being a woman and being violent. Was she still feminine if she hit and kicked and killed?

She finished her whiskey and poured another.

Anna looked at the men around her. She considered the empty leather holsters on their hips and thought about the Lugers they must have left behind in their bedrooms and offices. They didn't have their weapons and yet they were in their starched SS uniforms. Maybe she should have worn her uniform tonight? No, she shook her head, she had been instructed not to. Her gaze fell down her long red dress. It looked like she was ready to dance in a club on Kurfürstendamm or maybe stroll along the River Spree with a handsome cut of manhood at her side.

That heavy thought kept tumbling in her head, though. What did it mean that she had permission to be violent when all her life she had been told to be ladylike? Although she was allowed to taste the power of a uniform, there were clearly borders she wasn't allowed to cross. Why else would they refuse to give her a pistol? It suddenly seemed like she had no power at all. But if she had a gun, Anna wondered, would she be man enough to use it? Could she send brass and fire into someone's skull? How would men feel about this? Would she still be ladylike or would she become something else, something ugly and obscene?

Anna stared at the empty holster on Keller's hip and shook these strange thoughts from her head. She smoothed her dress and resurfaced to the conversation.

"That's the last communiqué I got from Prinz-Albrecht-Strasse. They've tasked me with finding a cure for these wounds. I mean, can you imagine? As if I didn't have enough to do already," Keller said scratching the base of his neck. The peaked cap on his head tipped forward and was in danger of falling off. He righted it and finished his glass of champagne.

"I'm sorry," Hans said shaking his head. "Berlin may run the camps but they don't know what it's like…not really…not day-to-day."

"Agreed," Keller said, gesturing with his empty glass. "I mean, I can understand the need to find a solution, but this communiqué is taking valuable workers away from my factories." He paused and bit his lip as if reconsidering his argument. "But then again, if it saves lives at the front it's a small sacrifice to make, I suppose. The wounds our boys are getting from shrapnel are bad enough but to cope with infections…? Maybe it makes sense to have our doctors do experiments. They can test new drugs and see how quickly the body heals. The regeneration of muscles and nerves, that's what I'm talking about. Did you know, there's even talk of bone transplants?"

"Is that so?" Hans said, eyeing Anna.

"Indeed. We've already experimented on a number of prisoners—cutting into them, that sort of thing—and toxins have been injected into their muscles to mimic the infections at the front. Fascinating process."

Hans cleared his throat and rolled his eyes towards Anna.

Keller raised his arms. "Ah, my goodness! Where are my manners? All of this boring talk. I'm so sorry, Johanna," he said, giving her his full attention. He reached for the Irish whiskey and splashed a full measure into her glass. He replaced his empty champagne flute and picked up a crystal tumbler for himself. Firelight danced in the cross hatching as he poured. He lifted his glass. "Prost."

Her whole body felt cozy and her lips were numb. She felt full of helium as she touched her glass to his. "Prost."

Keller leaned into her ear. His mouth was close to her gold earring and his breath was warm. "Come outside. We might see the northern lights. Do you know much about them?"

Anna nodded and, as she did so, she felt her wavy hair move against her cheek.

Keller took a stride backward and almost immediately transformed into someone else. A cloud of power formed around him. "Attention," he shouted. "Attention everyone."

The talk in the house plunged into chattering, then mumbled into silence.

"Thank you for being here. It's a treat having you in my home, especially after such a long day. You've been very patient, particularly with so many treats on the table." He waited as all eyes traveled to the meats and cheeses and fruit. "It's my pleasure to host you. And now, everyone…eat!"

The room seemed to shrink as women in fine dresses and jewelry moved closer to the table. SS officers followed behind, graciously allowing friends to butt in front of them. They smoked and pointed at what was being loaded onto china plates. Another log was dropped into the fireplace and Mozart was on the radio. A breeze came through on open window and this made the drapes flutter and dance. Anna stepped forward and had her eye on a raspberry chocolate bonbon. It had been months, maybe a year, since she had something so rare. She planned to place an entire orange on her plate. She also considered the deviled eggs and white sausage. She had never tried caviar. What did it taste like?

"Come with me," Keller said, taking her by the elbow.

"But—"

"There'll be more." His grip was firm and she let herself be steered through the crowd. His hand was on the small of her back as they moved away from the crowd, through a small kitchen that had several prisoners cooking over a stove, and he opened the back door with an outstretched arm. "After you," he said.

It felt colder outside, and she realized—while rubbing her bare forearms—that she had gotten used to the crackling fireplace. They walked down wide stone steps and Keller pointed to a clearing in the trees.

"See that," he said, gesturing up ahead. "Someplace quiet."

As his shadow crunched over twigs and leaf moss, she followed. She wanted to remove her heels and walk barefoot, but she considered the undergrowth and hidden roots. Better to walk slowly, she thought. He marched on, calling back for her to keep up. Tree limbs swayed and cracked overhead. Behind her was the glow of the camp. She closed her left eye to keep some of her night vision and she wondered if, really, she ought to be following him into the dark. She didn't know him well. And just when she was thinking about turning around, he stopped. The flame of a cigarette lighter flared like a dancing spirit and she watched his face emerge, red and shadowy. There were a few puffs. She glanced back and saw the lighted windows of the villa. They weren't too far away, she considered. Maybe it was safe.

"You know," he said loudly, venting smoke, "I was studying your file this afternoon. Your full name is Johanna Regina Hartmann... should I be calling you Johanna? I heard Binz call you 'Anna' this afternoon. Do you go by Johanna?"

She shook her head. "No one calls me that. Not anymore. When I moved out of the house—" she paused. "I go by Anna now."

Keller nodded and flicked ash into the air. "I see. Change of name. Change of person."

She scanned the black sky, salted by stars, and saw no sign of the Northern Lights.

"That reminds me," Keller said, clearing this throat. "I need another prisoner."

"For a trip into town?"

"No," he said inhaling smoke. "Another volunteer. Do it first thing tomorrow morning, yes? Before roll call, so the number isn't counted."

She scrunched up her face in confusion. She didn't want to ask for an explanation because that would make her look foolish. It took her longer to respond than she would have liked—the crickets sang all around them—and he offered the answer for her.

"So they aren't counted among the living," he said. His silhouette scanned the skies. "That which isn't counted, doesn't exist. Understand?"

Almost by instinct, her hand went to where her truncheon should be. "I know just the prisoner. She'll be happy to join her friend. Should I take her to the Bunker?"

"What a beautiful evening," Keller said, doing a slow spin. He dropped his cigarette onto the grassy dirt and crushed the red glow. "I should take more night strolls like this. Good for the soul."

"Should I take her to the Bunker, sir?" she tried again.

"What? Oh, yes, yes." He turned his back and pointed at the horizon. "Oh my God, see that there, Anna? See that? The Northern Lights are coming out."

She didn't move.

An eerie blue green lifted in the distance. It twisted and swirled in bands of light just above the trees. Ribbons of bright green shimmered and melted. It looked like a mountain of coiling light. Flares of red reached across the sky, feathering.

"You must be cold," Keller said, taking a step back. He put an arm around her shoulder and began to rub. "Beautiful," he said leaning in to smell her neck.

When he kissed her, his tongue tasted of beef and cigarettes.

CHAPTER SIXTEEN

59

Svea felt ugly. She looked at her grey skin and considered the lice in her armpits. Her hair was tufted and, if she touched her cheeks, she could feel how sunken they were, how gaunt and withered she had become. The wound on her left arm from the selection was scabbed over and there was dirt beneath her fingernails. She felt hollow, as if the best parts of her had drained away.

She climbed down from her bunk and thought about the new prisoners that had crowded into their barrack. One of them had taken Julienne's place and she was gorgeous, like something out of an oil painting. Her hair had been shaved, of course, but her skin glowed with nourishment and vitamins. These new prisoners moved around in mute shock and Svea felt as if she were traveling back in time to watch herself. One of the new prisoners acted like she was at a poorly run hotel instead of a concentration camp. This woman just gawked at the Northern Lights and kept saying how pretty they were. How beautiful. When someone told her to shut up and go to bed, she just kept staring. The woman sat there for hours looking up at the twisting light. And now, she was dead on the floor. She had hanged herself with a belt.

There was always one, she considered. Whenever new prisoners arrived, there was always one who took her own life before the sun could rise. She grabbed the woman's wrists and began to pull. It was her turn to stack the freshly dead in the washroom—they all had to do this job eventually—and as she pulled the young woman over the stone floor she watched her head loll and flop. Someone had loved her, Svea thought. Someone had brought her into this world and cared for her and hugged her, and now she was being dragged past rows of sleeping women as if she were a sack of grain. She was just another body, just another corpse for the wooden cart and the furnace.

Someone would miss her though. Svea looked at the woman's left hand and saw no indent of a wedding ring. Perhaps she wasn't married? Svea pulled her into the washroom and brought her to rest near an Italian woman that had also taken her own life during the night. She fit them together like tinned herrings. The Italian was badly bruised on her forearm. Svea had seen this new prisoner—who didn't know the ways of the camp—being hammered with a truncheon. The Aufseherin, Hartmann, battered her truncheon down onto this poor Italian prisoner and she didn't stop, not even when this fresh fish fell to the ground, not even when she held up her forearm and begged for mercy.

Svea swallowed and tried to compose herself.

If she had a thousand lifetimes, she could never forgive them. Being young was no excuse. They *chose* to join the Aufseherin. They *chose* to lace up the weapon of their boots. They *chose* to kick and hit and stomp. After all, Svea thought moving back into the barrack, she was young like them and she was German like them and—"For God's sake" she muttered aloud—she could have joined the Aufseherin if she had wanted to. But she *chose* not to. Being young was no excuse at all for joining. She didn't feel pity for any of them and, after the war, they deserved whatever was coming to them. She burned to live just so that she could testify against them. She imagined a courtroom with oak panels and gold balustrades. She would stand in the dock and it would be her, Svea Maria Fischer, who would point her steady finger at Hartmann and say, "She's the one. I saw what she did at Ravensbrück. I saw it all."

Svea reached for another body. This one was bony, light, and the woman's wrists were cold. It was like touching rubber. Svea pulled, and the trinket was so light that she didn't need to use both hands. She tugged and moved forward like she was dragging a basket across the floor.

Anger churned inside her and she returned to the courtroom in her mind. She would talk about how Hartmann had taken Julienne.

"My friend made the camp tolerable," she imagined saying to a judge. "Julienne gave me something to live for and made Ravensbrück almost bearable. That French girl gave me somebody to care about beyond myself and—"

Svea shook away the poison of the future. Even if there was a trial, she wouldn't be around to see it. Be here now, she thought.

The body behind her thumped over the wooden sill of a doorway and was fitted neatly with the others. Svea looked at the dead. There was always a chance of finding better shoes or a cap. Maybe even a bra. She glanced at the gorgeous woman who had hanged herself in the night. It was a good leather belt, Svea thought. New and strong. Why not keep it? She bent down, unlooped it from the woman's neck, and fit it around her own waist. She snugged it tight.

The siren for roll call shrieked into the dark morning and she stood there with her hands by her sides. Only seven women had died during the night and Svea knew it was a result of the selection from yesterday. Anyone that was too weak had already been taken away. A thought came to her. Maybe she could approach Zofia later this morning about news of Julienne? She let prisoners stumble-shuffle past her as they made their way to large metal buckets. They squatted. They pissed.

She smoothed her striped dress against the bony wings of her hips. With so many new prisoners, they wouldn't yet know how to pace themselves through the day. Most of them also wouldn't know to stand near the center for roll call because it meant you were less likely to be hit. None of them would realize that you should never be first for the soup pots. It was better to wait and try to get the dregs of vegetables at the bottom.

Just as she was imaging this, the front door was unbolted and a team of Aufseherin rushed in with flashlights. Beams of white slashed through morning shadows. Truncheons were brought down against the triple-layered bunks.

"Get up!"

"Move it, move it!"

The white beams continued to cut and swing, falling on beds, the floor, rafters, chests. Why were the Aufseherin inside the barracks? They usually waited outside and hit them as they exited.

"18311!"

Svea froze.

"18311!"

The beams moved across numbered shoulders. The Aufseherin didn't look at faces—they looked at numbers.

"18311? Come here or I'll kick your teeth in."

It was Hartmann. Svea thought about hiding beneath a bunk bed but, already, flashlights were slashing the floor and searching for anyone who might scurry away.

"18311! Show yourself!"

As Svea stepped forward, it felt like she was being pulled against her will. The longer she waited, the more pain they would bring later.

"18311!"

Svea came to attention before Hartmann. When she spoke, her voice cracked. "Prisoner 18311 present, Madam Overseer."

The other Aufseherin immediately stopped searching. Quiet fell.

"Follow me," Hartmann said, turning for the wooden door.

At first, Svea didn't know what to do. She expected to be hit, and it was strange to find the guards simply stepping aside and letting her follow Hartmann. The fact that they weren't hitting her was worrying. She looked at their dark shadowy faces and felt a hand squeeze her shoulder.

"Go," a familiar voice whispered. It was Zofia. "I will find out what is happening."

Svea's legs felt like rooted trees as she half-stumbled for the door. She tried to swallow but couldn't make any spit. What was going to happen? She glanced back at Zofia but couldn't see her anymore.

Stepping into the cool blue dawn felt dangerous. Each step seemed like she was on a tightrope and she listened to the cindery gravel beneath her clogs. The Aufseherin clustered around her and, although she wanted to know where she was being taken, she knew it was stupid to ask. Had they found out she was Jewish? Maybe they were going to take her to another camp? Would she be able to survive with a yellow winkel? As they walked to the front of the Appellplatz, she glanced at the huge gate. It was closed. To walk through it would mean—what exactly? Was it better or worse to be taken from the camp? Lights were on in the kitchen block and she heard the SS laughing over their breakfasts in the nearby canteen. A few of them were outside and they wobbled on drunken knees. One of them held a bottle of Dom Perignon.

A flock of geese drifted overhead in a sloppy V and she watched them flap on, free. Her eyes went to the crematorium chimney.

The Aufseherin veered her to the left and it was obvious they were taking her to the Bunker. A wave of terror crashed over her. Those that went inside rarely came out. It loomed before her.

"Faster," Hartmann snapped as if Svea were a dog that wasn't keeping up.

They moved beneath the lime trees as the second siren for roll call sounded. For perhaps the first time since her arrival in Ravensbrück, she wished to stand at attention for hours and be bored. Boredom was a luxury, she thought. If she managed to step away from the camp and enter a new life she would never take boredom for granted ever again.

When they came to the wooden door, Hartmann used the side of her fist to knock. *Thud, thud, thud.* There was the oiled clank of a lock and the heavy door glided open, silently. A rectangle of light spilled out onto the ground. Svea had expected it to be dark inside and she had to blink to adjust her eyes.

"In," Hartmann said, prodding with a truncheon.

The floor was tiled and Svea didn't have traction due to her clogs. They entered a hallway with harsh ceiling lights and she could hear a scream from somewhere up ahead. When a wooden staircase appeared before her, Hartmann motioned for her to go down. The metal frame that supported the wooden treads squeaked under their combined weight. They descended into a basement corridor. A wide one. They walked past heavy wooden doors—prison cells—and she heard whimpering. They came to an abrupt stop. A white 59 was painted on a door and one of the Aufseherin pulled out a thicket of keys. She fumbled and dropped them.

"Hurry up."

"I'm trying. It's dark down here."

"You should've gotten it ready back there," Hartmann said, nodding towards the light.

"We're the same rank, Little Nurse. Just because you got asked to a party last night doesn't mean—"

Another guard brought out a cigarette lighter and flicked the thumbwheel.

"Is that better?"

"That *is* better. Thank you."

A stubby key was inserted into the lock and the door swung open. Svea was pushed into the darkness and she tripped, nearly falling. She turned around and expected the door to slam shut but, instead, the four guards stood in the framed pale light.

"Take off your shoes." There was a pause. "And your belt."

Svea kicked off her clogs and felt cold concrete on the soles of her feet. She didn't want to give up the new belt but what else could she do? She had owned it for—what?—fifteen minutes? She unlooped it from her bony waist and bent down for the clogs. Wordlessly, she gave them over.

And then the door closed, dragging all light with it.

CHAPTER SEVENTEEN
Inside the Bunker

The darkness was so total, so absolute, that Svea couldn't see anything, and after a while she didn't know how long she had been in the cell. Time stretched like rubber. Had she been locked away for an hour? Three hours? A day? Without the rhythm of camp life, it was hard to know where the minute and hour hands rested. It was like being blind to time.

The floor was cold and there was the smell of wet metal. In the first few minutes of the door slamming shut, she felt her way around the cell. It was four and half paces long by two and a half paces wide. A bed was bolted to the floor—she had stubbed her toe on it several times already—and pipes were anchored to the wall. They were warm. Perhaps they carried water or steam?

Worst of all was the whimpering from the cell next to her. No, she reconsidered, that wasn't the worst thing of all. The worst thing was not knowing what was coming next. Was she going to starve to death in the cell? Were they going to beat her? Torture her? Although she couldn't see her body, she was aware of the pain that could visit it. There were rumors of a flogging bench somewhere in the Bunker. Women were strapped to it, half-naked, and a special whip made of ox hide was brought out. It was, as one of the Aufseherin had said, "Very durable."

Had it been used on Julienne?

Svea sat on the bed, which was an unpadded wood plank, and she imagined her friend naked to the waist, strapped to the flogging bench. It was said that twenty-five lashes were standard and that a doctor was brought in to monitor for cardiac arrest. If a prisoner fainted, they were revived with a bucket of water. And if they were in danger of dying, the remaining lashes would be doled out the following day. Svea wondered if she would be stripped naked and strapped to the bench. How many lashes could she take before—

The whimpering continued and she went to the corner of her cell. *Her* cell, she almost laughed. And to think she had longed for privacy not that long ago. Now that she had it, she ached to be in a crowded barrack.

"Hello?" she asked the wall. Maybe she was imagining the whimpering? "Is anyone there?"

The noise stopped.

"Can you hear me? Hello?"

There was no sound so Svea tried French. *"Bonjour? Pouvez-vous m'entendre?"*

After a long lingering minute, she heard movement. A scraping.

"Hello?" she shouted. "Julienne?" She paused and pressed her ear to the wall. "Julienne? Is that you? It's Svea!"

A voice shouted from another cell. "Shut up! They'll beat us if they hear you."

"Julienne?"

The voice—high and sharp—was louder. "QUIET! You'll get us whipped."

Svea moved to the door in a fit of rage. She took breath into her lungs and felt her vocal cords tighten. She wanted to shout at the voice to mind its own damn business but, she reconsidered, maybe silence was better. What if Julienne *was* here? It was certainly a possibility because she'd seen her friend get dragged into the Bunker. Yes, she nodded. She had to be here somewhere. It was worth chancing it.

"Julienne! It's Svea! Are you here?"

"SHUT...UP!" came the voice across the hall.

Maybe it was foolish to continue but she couldn't help herself. The one person that made Ravensbrück bearable could be yards away. She only needed to fill up her lungs and yell words into the darkness. Maybe there would be an answer.

"Julienne? It's Svea...it's your Svea."

"Shut your fucking hole!" came another voice.

There was another sound, a worrying sound. It was a clanging of metal bars. Heavy boots thudded against concrete. "Who's talking?" a voice demanded. "Who the hell is talking down here? Who wants a trip up the chimney?" It sounded like Hartmann or maybe like that Aufseherin who ordered them to sing. Ahoy, ahoy.

"Who the hell just spoke? Was it you, cell 57? Or maybe you, cell 60?"

Svea couldn't remember which cell she was in and she backed away from the door. Light leaked from the threshold, it spilled across the dirty floor and illuminated her toes. It was so bright that she had to shut her eyes.

"Which one of you cunts was talking?" A truncheon banged on a door. "Was it you?"

The sound of boots came closer and Svea watched the carpet of light turn into murky shadow. The boots continued down the corridor and the light returned. Pipes in her cell gurgled with a rush of water and she stood there, holding both hands over her heart. There was a rattling of keys and a cell door across the hall groaned open. A woman began to beg for mercy. She sounded Russian.

"Please, no. It was not me. I wasn't for doing the shouting, Madam Overseer. Please. It was not for me doing the shouting."

There was the snake-like hiss of a whip and a shriek of pain. It was full-lunged screeching—animal squeals—and Svea backed up, her nerve endings prickling.

"You must be QUIET!" The whip hissed. Another shriek. "Silence!" All the while, the screaming continued.

Svea plugged her ears but after a few seconds she decided that someone should witness this woman's suffering. A thought cut through her—what if she, Svea, had brought this on? If she had just been quiet, maybe this wouldn't be happening? She placed a palm on the door.

"Stop!" Svea screamed, slapping the door. "Stop hurting her." What if it was Julienne? What if she had brought this down on her? No, she reassured herself. It didn't sound like her. The woman didn't have a French accent. Surely she was Russian.

"Stop!"

Minutes passed and although the screaming had stopped, the whipping flick of the snake continued. There was panting now. Heavy, brutal, measured. When the whip stopping snapping, the Aufseherin cleared her throat. She spat. Svea could hear it. Was the prisoner dead? Svea leaned against the door and felt dizzy. The cell began to spin.

"Let that be a lesson to you all," the guard yelled to the corridor. She locked the cell and added, "She won't be getting up anytime soon."

The boots moved away, a light was snapped off, and darkness filled Svea's cell. No one dared to whisper, not even Svea. She dropped to the cold floor and began to weep. She placed both hands over her mouth and stifled a scream.

≫

Time stretched. It blurred and drifted. Her stomach grumbled for a bowl of watery turnip soup and she imagined chewing a chunk of moldy bread that was handed out after morning roll call. Her tongue was leather. Her lips were cracked and possibly bleeding. She trembled. What little glucose she had left in her body was probably gone, and this meant amino acids were being stripped from the fabric of her muscles. Her brain was yelling for fuel. Maybe this was how they planned to kill her? To starve her to death in the darkness. But why? What had she done?

Svea shivered and tired not to think about the prisoner across the hall. The body had been hauled away long ago— "Another log for the fire" an Aufseherin had said—and silence filled up the hallway like they were somewhere deep beneath the ocean. Darkness. Pressure. Cold. It was like being in the sunken wreck of a battleship, she thought.

Svea opened and closed her eyes to see if there was any difference in her vision. When her eyes were open, it was like being in a sunless cave, and when they were shut, she could see purples and greens. Color was splashed across the inside of her eyelids and she watched them drift like oily vapor. She slept. Or at least she thought she slept. Without a watch it was hard to tell if she dozed for a few minutes or if she sank into hours of sleep. It was the only good thing about being imprisoned— she was able to sleep. But whenever she considered that the steel door could fly open at any moment, she stayed awake and alert.

Images and conversations from her old life flickered in the movie house of her mind. She allowed herself to think of Peter; how handsome he was, how well dressed. His eyes had a way of shining

145

when he smiled, his lips were soft, and the way he furrowed his brow when he concentrated on an engineering problem made her catch her breath. He was pretty. She knew that men didn't like to be called pretty because it made them feel like they weren't somehow men, but Peter was pretty. Oh, his smile. She drifted into the past and met him on a dance floor. The music was slow. She leaned into him and felt his kiss on her forehead. Then they were back in their flat. She allowed him to lead her into their bedroom where her blue dress fell to the floor in a pool of fabric. She unhooked her bra and, naked, she crawled into bed.

Boots stomped down the corridor and a light snapped on. She sat up and heard two people—a man and a woman—talking in the corridor. As the voices got louder, and as they stopped in front of her cell, she stood up and searched for her cap. It had tumbled off her head hours ago and she couldn't find it in the darkness. Now that someone was entering, she would need to come to attention with it or risk a beating. Where was it? She searched the floor and found it in the corner. She jammed it onto her head and stood up. The stone floor was cold against her feet and she curled her toes. Whatever happens, she thought, let it happen quickly.

A key jangled and the door opened. Light poured in, making her blink, and she came to attention. She recognized the shape of *Oberaufseherin* Binz, who had a certain way of standing with her legs set widely apart. Her blonde hair curled out from her cap and, as usual, she wasn't wearing any earrings. Her brow was furrowed, as if she were in a constant state of anger.

"Madam Overseer," Svea said with both arms at her sides. "Prisoner 18311, present." She didn't look Binz in the eye because that was forbidden. Svea did, however, look for a whip. Perhaps one made of ox hide. Binz only had her truncheon, and it was snug in its holster.

"Madam Overseer?" Svea asked, letting a question mark fall between them.

Binz stepped aside and let a doctor in a white coat appear.

"Follow me," the doctor said, almost happily. He motioned with a finger. "Hurry."

It felt strange to leave the cell and it felt even more strange to walk in a straight line for more than five paces without bumping into a wall. As her eyes adjusted to the overhead lights, she studied the doctor. He had a clipboard and, every now and then, he glanced back at her.

"She's not hurt?" he asked Binz.

"No. Hasn't been touched."

"Good," the doctor said, climbing the stairs. He led them to the exit and held the door open for Svea. "This way," he said with an extended hand.

She was surprised to find herself outside in delicious daylight and she took a moment to look around at hundreds of prisoners digging a drainage ditch. Lime trees shook in the wind and the sun was directly overhead. So it was noon, she realized, squinting up. Her knees were weak and she had trouble keeping up with the doctor. Binz gave her a prod in the back. It was painful to walk on the cindery ground without wooden clogs. Diamond bits of black rock stuck to her feet. Where were they taking her? When they passed the kitchen block, she enjoyed the smell of soup, bubbling. Stacks of bread were being unloaded from a truck. The truck, she noticed, had gold lettering on the side. HIMMEL MARKT. She looked away and focused on the doctor's shoulders in front of her. Pots banged together and water rushed into a sink. It would be a good job, she thought, working in the kitchen. A happy thought flared into view. What if she was being given a new assignment? What if she was going to cook for the SS or do laundry? At least she wasn't going to the main gate, which might mean death. "The only way out of this camp"—she let the rest of the saying drift away like coal smoke.

She breathed in fresh air and tried not to think of Binz following behind. What did it mean that the head Aufseherin was trailing her? Why was Binz involved?

Women struggled with the concrete roller and she looked away, feeling nothing. Rocks continued to bite into her naked feet.

When it became clear they were going to the Revier, she felt her heart quicken. She had to force herself to enter the camp hospital. She was pushed in by Binz. Fluorescent lights were bolted to the ceiling and rows of beds were pushed against the walls. There was the smell of chemicals and unwashed bodies. Her friend, Hannah, once had to help a prisoner with dysentery get to the Revier, and when she saw it she thought it was the morgue. Svea looked at the ordered beds and saw unmoving bodies. Their mouths were open and they stared at the ceiling. These women were thin, just skin and bones. "Husks waiting to die," Hannah had said of the Revier.

Svea wanted to turn around and run away but Binz was blocking her path. This tank of a woman had her truncheon out, and she stood in the doorway.

"Follow me," the doctor said merrily. He placed a mask over his mouth.

The three of them moved into a large white room that had an operating table. It had stirrups and leather restraining straps. The doctor patted it.

"Up, please."

Svea looked around and didn't understand what was happening.

"I'm going to examine you," he explained, tapping the table again. "Up, please."

Binz closed the door and stood in front of it. She tapped her truncheon against her knee. "Do as he says," she motioned.

"Examine me for what?" Svea asked, feeling naked even though she still wore her uniform.

"Do as you're told," Binz said with a hint of boredom.

Svea smoothed her dress and noticed a cabinet full of vials. There were also jars of gauze, sponges, needles, laryngoscopes, and muscular charts on the walls. A desk in the corner had a typewriter and there was a bookcase full of black binders. These were all things she would have used if she had become a doctor. This could have been her life if it wasn't for National Socialism. But now a surgical table was in front of her.

"What are you examining me for?"

"Up," the doctor said, reaching for a bottle of iodine.

She looked around for clues that might tell her what was about to happen. A clipboard had the word SULFONAMIDES written across the top and—she had no idea what to make of this—there was a small mound of wood shavings and broken glass.

A knock came on the door and three other doctors entered. They also wore white coats and masks.

"Hurry up," the doctor said, uncorking the iodine. "On the table, please."

Later, Svea wouldn't remember walking to the operating table. She wouldn't remember if she did this by herself or if she was dragged by the doctors. What she would remember though was the tightening leather straps on her ankles and wrists. She would remember staring at harsh overhead lights and she would remember crippling helplessness, as if she were caught in a spider's web. She strained against what held her down. She tried to move, but was pinned fast.

"What are you going to do?" she shouted. Sweat prickled her forehead and her eyes darted around the room. A stainless-steel table with instruments was brought over. Gauze. Scalpel. Thread.

"It'll be over in a minute," one of the white shapes said, splashing iodine onto the lower half of her right leg.

"The *peroneus longus* is here," the doctor said, tracing a line below her kneecap. "Cut here."

"Please. You don't need to do this. Stop! What are you going to do?"

They stared at her leg, and one of them reached for a scalpel.

CHAPTER EIGHTEEN

Bone and Glass

The pain was blinding. Even now, laying in a hospital bed, it felt like knitting needles had been driven into her knee. She looked down at the gauze and saw dark umber. Pus was blotting up from the bandage and, when she tried to move, it felt like volcanic fire erupting inside her tissue. She wasn't tied to the bed, but there was hardly any need to strap her down because the very idea of putting weight on her right leg made her shrink.

Images flashed through her mind. The doctors. The lights. The scalpel. Wooziness. The clink of something being dropped on the table. They had used some kind of anesthetic that made her feel as if she were in syrup, but it hadn't taken affect by the time they started cutting. When she felt her skin slitting open, and when she looked down to see the inside of her leg, open to sunlight, she passed out. When she came to they were stuffing something in the wound. Glass and wood shavings. She screamed and kept on screaming until a wave of pain pulled her into unconsciousness. Her brain was trying to protect her and yet, when they started to suture her skin back into place, she revived and started screaming again. She begged for more anesthetic. They didn't look at her, not once, and in spite of the scorching agony that flared from her knee, she tired spitting on them. Her mouth, however, was too dry. After a moment—a moment where she felt herself panting hard and grunting under the weight of so much pain—her mind flicked a switch and everything went dark. Svea sank into the abyss.

She had no idea how long she had been out. Shadows stretched across the white walls of the Revier and the fluorescent lights were still on. She tried not to think of the pain. She had read about Buddhist monks who willed themselves not to be hot in the heat of a jungle day and she knew people that could be hypothesized into believing they were elsewhere. And yet, no matter what she did or what she focused on, there was only the burning knitting needles of pain. Her head felt like it was stuffed with cotton and she ached for water.

Why had they done this? Was it a form of punishment? No, she remembered, almost happy to think of something other than the splintered glass and wood shavings that had been stuffed into her muscles, she remembered the Rabbits from several months ago. These Polish women had been operated on by SS physicians in order to see how their wounds might heal. Glass and wood had been cut into their muscles. At the time, she didn't concern herself with these women. There were more important things to worry about like beatings and finding food. What happened to these Rabbits? One day they were hopping around camp on their good legs and then they were gone. Simply gone.

A chill went through her body. She was a Rabbit now. Would she only stay alive for as long as the data of her body was useful to SS physicians?

She looked down at her leg and tried to tighten her muscles. Pain blazed through her. She tried to wiggle her toes and move her ankle and stiffen her calf. Much of her lower right leg was numb and she was sure they had cut some nerves. She imagined pulling off her skin and looking into the hidden rigging of her knee. Something was in her calf muscle—she could feel it slicing around—and she wondered when they would take it out. Would they take it out? And if so, would she heal? *Would* she walk normally again? She thought about that prisoner with the broken arm and how it was easier to shoot her than fix her. Svea studied her leg and knew the wound would keep her alive until they had no more use—

She turned from the poisonous thought and squinted at the woman in the bed next to her. She was breathing, raggedly. Her lungs were full of mucus. She wheezed and coughed.

Svea felt her lymph nodes and, sure enough, they were swollen. She had a fever too. No wonder, she thought. Her body was trying to fight off an infection. Had the doctors dipped the glass into anything before they inserted it into her? Staphylococcus maybe? From some foggy memory on the operating table, she recalled one of the doctors chipping her upper shin with a hammer. These people weren't doctors, she thought. They were butchers.

Her eyes narrowed and a pure hatred washed over her. It scoured away the pain.

She woke up to find doctors gathered around her bed. They didn't say a word to her. Instead, they simply lifted the bandage on her leg without warning. A jolt of pain sizzled up her back, which made her flinch.

"Don't move," one of them said without anger. He used a pencil as a pointer. "See here? We've done a little osteoclasis and grafted material directly into the *peroneus longus.*"

They wore white coats over their SS uniforms. Their peaked caps with the Death's Head emblem perched squarely over their foreheads. They leaned over her leg and murmured in the coded language of medicine, not realizing that she understood what they were saying.

"Osteotomy, combined with debris similar to that found in battlefield conditions, is offering new possibilities for treatment. This one has sulfonamides in the wound."

"Antimicrobial," another doctor hummed in agreement.

"Do they all have sulfonamides?"

"No," the head doctor snapped, as if annoyed at being interrupted. "We're confident that once the wound begins to—stop moving!" he ordered Svea. "The stitches are still fresh and I've made them strong so the skin can heal. Once we have that underway, we can graft. Grab me the powder just there, will you?" He nodded towards a metal table.

Another doctor reached for a tall plastic bottle. The head doctor— neat, clean shaven, sharp ferrety eyes—flicked powder onto her leg and lowered the bandage. He didn't dress the wound anew. Instead, he fitted the bloody pus-stained gauze back into place.

"We don't clean the wound?" one of the others with clipped blond hair asked.

"Oh no. We're trying to simulate battlefield conditions. Our soldiers are lucky to get a wound dressed more than once a day, so it is the same here."

The head doctor glanced at Svea's shoulder for a long moment before writing something on his clipboard. It seemed like he was studying her winkel, her number. "If you'll follow me, I'll show you the operating room."

As the doctors leaked away, Svea heard one of them ask if the prisoners felt any pain.

"Does it matter?" the head doctor said without anger.

There was polite talk as they moved down the tiled hall. One of them stopped to light a cigarette. He puffed a few times, waved the matchstick into a wisp of smoke, and dropped it on the floor.

Svea clenched her fists against a tidal wave of pain, she gritted her teeth and looked around for gauze. Her eyes flicked around the room. Beds. Dying women. Empty cabinets. Bedpans. Blankets. Maybe she could dress the wound herself? Maybe she could cut up a blanket?

On the other side of the rectangular room was a glass cabinet with a large Red Cross. It looked like there was a box of gauze inside. How could she get to it? Maybe she could hop? She looked at a skeletal woman lying in a bed near the glass cabinet. Svea propped herself up and cleared her throat. "Hey. Hey, you. Can you throw that box of gauze to me? Please?"

None of the women looked up or showed any sign of hearing her. Instead, they stared at the ceiling. There was a smell coming off them. It was sweet, almost floral. Svea had been around plenty of dying people and she knew how the body began to shut down. She was sure the woman near to the glass cabinet was nearly dead. Her chest rose, falteringly, and sank. Svea looked at the other women and saw that they, too, would soon be on their way to the ovens.

The front door of Revier suddenly banged open and two Aufseherin marched in with a pregnant woman between them. A new arrival. She wore a patterned dress and held a frilly hat in one of her hands. Her hair was caught in a long braid that hung down her back like a bell rope. As she walked closer—looking in horror at the withered bodies in the beds—one of the Aufseherin pointed ahead.

"Through that door. It's a simple exam," she said brightly. It was the one who was beautiful and had a natural spring in her step. Black hair. Pretty skin.

The pregnant woman with a large belly moved through the wooden door and into the operating room. Svea knew what would happen next. The woman would be strapped down and her baby would be made unborn. Infants were not allowed in Ravensbrück and, for those rare toddlers that were brought in with mothers, Svea had heard rumors of a "Children's Room" somewhere in camp. The children were left to starve. That was the rumor. Could it be true though? Surely not even that level of barbarity could exist here.

She let the thought sink into her imagination, but it bubbled up again and she found herself holding her own belly. Abortion was illegal in the Third Reich and if a doctor performed one he would be arrested and tossed into prison. Now though? All things were possible at Ravensbrück. What was illegal outside of the main gate was legal inside the camp. Abortion. Infanticide. Murder. Medical experimentation. Anything that was forbidden could flourish and thrive behind the barbed wire.

"It's just an exam?" the woman asked, still holding her belly.

"Yes," the pretty guard smiled. "To make sure everything is okay."

The door closed and Svea knew the woman had no idea what waited ahead. She turned away and thought about her own little lost lamb. Once, a lifetime ago, her body had been home to a daughter. And then one evening, when things were still normal and happy, she felt a cramping. She was having a bubble bath at the time. The blood. The body. Yes, she had been a mother, once. And although she was only twenty-five, a whole lifetime had been stripped away from her. A planned life. Music. Peter. A career. Her whole future, smashed to the ground like a china plate. What would she have become if Ravensbrück didn't exist?

She looked down at the bandage. The yellowy pus was heavier now and there was more blood. She looked around for crutches but couldn't see any. A thought took her over. She squinted into the idea and let it possess her. Maybe…? Yes, she was still in her uniform, so maybe she could hide somewhere? In the kitchen or the laundry? It was preposterous and dangerous, but she needed to do something. She couldn't just lay in bed and let them take everything from her.

And then something wonderful happened.

"I've been waiting to come over," Julienne said.

Svea blinked.

"You must be in pain," Julienne said, squeezing Svea's forearm. "Are you okay? What can I do?"

"Is it…? Is it *really* you?"

Julienne looked around for doctors. "If they find me talking to you—"

"How did you get here? I thought you were in the Bunker."

"Shh. Listen. I have been in that bed far over there, and I saw them bring you in and I wanted to say something but we are not allowed to speak in this place." She leaned in and caressed Svea's forehead. "With that poor mother in surgery right now, I knew I could take a chance." Julienne's eyes went to the damp bandage on Svea's knee. "You are in pain, yes?"

There was a scream from the operating room and they both looked at the door. Adrenaline prickled Svea's nerves and she worried about an SS officer or an Aufseherin coming in. She looked at Julienne's knee, which was also bandaged. "You can walk?"

Julienne put a finger to her lips. "Shh. Shh. They strapped me to that table and cut without anesthetic last week. I heard you screaming, Svea, and I felt so badly for you." Her eyes welled up. "But listen, quickly, I will explain. They did not put debris in my leg like they did to you. They cut my nerve. I cannot feel the middle of my leg. She is numb."

"But why—?"

"The doctors told each other it was to see about regeneration. Maybe my nerves, maybe they will grow back? But maybe not. I am healing, which is something, yes?" Julienne stopped rubbing Svea's forearm and began to back away.

"Don't leave," Svea said, reaching out.

"No, no. I am just showing you that I can walk. See?"

She moved back and forth, and although there was a bloody bandage on her left knee, she could walk with a limp.

"If I survive this place," Julienne said, staring at her knee, "I will never dance again."

The two women looked at each other and offered weak smiles.

"How can I help?" Julienne asked. "You have been so good to me, and I have not been useful for making you feel better. I tried with that bracelet but that only caused you more pain. What can I do to help?"

"Don't leave," Svea said. She wanted to add that just seeing her friend's face again made her feel better. She had a reason to lift herself up and there was a budding sense of purpose again. "Stay," she said. "That's what you can do."

There was another scream, but this time it wasn't filled with pain—it was full of the realization that something precious was being destroyed.

Julienne stared at the entrance of the Revier for a long moment and then looked at Svea's leg.

"Can you hop?"

"I haven't tried to stand yet."

"But can you?"

Svea raised both eyebrows at the thought. "No…I don't think…"

The screaming turned into wails of grief.

"Lean on me. Let us leave the Revier, together."

Svea considered what would happen if they were caught. No, she corrected, not *if* they were caught, but *when* they were caught. Although the camp was full of thousands of women, they both limped. Where would they go? Where would they hide? What if there was another selection and they had to run?

"Svea. Look at me. If we stay here, we die."

There was a determined look in Julienne's eyes—one that Svea hadn't seen before—and she found herself nodding. She looked at the wasting bodies around her and realized that in two weeks, maybe three, that would be her struggling for breath, that would be her lungs full of mucus, that would be her body shutting down. She looked at her knee and considered the dazzling pain that would light up her nerves if she tried to walk.

"Lean on me," Julienne said. "If we are quick, maybe we can find a barrack and ask for help? Pity is not dead in this camp. After all, you helped me."

Something shifted inside Svea. She propped herself up and nodded to the glass cabinet. "See that box of gauze? Bring it to me."

Julienne shuffled and limped over to it. She moved in a hobbling glide, like her right leg was attached to a rail on the floor, but at least she could move. And she moved surprisingly fast. She swung open the glass door of the cabinet and reached for the brown box. She turned around and waved it back and forth. "Empty," she said, putting it back. She closed the glass door carefully. It clicked shut.

"If we want to leave, we go now," Julienne said, hurrying back in her hobbled glide. She held out both arms as if she were going to pick up a toddler. "Do not think, just stand. Fall into me."

Svea stared at her bare feet and, while gritting her teeth, she swung both legs over the edge of the bed. The pain was ferocious. A shock of agony made her catch her breath—it made the world funnel into darkness—and she got lightheaded. Two strong arms lifted her up, and with the world now sliding sideways she propped her head against Julienne's shoulder.

"Put your weight on me," her friend whispered. "I have you. Yes, good. Now move your left leg…yes…now the other."

She didn't dare place weight on her ruined knee. Instead, she hopped and let the dead leg drag behind her. In this way, the two women shuffled and hopped for the grey doors of the entrance. It felt good to lean on Julienne and she braced herself against the metal frames of passing beds. The dying women in ordered rows of the Revier stared at the ceiling and breathed on.

When they reached the front door, Julienne nudged it open and looked outside. "There is a step down," she said. "It will hurt."

Svea sucked air into her lungs and prepared for a voltage of suffering. She hopped down the step—overwhelmed by pain—and felt Julienne grab her. Now that they were outside, they had to keep going. There would be no excuse for leaving the Revier without permission. Svea ignored the pain in her leg and focused on what needed to be done. She studied the camp and considered their options.

A barrack was across the way and a team of prisoners were cleaning the windows. A flash of sunlight was doused by a wet rag. A group of Availables scrubbed the kitchen block with wire brushes and bleach. Hundreds of uniformed women were hard at work, cleaning, digging, repairing. Her eyes moved quickly, scanning for danger. A group of Aufseherin were busy tormenting prisoners that had to pull the concrete roller. Laughter brought other guards scurrying over. They clustered around, magnetized by their power to hurt. Their backs were to the Revier.

"You are okay," Julienne said in a calm voice. The two women rested against each other, their weight shared. The lime trees shivered in the wind. A twirling gust lifted cinders up from the ground.

"Now what?" one of them asked.

There was a shrug and then, wordlessly, they hop-shuffled into the unknown.

They would be easy to find.

CHAPTER NINETEEN

The Place of Least Danger

Anna stood with her hands on her hips and inspected the ragged women filing past her. It had been a full day since those dirty little pieces had dared to stroll out of the Revier, and she was determined to find them, especially 18311. She chewed on her lower lip and squinted at the edge of camp. They had to be somewhere.

She studied the numbers that paraded before her and wondered if they had gotten rid of their old uniforms and adopted new numbers. It would be easy to do. All they needed was someone freshly dead and they could slip into a new dress. If they hid in a barrack at night, there would be plenty of opportunities to find a cold body in the morning.

Anna dropped her hands to her side and began to walk. She looked at shoulders and ached to find the right series of numbers.

49821

73032

60870

77991

The prisoners all looked the same. Skeletons in dresses. Dirty faces and pale eyes. Tufted hair. Lice. Worst of all, she never caught the civilian name of 18311—the name she had used before the camp—and Anna wished she knew what it was because she could shout it out now. It might be enough to make the thing turn to hear her old name. Maybe, Anna thought, maybe she could find out more information in the Administration building. They would have taken a photo of 18311 when she was admitted. Her real name might be on that document.

Anna closed her eyes and tried to see 18311's face. The pretty green eyes. The turned up nose. In another setting, she would have been pretty. She had a Berlin accent. 18311 wasn't a Jew or a communist because she had the black winkel of an antisocial. A prostitute maybe? Yes, she considered, she could always visit the Administration building and do research. What was hiding in this prisoner's past?

The morning was chilly, even for early June, and she looked at the fishbone clouds overhead. Pale colors streaked the sky as she walked over the pebbly ground. There was a pleasing scrunch beneath her boots. The prisoners scurried to the sock factory and mat weaving mill. They all looked down, afraid to make eye contact. A pleasant feeling filled Anna at this and she adjusted her dark grey cap. She moved a strand of hair behind her ear. She burped and tasted the eggs and toast of breakfast.

She ignored the numbered shoulders flowing around her and focused, instead, on bare knees. Even if the bandages had been removed, the gash would give 18311 away. The limping too. Anna studied kneecaps and calf muscles. She scrutinized gait and posture. Everyone had their own peculiar way of walking, she noticed. She hadn't really considered it before, but after an entire day of watching the movement of others she came to realize that each person's walk was as individual as fingerprints. Sniffing for clues like this made her feel like a detective. She liked the idea that she was seeing things that were in plain sight, but no one else noticed. Anna considered her mother's pigeon-toed step and her father's heavy stride. The prisoners swung their arms different too. They bent forward as they walked or moved in a scuttle with their heads down. How did 18311 walk before she had been turned into a Rabbit?

Anna stopped walking.

Where *was* she? The two prisoners had to be somewhere. You couldn't just disappear into thin air at Ravensbrück. Anna let her eyes glide over barracks and factories and washing facilities. Could they have escaped?

"Any luck?" Ruth asked, appearing next to her.

Anna shook her head. "Not yet."

"They weren't at roll call."

"Would you show up at roll call?"

Ruth shrugged. "Who knows what parasites think?"

The noise of the camp settled between them. There was the sound of wooden clogs skittering over pea gravel. There were doors opening and banging shut. The sound of boilers heating in the kitchen block. Coal was dumped near the laundry facility. The main gate—opening—clanging shut. And always the shouting of orders. There were over 30,000 prisoners in Ravensbrück and there were plenty of places to hole into, Anna thought. Binz had assigned twenty Aufseherin to find the two prisoners and she had promised a bottle of cava from Barcelona to the guard who sniffed them out first.

Anna took a deep breath and considered the camp. Where would two rats make a nest?

"Where do you think they are?" Ruth asked.

Another voice joined them. It was Lotte. "Still haven't found them?" Her perfume made Anna turn towards her.

"Not yet."

"What'll happen when they're found?"

Anna jumped in before Ruth could answer. "I'm getting that bottle of cava. That's what'll happen."

"We should share it," Lotte suggested, pacing back and forth. She had a confident gait and walked with both arms crossed over her chest. "I've never had cava. Is it good?"

Anna used her truncheon as a pointer. "See there? They could be in that line of barracks at the back."

"Or there," Lotte said, nodding to the sock factory.

Anna ignored them and went back to scanning the possibilities. If *she* had a ruined knee, where would she go? Not far, that's for sure. The kitchen had already been searched. Same with the laundry. Anna had lingering suspicions about the laundry, though, because there were huge piles of clothes that needed to be sorted. It would be easy to hide beneath a mound of uniforms and wrap yourself in silence.

She looked at the high walls. Surely they hadn't managed to escape? No, she shook her head. Even if they did, who would protect them?

"There are plenty of places to hide," Lotte said, still pacing. She kept her arms crossed over her chest as she swung out her legs slowly, lazily.

Something inside Anna snapped. They would never find the two prisoners if they just talked about it. She marched towards the laundry in a heavy stride, much like her father, and this made the others hurry to catch up.

"Do you have an idea?" one of them asked. It sounded like Ruth but Anna didn't turn around. She was happy that the stupid nickname they called her had been sent up the chimney over the past few days. No one called her Little Nurse. Not anymore. Anna gripped the handle of her truncheon and liked how it felt warm and familiar. She moved quickly and enjoyed the swish of her grey culotte skirt around her knees.

She hopped up the steps of a brick building and watched prisoners scramble to attention. They snapped off their caps.

"Madam Overseer," they said, mostly at the same time.

"That pile of clothes," Anna said, waving the magic wand of her truncheon. "Make it disappear. Move it to that corner. I want each dress, each blouse, and each pair of underwear moved one-by-one." She looked around for a rake or pole. "And get me something long," she said, going over to an enormous pile of civilian clothes that needed laundered. "Hurry."

Ruth and Lotte scurried in behind her.

"Well?" Anna asked the prisoners. "What are you waiting for? Move that pile of clothes to that corner." To make her point, she brought the truncheon down onto a prisoner's hip. There was a howl of pain, which was followed by a burst of movement. The dirty women of the laundry rushed to move the clothes from one side of the white-tiled room to the other. They moved quickly, urgently. The smell of powdery detergent was in the air. One of the prisoners dashed over to a chemical delousing bath and reached for a pole. The prisoner came to attention with it like she was holding a medieval pike.

"Madam Overseer," she said smartly.

Anna tucked her truncheon into her belt and took the metal pole. Good, she thought. The pile of clothes seemed to melt as the prisoners moved it from one side of the room to the other. It was still several meters high when Anna went over to it. She stabbed it with the pole. She thrust it in and out like she was attacking a boar. She ripped a several dresses. She snagged a bra.

"Interesting." Lotte nodded. "You think one of them is hiding beneath that?"

Anna kept poking and thrusting. She hoped to hear a yelp of pain or see blood on the pole. Furious, she threw it aside and watched it clang against the floor.

"Have they been here?" she asked the room of prisoners. Her voice softened. "You can tell me. I'm not going to punish you for telling the truth."

The prisoners said nothing as they continued to melt the pile with frantic movement.

"Were they here?"

One of the prisoners came to attention. It was the red head who offered the pole.

"Madam Overseer," she said. "I am pleased to report that my work detail has only been here this morning." The woman stared at the wall over Anna's shoulder—she did not make eye contact.

Anna stepped closer and was curious to see if the prisoner would look her in the eye. "Who do you think I'm looking for?"

"*We're* looking for," Lotte corrected.

"I am not understanding the question, Madam Overseer."

Anna slapped the woman across the cheek. She waited for the Russian prisoner to right herself. "There are two Rabbits on the run. Have you seen them? Are they here?"

The woman began to shake. When she spoke, the woman's accent was heavy. "I report only that we have been here for the morning. No one else is here, Madam Overseer."

Anna glanced at the woman's number and saw a red winkel. A communist. Next to the Jews, the Soviets were the greatest threat to the Reich. You couldn't trust any of them. Anna glanced around and was aware of the wet floor beneath her boots. Steam was in the air and the prisoners were sweating. She noticed that their hands were badly pruned from having to dunk clothes into water. She felt like a detective and imagined clues rising up into place. Maybe these prisoners weren't hiding the two rats, but they were getting help from *someone* in camp. Maybe they were being handed off between barracks?

"Yes," she said to the humid air. Others must be helping them. Call it a hunch, but she was sure of it. And in that moment, she felt like Inspector Karl Lohmann in *M*. She had seen that movie in Berlin and loved how Lohmann tracked down the killer. He moved through darkness and rooted out a lurking evil.

"Yes what?" Ruth asked. "Do you have an idea?"

Anna turned on the squeaky wet floor and stepped back into sunlight. The day was bright and clear. Things were beginning to lock cleanly into place. Maybe, just maybe, an entire barrack would have to be punished?

That would flush out the vermin.

≋

Svea placed her head against a roll of fabric and tried to ignore the whirring and clacking of the looms. It was deafening. Shuttles flew back and forth as weaving lines slammed up and down. There was the smell of oil and wool. She tried not to think of her throbbing knee or the cold concrete against her calves or how much her pelvis ached from lack of movement. She looked at Julienne, who was either asleep or trying to block out the cascade of looms.

They were in the weaving factory, which was at the back of camp. They were on the floor, beneath a window, and all around them were upright rolls of fabric. It reminded Svea of being in a childhood fort. Instead of chairs and pillows, they were hunched behind columns of woven wool. There was absolutely no room to move and Svea wondered how much longer they could hide. They had been there for—what?—most of the day now.

She glanced up at the window and worried that a face might look down upon them. From the outside, it would look like rolls of woven wool had been leaned against the window but, if a guard took a few steps forward and pressed her face against the glass, if an Aufseherin looked down, they would see the top of her head.

Svea pressed against the cold concrete and watched a bluebottle fly hopscotch across the window. It buzzed and battered itself against the dirty glass. The fly stopped trying to get out and started cleaning its legs. The whirring and smacking and stuttering continued. There was a rhythm to it, and Svea felt like she was in a dancehall listening to drummers beat out a tempo. You just needed a few blaring trumpets and you'd have something almost like swing. She imagined herself spinning into Peter's arms. Sparkling notes tumbled around them and her legs moved in healthy little kicks and spins.

She looked down at her knee and, slowly, against her will, she was pulled back to the present.

She had never been in this part of Ravensbrück before and she couldn't decide if feeding lines of thread into a loom would be easier or harder than sewing socks. "Women's work," men called it, as if it were somehow lighter. She closed her eyes and winced at the pain in her leg. She tried to remember her biology classes at Humboldt University. Would her body absorb the debris that had been sewn into her muscle? Or was she doomed to be like that woman with a broken arm? They couldn't stay hidden forever. She dared to look at her leg again. My God, she thought, it felt like it was rotting away. It was already twice its normal size and slowly turning grey-green.

She looked at the leaning columns of wool and felt like a child. There was a helplessness to it and, at times, she felt like she was being cared for by a team of mothers. Prisoners brought them crusts of bread along with mugs of cold soup. She didn't know who these women were but they showed up, silently, and scurried away as soon as the delivery was made. One woman with grey eyebrows and a yellow winkel tended to her wound. The stinking bandage was peeled away and a swath of wool was wrapped around her knee. The woman pulled out a white pill and mimed for Svea to stick out her tongue. When she did this, the woman placed it onto her tongue. Svea made spit by sucking her front teeth, and then swallowed. The pain was dulled for the next few hours. It leaked out of her body and, in its place, was a warm drowsiness. The same white pill had been given to Julienne, and she too melted away.

Somehow, these prisoners managed to get new uniforms for them. At first, Svea wasn't sure how they did this, but she remembered the dead stacked in the washroom every morning. It would be a small matter to steal a dress off a body. Several hours ago, when a woman arrived with two stained uniforms, Svea remained in a sitting position—with her legs straight out before her—and her old uniform was slipped over her head. She was naked except for grey splotchy underwear. She had lost so much weight that her breasts sagged as if she were an old lady. When a different uniform was slipped on, she glanced at her new number. Now she was 42813 and she had a green winkel. She was a criminal. She tried to imagine what 42813 might have done to land herself in Ravensbrück. It could have been anything from murder to petty theft to breaking the race laws of the Third Reich. Whoever 42813 had been, it was certain that her body had entered the ovens. The alchemy of fire. Maybe she was already climbing up the chimney and scattering into a graveyard of sky. Maybe part of her was drifting over Lake Schwedt.

Svea looked at Julienne, who was dozing with her mouth open. She had a new number, too. She wore a black winkel and was 56210 now. Of course, Zofia had organized it all. If anyone deserved to survive Ravensbrück, Svea thought while adjusting her wool bandage, it was that good woman from Poland. Maybe she would make it out? She was certainly resourceful enough and, maybe, maybe in some distant future, maybe she would stand in a courtroom and point her finger at the Aufseherin who had tormented them.

The bluebottle fly continued to bump against the top of the window and Svea wished that she could swat it. She glanced at her damaged knee and worried the fly might crawl into her bandage while she slept. It might be drawn to the pus, as if it were honey. She had shooed it away many times already, so what would happen if it crawled inside her knee and laid maggots?

She started to whisper the Ten Commandments in order to refocus her mind. "A mantra," she murmured with closed eyes.

Never forget you're fighting a battle.

Mind your health.

Serve the community altruistically.

That commandment hung in her head. She thought about how they helped each other and supported each other whenever possible. It was something like a sweet miracle, this kindness. She wondered if the men were like this in their barracks? Did they lift each other up or did they only look out for themselves?

A noise came. Svea turned around and felt a flare of adrenaline. Had they been found? Had an Aufseherin peeked through the window while she was sleeping? Was she going to be dragged out and whipped?

But, no. It was Zofia. And as she crawled in, Svea laughed with relief. "I'm glad it's you."

Zofia leaned in. Her lips brushed against Svea's earlobe. She had to shout above the looms. "I do not have long. Good news. I can get one of you into the Siemens Camp." She pulled back and held up a single finger. "One. It is a rare opening."

"Can't we both—?"

Zofia shook her head. "One."

They both looked at Julienne, who was still fast asleep against the concrete wall.

Zofia returned to Svea's ear. "It is either you or Julienne. You must decide who goes."

The Siemens Camp, Svea thought. What a luxury. Prisoners had their own beds, and showers, and adjustable chairs at their work stations. That's what she had heard. It was the place of least danger.

Now it was Svea's turn to place her lips against Zofia's ear. "Why can't we both go?"

Zofia's soured with irritation. "My contact said one. She is risking much to make this happen. Talk to each other. Let me know your decision."

Now it was Svea's turn for frustration. After everything they had been through, how could they be separated now? Svea spoke without thinking. "Send someone else. I want us to stay together."

"Don't be stupid. And do not be selfish."

Svea didn't know what to make of this. Selfish? How was this selfish?

Zofia leaned in again. The clattering looms thundered around them as Zofia pointed at Svea's knee. "You are easy to spot, but Julienne has a chance. Her limp is slight. She can blend in. You?" Zofia shook her head. "If you care about her, give her a chance. The work is lighter in the Siemens Camp."

Svea's stomach dropped. Could she save Julienne by losing her? And if she let her go, it meant losing the one thing that made Ravensbrück almost bearable. Svea crossed her arms. She shook her head. Another idea came to her and she motioned for Zofia to come closer. "How long…how long can you keep us hidden? Until I'm healed?"

Zofia tapped her wrist as if pointing to a watch. "Decide soon. We do not have much time."

She wormed out of the cramped fortress of fabric and hurried away.

Svea stared at her sleeping friend and couldn't imagine losing her a second time. Selfish, she thought. How was it selfish to stay together? She watched her friend's chest rise and fall.

Long minutes passed—perhaps half-an-hour—before Julienne's eyes fluttered open.

What? she asked without speaking a word.

Svea thought about not telling her about Zofia's visit. She could always let a lie of silence take over. She could always seal her lips and keep her friend by her side. How was it selfish to want to care for her?

What? Julienne asked again with raised eyebrows. "What?" she mouthed. "Tell me."

CHAPTER TWENTY

The Hunt

She wasn't angry about searching for the prisoners, and instead of feeling like a detective sniffing for clues, she now began to think of herself as a hunter. She imagined being in the Black Forest with a long rifle and somewhere—somewhere hidden in the trees—was a legendary buck. A ten-pointer. She imagined walking over fallen twigs as she scanned the area for signs of life. She would move in a crouch and let the snout of her rifle lead the way. She would study the ground for scat, bedding sites, and tracks. To stalk prey with a gun, like a man, made Anna smile. She would hold the barrel in her left hand and her right finger would hover over the trigger. The safety would be off. She would be ready for the kill.

They were near the rail line and she looked down its length. The smell of creosote lifted around her as she walked over the wooden sleepers. They stood before the warehouses of Ravensbrück and weren't sure what to do next. They had already stalked many of the barracks, the laundry facility, the kitchen, the carpentry and plumbing shops, the sock factory, the mat-weaving facility, the garage complex and, now, they were walking the perimeter of camp in the hope of chasing down the path of the two trinkets. Where had they slithered?

"You have to think like them," Anna said stepping away from the tracks.

"I'd rather not," Lotte said, lighting a cigarette. She puffed and flicked the spent match into the rail bed.

"You're keen to get that bottle of cava, aren't you?" Ruth laughed. "It's a fool's errand, you know. They'll be dead soon enough. Who would dare to hide them from us? I mean…would you?"

Anna looked beyond the rail line. The camp lifted with noise and she felt keen to get back inside. It was her camp. It was her realm. Thunder drummed on the horizon and she looked at a boiling green sky. A splinter of lightning pounced far away—a moment later came a crackling. The air felt cooler and the wind began to shake the trees. The barometer was falling and she held out her hand to test for rain. Was that the right word? she wondered. Barometer?

"We should get inside," Lotte said, nodding towards the thunderhead.

Anna said nothing and kept looking at the walls of the camp.

"Lightning," Lotte explained. "Rain I can handle, but I don't want to be outside when thousands of volts come shooting down from the sky."

Anna ignored her. "I don't think they escaped. We should focus on what's inside the walls. Being out here was a mistake."

She imagined holding a rifle on the Serengeti. She stood with one leg forward. She made a hard face and felt like a man, cocksure. All she needed to do was squint down the barrel and pull the trigger. She held death in her hands and could send brass flying into skulls whenever she wanted.

Another blast of thunder rolled overhead and she looked up at the churning sky. Trees shook and creaked around them. Goose pimples sizzled on her forearms due to the dropping temperature.

"We should get inside," Erna agreed nervously.

"Anna...?" Ruth asked. "Inside is a good idea."

She studied the looming storm and watched lightning pulse in bright bursts. Rain started to fall. Slowly at first, then faster in fat patterings. The wooden sleepers of the rail line were already dotted with wet.

"Fine," she agreed, stepping in front of them. "Inside."

Four huge wooden warehouses were next to the tracks and she led the way towards one of them. She stepped onto the concrete loading dock and hurried into the cavernous space. The other Aufseherin followed, pushing in. A moment later a wall of rain dropped from the heavens. Thunder roared and boomed. Hail clattered on the roof—it sounded like small arms fire. Pine trees swayed at dangerous angles. Anna found her eyes moving through the heavy rain to the crematorium chimney. Tarry smoke tumbled up into the sky and it was flung about in the wind. It seemed to dance. It pirouetted like an oily ghost. But no matter how hard the wind tried to bat it away, the smoke continued to rise.

A bolt of lightning sizzle-cracked near a tree.

"We should move away from the door," Lotte said, already backing deeper into the warehouse.

Rain came sheeting down and a puddle began to form on the concrete floor. They hurried into unlighted space and stood next to a mountain of clothes. The entire warehouse was filled with trousers and blouses and sweaters and dresses. A monstrous pile of shoes was in the middle and Anna noticed that each pair was carefully tied together. Hail continued to batter the roof and she looked out the large door. The rain seemed to be moving sideways now. If those two dirty Rabbits were outside, they would have wet fur, she considered. Maybe they would die from the cold before she could hunt them down? The thought filled her up with vinegar.

"Anna?" Erna asked.

She realized that she had been lost in a world of her own thoughts and didn't know what the others were talking about. It hardly mattered though, especially when she saw Lotte smoking a cigarette.

"Are you kidding me? Put that out," she ordered. "What are you thinking? Do you see where we are?"

They looked around at the impossibly high piles of clothes.

"Imagine if this caught fire," Anna said, offering a sweep of her arm.

Ruth laughed. "With *this* much rain coming down?"

"That's not the point," Anna flared. "All of this is bound for Berlin to clothe those that have lost their homes in the air raids. And you're in here smoking? Put that out. Put that out right now."

Lotte took a long drag and seemed to weigh whether or not to listen.

"Put it out. Fire spreads quickly."

A moment passed and, as the two women stared at each, thunder rolled and hail continued to clack off the roof. In a flashing moment that surprised even her, Anna snatched the cigarette from Lotte's lips and dropped it onto the concrete. She ground the embers into ash and then, slowly, turned around to look at the others. She squared her shoulders and studied them.

A nervous look came over Ruth. Her bright eyes darted to the floor as Anna continued to stare. Ruth still didn't wear makeup but she hardly needed to. She was a natural beautiful. A spray of freckles was across her nose and cheeks. Anna turned to Lotte, who was using a new perfume. Although Anna had seen her kick prisoners in the stomach, there was something soft and pudgy about Lotte. Anna then looked at Hilda, who had been quiet throughout all of this. It was surprising because she was always demanding the prisoners to make noise, to sing, as if the dirty pieces were some kind of personal radio. Anna was beginning to hate how this woman always talked about classical music. Mozart. Wagner. Beethoven. It all sounded the same to her. No, she preferred folk songs about the forest and farming.

And lastly, she looked at Erna. Happy Erna. Easy Erna. Stupid Erna. Whenever she talked about the future it was always about finding an Aryan man and making future soldiers with him. A woman's place was in the home, she said during their fireplace talks. Erna hoped to find an SS man and make him look her way. But she was frumpy and awkward. Anna just couldn't see this barrel of a woman with an officer. Plus, there was the unattractiveness of how she raged against the prisoners. She was called "The Beast" for how she marched towards her victims and flailed away until blood and bruises lifted up. Erna cursed, her face reddened to the color of merlot, and her eyes bulged as she worked the truncheon. The Beast would never find a good man, Anna thought. What man would want such a ferocious girl? Men wanted grace and elegance. They wanted slinky dresses and nice smiles. What Erna offered was too savage, too dangerous, too unladylike. That was the thing about being an Aufseherin, Anna considered. You had to know when to be violent and you had to know when to be a poised woman in a red dress. You had to know when to flick the switch and make yourself pretty.

She stood there, staring at them in disgust. Oh sure, they had started off together, but that didn't mean they were in it together. She was on her own. She would prove herself, and then maybe one day Keller would—

"What should we do now?" one of them asked.

Anna cupped her hands behind her back and glanced out the door. It was a good question. They were *supposed* to be hunting but here they were hiding from a little falling water. It was something the prisoners would do, this hiding, and she didn't want to be helpless. Not anymore. She was a guard, she was powerful, she was a huntress. It wasn't right that she was hunkered down like a Rabbit.

"What should we do?"

171

Anna didn't turn around to see which one of them had spoken. Instead, she looked at the piles of clothing and, absent-mindedly, she began to finger the lapel of her uniform. It was rough and the stitching felt good against the pad of her thumb. Wool, she thought. Looms, she thought.

"Do you want to know what we're going to do?" she asked them. "We're going to check the weaving factory again."

Ruth snickered. "You really want that bottle of cava."

"It's not about the goddamn cava," Anna snapped.

"Oh, Little Nurse, tell me what it's about then?"

"Call me that name again, and I'll break your fucking nose." She stared at Ruth, she drilled holes into her. Seconds passed. The soft woman with a spray of freckles across her cheeks looked like she was going to say something, but she laughed nervously until finally, eventually, she glanced down and looked away.

Anna didn't allow herself the smile of victory. Instead, she turned and walked into the rain. As water needled all around her, and as thunder rolled out towards the hills far beyond the camp, Anna didn't mind any of it a bit. She let the storm rage around her.

"Follow me!" she shouted. And she didn't look back.

～

Svea was in the lowest bunk and she studied the wooden planks above her. Sunlight had long ago slid down the walls and the world was saturated in dark blue twilight. Searchlights thwanked on and they roamed the camp like sniffing dogs. She rested and listened to the sounds of the barrack. Women were murmuring, there was a laugh, the sound of kissing.

Her blue and white striped dress was still damp from the powerful rain of the afternoon. As soon as the storm started, she and Julienne were hustled away from their hiding place and brought to a nearby barrack. The rain waterfalled down with such force that she couldn't see more than one hundred yards in front of her and the wind made the lime trees stagger about. A bolt of lightning flashed so close that she felt the hair on her forearm lift up—there was a shock of white—and thunder fractured through her chest. None of the guards were out and she knew that's why they were being moved. When they stumbled into the barrack, water was leaking from the roof and she was grateful to be shown a lower bunk. Julienne crawled in next to her. Zofia said she would return to the barrack later and then slipped away for the sock factory.

That was hours ago and now Svea was shivering in the cool night air. Her dress stuck to her chest, her stomach, and there were bits of straw stuck to her arm. At first, she and Julienne held each other to stay warm, but eventually her friend rolled away. They were given another white pill—she didn't recognize the prisoner that offered it, nor did she know any of the women in this particular barrack—could they betrayed her?—but she took the pill and trusted the future. The pain in her knee dimmed like a dying lightbulb and Zofia's words swam in her head. *Give her a chance. Let her go.*

She closed her eyes and decided that, yes, it was okay that she hadn't told Julienne about the Siemens offer. What harm was there in being quiet? Of course, it wasn't just any offer: it was an offer to live in the place of least danger. And anyway, she argued with herself, she liked having someone to care for, someone to talk to, someone that made her feel necessary. Julienne made Ravensbrück endurable. Svea opened her eyes at the thought of life being better in the Siemens Camp. The prisoners had showers. They had food. They might even have blankets and clean beds with coil springs. How could she deny Julienne this?

Svea propped herself up on an elbow and looked down at the wool bandage on her knee. They would be found eventually. It was only a matter of time. Even when the wound healed she would have a limp. There was no way she would survive another selection. But Julienne…

She looked at her friend's knee. They had snipped her nerves and maybe they would grow back. Regeneration. Julienne didn't hop like Svea. She shumbled along as if she had strained her knee. It wasn't noticeable at first and, of the two of them, it made the most sense that Julienne should go. Svea laid back again and wanted these slippery thoughts to go away. A choice had to be made, though. It was a choice between what made her happy and what was right. Maybe they could both go to the Siemens Camp? Maybe Zofia would bring good news for two?

The other women in the barrack had been busy picking lice off each other, and they now began to worm their way into bed. Two more entered the bunk—they spoke Italian—and this made Julienne press into Svea. Her body was warm and Svea placed her forehead against the back of Julienne's shoulder. She felt the rhythm of her friend breathing. A searchlight cut into the barrack and caressed the far wall.

When the beam moved on, Svea heard the soft padding of bare feet. She turned to a shadow at the foot of the bunk.

"Follow me," Zofia whispered. It was an invitation rather than an order.

Svea wiggled to the end of the bunk and heard grumbling from the two Italians. Julienne started to get out of the bunk too.

"You stay," Zofia said. This was an order.

It was painful to shimmy to the edge, and she was grateful for the pill and the strong arms of Zofia. She leaned into her friend as they moved for the washroom, which was the only place where they could find some privacy. When they entered, she saw what looked like a sack in the corner but she knew it was a body. A metal bucket was near the door and she could smell the pong of urine.

"Do you need to...?" Zofia asked, motioning to the bucket. "I can support you in the squatting down, if you like."

Svea thought about having to get up in the middle of the night and found herself nodding. "Yes. Thank you.'

She placed her back against the wall, lifted her dress, and Zofia peeled off the soiled underwear. And then, together, Svea allowed herself to be lowered. The pain was tremendous and she gritted her teeth to keep from shouting out. When the stream came, she heard it ringing off the side of the bucket. She adjusted herself and the ringing turned into a deeper rush. She felt it spatter against her ankles. When it was over, Zofia slid the torn grey underwear up Svea's legs. It was still damp from the rain.

Zofia stepped away from the bucket and leaned against the wall. "So...what have you decided?"

"About what?"

There was a sigh. "No games. What have you two decided?"

Svea couldn't bring herself to say the words. She simply nodded towards the triple-layered bunks. "Her," she whispered.

There was a pause. "Yes." There was another pause before Zofia added, "You are a good woman."

They stood in the dark and let the weight of the decision dissolve around them. They both knew what this meant. Zofia turned to go, but Svea reached out to stop her.

"How will you get her out? She can't just walk out of camp."

Zofia's voice was soft. "She will ride on the dead tomorrow morning. In the wooden cart. Understand? Everyone looks away when it is moving."

"But how will——?"

"I have a contact in the Administration building. She is a prisoner who cooks and cleans. The SS, they trust her. She has arranged a transfer to the Siemens Camp, which is down a path away from the crematorium. Once the wooden cart gets outside the main gate and turns for the ovens, my contact will be there, by the garages."

"Do you think she can do this?"

"She has helped in the past."

"You trust her?"

"Trust," Zofia said, as if tasting the word for the first time. "Like I say, she has helped in the past. That is enough, maybe."

An owl hooted from beyond the walls of the camp.

"I must go. I will tell Julienne so that she can prepare herself." Zofia took a few steps and stopped herself. "I am glad you decided this way. If *you* had decided to go, I would not have accepted that. Julienne has a better chance. You are doing the right thing, Svea from Berlin. You are a good German."

When she left, Svea stared at the washroom. So it had come to this, she thought. Her eyes moved to the drain. Ravensbrück, she reasoned, was like a monstrous magic trick. Hundreds of women disappeared every month. Helena. Lorelei. Maria. Sylvia. Constanza. Margit. Rosa. Charlotte. Katya. They all entered the camp and then vanished. The whole camp was one monstrous trick. Now you see me, now you——

She took a deep breath and leaned against the wooden wall. For a long time, she stared at the tiled floor and enjoyed the simple wonder of air moving in and out of her lungs. She closed her eyes and paid attention to the lullaby of her heart.

She heard Julienne's voice from the next room. "No!"

Svea listened to the darkness.

Yes, she imagined Julienne finally saying. It was the only answer that could be given.

Her uniform was finally dry. Anna had placed it before the fireplace during dinner and then, when she went to bed, she draped it over her radiator. The wool uniform was warm when she put it on and it felt good. She stood in the Appellplatz and enjoyed the morning sun. A full belly, clean clothes, and a new light of fear in the eyes of those who looked at her.

Yesterday, after she marched out of the warehouse, the others followed. With Anna in charge, they redoubled their efforts and returned to the Revier in the hopes the two trinkets had sneaked back in—maybe they were searching for bandages or pills. But, there was nothing. They went to the shoe repair shop, the painter's shed, the water treatment plant, and the motor pool. They searched cabinets and beneath cars and in piles of potatoes. They even searched places that were off limits to prisoners—the telephone exchange, an electrical substation, and the petrol station. They searched the kitchen and the coal bunker. But again, there was nothing. At her suggestion, they did find something promising in the weaving factory. Behind a number of fabric rolls—and below a window—they found crumbs and stains of blood. When Anna saw this, she roamed the entire factory for signs of her prey. In spite of their efforts, though, they came up empty handed.

It was a new day and once roll call was finished the first place she would go—the very first place—would be the weaving factory. She strolled through the ranks of prisoners and looked at kneecaps. She searched for wounds and bandages. She paused to lift up the hem of a dress with her truncheon. She walked down the line searching, searching, searching, and she didn't bother looking at faces or numbers. In fact, Anna assumed that 18311 had slithered into a different uniform by now. She had asked the others in her little crew—that's what she called them— her little crew—to do the same. Any talk of winning the bottle of cava had been strictly forbidden. *This is about finding the enemy*, she told them.

The rags in front of her reeked of filth. You'd think the rain would have freshened them up, Anna thought, wrinkling her nose, but this simply wasn't the case. One trinket was slouching a bit too much, so she rapped the woman on the bony wing of her hip. The slouching continued so she kicked the prisoner to the ground. The thing raised her hands and said something in the gibberish of her tongue. The creature was crying now and Anna looked into its yellow eyes, the wormy ghost of something subhuman. Anna gave out more kicks. She aimed at the leg and chest. A delicious sense of control filled her up and she looked around at the other prisoners standing at attention. It was good to be feared, she nodded.

"Rentz!" she shouted.

Lotte hurried over.

"Make this thing stand up."

Anna walked on and heard the thud of a boot. There was a crack and a shriek. She didn't look back. Instead, she kept moving through the ranks, lifting dresses, looking at kneecaps. Anna glanced over her shoulder. The Russian was standing again—tottering, really—and Lotte had moved on to torment another body.

She scanned the entire Appellplatz. Where were they? At this rate it would take hours to find the rats. Maybe she could make the entire camp run in front of her like they had done for the selection? She would need to clear it with Binz, of course, but it wouldn't take long. Maybe half an hour?

She came to the end of the column and did a U-turn up a new column. There was a rumbling sound on her right and she glanced over to see a wooden cart piled with the dead. A team of prisoners pushed it as it crunched over the cindery ground. The bodies juddered and a lone prisoner sat on top, guiding the team towards the gate and looking ahead, giving muffled orders.

Anna looked away and kept searching for hurt knees. The first time she saw that cart of the dead she felt an oily queasiness in her stomach. She couldn't stop looking at the limbs and open mouths— she thought she was going to throw up—but she had hardened to such things now. It was a triumph over herself that the cart didn't bother her anymore. It almost pleased her that the cart loaded with the dead didn't even deserve her attention. It moved on. It moved away. She kept on walking, eyes down, looking for anyone that might have a limp.

And then a thought hit her.

She looked up in surprise and stood there blinking for several seconds. Of course, she thought, touching her forehead. The dirty trinkets wouldn't be at roll call. They would be—

She looked at the barracks.

The thought came into sharper focus. Why hobble out for roll call when you could stay hidden? It made her grimace. Here she was, doing roll call, because that was expected and routine. What she ought to be doing is searching the barracks now that all the prisoners had been drained into the Appellplatz. How could she be so stupid?

She took off at a run and gritted her teeth. Routine had gotten in the way of creative thinking. She had been blinded by habit and wasn't living like a hunter. Anna ran on healthy knees and didn't look back, not even when members of her little crew shouted after her.

"What is it?"

"Have you found them?"

Anna pointed at the barracks on either side. "Check those."

She ran into Barrack 6 and heard her boots thudding against the floor. She looked to the left and right. Columns of triple-layered bunks stood before her and she jogged between them, jumping up every now and then to see the top bunk. She stopped and took a deep breath. Could she smell hiding rats? She narrowed her eyes. Morning sun filled the barrack and she walked slowly, listening. A bed creaked. She moved in a crouch and jumped up to see the top bunk. There was nothing. She went into the washroom and saw that it was clean—the bodies had been taken away—and she moved into the next wing of the barrack. One of the windows was broken and, for a moment, she thought about searching for contraband. Jewelry. Watches. Radios. Books. But there was no time for that. Roll call would last at least another hour and during that time she could make a clean sweep of the barracks. And if nothing was found, well then, she would turn her attention to the blood stains in the weaving factory. It was only a matter of time before 18311 was found. And punished.

When she finished searching the straw beds—which were in horrible condition—stained with shit and piss—full of lice—she ran out of Barrack 6 and considered where the others were searching. She stood in the doorway of Barrack 8 and yelled, "Anything?"

"No," Hilda shouted from down the hall. "Still looking."

Anna held her truncheon and, as she ran past the clapboard building, she let it thump and bump against the wall. It would cause terror, she thought. If 18311 *was* hiding, she would hear the clunks getting closer.

"I'm checking the next one," she shouted more to herself than the other Aufseherin.

And so it went, barrack after barrack. They leapfrogged from one empty space to another, and although they found hidden necklaces and rings, they didn't find either of the two prisoners.

Anna stopped and wondered if they were hiding separately.

She did a little turn and considered all the places they had checked. There was nothing for it, she told herself. They had to continue searching the barracks until roll call was finished and then maybe she could approach Binz about having the entire camp run past her. It would slow the factory work by an hour, and Administration might not like that, but what if she went to Keller directly? He liked her and perhaps—perhaps showing some initiative would be good.

"Especially if I found her," she told herself.

"What was that?" Erna asked.

"Nothing. Keep searching. I'll take Barrack 15. The rest of you move up the line. We'll meet at the end, just there." She took off at a slow jog and added, "If you find her, tell me immediately."

She went into Barrack 15 and searched the lower bunk, the middle bunk, and hopped up and down to see if anyone was in the top. As she moved, she wondered if there was a better way to search. Anna thought about the pain 18311 must be in. If she were to shake the bunks, maybe the jolting would make the prisoner squeal?

Anna slid the truncheon into her belt and began moving from bunk to bunk, shaking them. Bits of straw fluttered down and the nails squeaked. She moved quickly now and looked at the lower and middle bunk while she shook each triple-layer bunk. If there was a prisoner, she told herself, she would feel them. She had gotten used to how much she could rattle the bunks—how much they weighed— and if there *was* someone on top, she would feel that extra weight.

She moved into an empty washroom. Shit was on the floor from where the bodies had been piled. She ran into the other wing of the barrack and began looking, shaking, looking, shaking. It happened on the fourth bunk. She shook, and it felt more sturdy. She shook again and heard a stifled yip of pain. She put her boot on the second bunk and lifted herself up. There, huddled against the wall, was a prisoner.

"Get down," she yelled.

Anna reached for the thing's ankle and saw a bandaged knee. She froze. It was her. 18311. It was the missing Rabbit.

"Get down," she roared. She reached for her truncheon and began hitting the bare feet. The prisoner huddled closer to the wall. Anna jumped down and hurried to the other side of the bunk. She climbed up and grabbed a fistful of the prisoner's dress. With a grunt, she pulled and watched the thing tumble to the floor. There was a squeal of pain and when Anna saw the trinket's face she couldn't help but smile.

"Found her!" she yelled. "*I* found her!"

The look on the trinket's face was hard to read. There wasn't exactly surprise. It was something more like resignation. 18311 didn't look afraid, and when Anna lifted her truncheon to make the thing flinch, there was a turning of the head. There was no begging for mercy. There was no whimpering.

"Where's your friend?" Anna said in a cool voice. "Who's been hiding you?"

The Rabbit in the trap said nothing.

This strange calm reaction filled Anna with rage. She took a step forward and kicked the prisoner in her broken knee. There was writhing and weeping and great sobs of pain.

"Where…is…your friend?" Anna asked slowly, evenly.

There was no answer, just sniffles of pain. The prisoner clutched her knee and tried scooting away. The bandage on her leg bloomed with red.

Anna took a step back. "Don't worry. I'll find your friend. As for you," she said putting her truncheon away. "You'll be smoke in an hour."

Now there was worry. Now there was fear.

Anna couldn't help but beam. This was a praiseworthy first step in her career, and to think that she had only entered Ravensbrück a few days ago. What a transformation. A bright future surely did await up ahead for her. Or maybe it had already arrived? This was something she could look back on with pride. Oh yes, there would be a celebration tonight. She might even wear her firecracker red lipstick.

But, she wondered, how would she chill that bottle of cava from Barcelona?

CHAPTER TWENTY-ONE

What Happened in the Alleyway

Svea stared at a brick wall and considered the way the cement had set. It had squished out from the red bricks and curled into a gentle, stable, eternal wave. The memory of a day of building, long lost now, was right before her, frozen in time. A tuft of grass sprouted from a crack. It was a little sprig of green, pushing out. She marveled at how it quivered in the wind.

They were standing in a narrow alleyway and facing a wall. There were three other women and they had all been ordered to stare at the bricks. Svea wobbled and was worried that she might collapse into a heap. Her knee blazed with pain and she couldn't put any weight on it. A trickle of blood ran down her shin. She balanced on her left leg, hopping now and then to keep from falling over.

They had been brought outside the main gate—the three other prisoners helped her walk—they were taken to the left, marched past the garages, and then around a corner. The lake was in front of her and, if she turned her head, she could see the village of Fürstenberg. A church bell was ringing, it was calling out to a Christian god, and gulls soared lazily overhead. Two people fished in a boat and she watched how they flicked their rods. How strange, she thought, it was only a few days ago that she was on the other side of that lake looking at the camp. The church bell continued to bong and clang. The sound rippled across the water.

When they turned the corner, she saw the crematorium. It was smaller than she imagined it would be and she was surprised to see windows. There were two of them, and they were both wide open. She could see the ovens inside, as well as waves of heat distorting the air. As they moved closer, her eyes fell onto a massive pile of coal. It was meters high and there was a wheelbarrow next to it. She couldn't see any bodies but there was a low rumbling like distant thunder. Oily black smoke rolled up into the sky.

Most strangely of all, there was a table with a checkered cloth on it. A large pitcher of lemonade was in the center and it was surrounded by tall glasses filled with ice cubes. Blueberries were in a bowl and packets of cigarettes were scattered about. There was even a vase of daylilies. Two Aufseherin had set up this table of refreshments and, when the other guards saw it, there was happy chatter.

"How thoughtful," the guard called Hartmann beamed. She went over and sampled a blueberry. "Delicious."

"Freshly picked this morning," another Aufseherin said, adjusting the vase of flowers.

"And lemonade," the one known as The Beast said, coming over. There was a coo of delight.

It was such a strange domestic scene, and in any other place it might be cozy. Svea's eyes lingered on the lemonade. The pitcher was damp with beads of water.

They were ordered into the alleyway and her tormenter, Hartmann, shouted for them to stare at the bricks.

"Stand there and don't move."

That was five minutes ago. Svea hopped on her left leg and, as she tried to calm herself, she studied the bricks. Many of them were chipped and damaged at head height. She looked up and down the wall. Tiny shards of red brick lay on the ground. She looked at the women lined up on her left, and then at the checkered table on her right. An SS officer appeared and he clapped his hands together in surprised joy.

"Look at this," he smiled.

Svea's eyes went to his holstered pistol. She looked at the chipped bricks before her and, in that terrible moment, the pain in her leg floated away. She tried to swallow, but couldn't. Her eyes went back to the SS officer's pistol. She knew that she was going to die. And there was nothing she could do about it.

Death was no longer somewhere out there on the horizon. It was right before her and she couldn't deny it or push it away or get around it. Her heart began to tremble and she wanted to cry, but at the same time it felt like she had already left her body and that this was happening to someone else.

"Let's get this over with," the SS officer yawned.

He stepped into the alleyway and pulled out his pistol. The Aufseherin watched him. They craned their necks. Only men were allowed to kill with a gun, Svea thought. Only men were allowed this power. That's why he was here.

Her executioner moved behind her—his cologne hung in the air—and he made his way to the dead end of the alley. He cocked his gun.

Svea looked at the bricks and started to quiver. She looked at the little wave of cement and the tuft of grass. In a few minutes she would be gone but this green blade would still be alive. She glanced at the SS officer—both wanting to watch and not wanting to watch—and she saw him level his weapon at that spot where the spine meets the base of the skull. She wondered what the prisoner had done to bring her to this wall. There was weeping as the woman began to pray. She was Polish. She started to sing. Svea looked at the other women who would be killed with her, and she wondered who they were. They were going to die together and she didn't even know their names. They shared this and yet they knew nothing about each other. It wasn't right. She wanted to say to them, "I see you. You're not alone."

When the crack came, she jumped. The reality of what was happening made her whole body tingle. She leaned forward to look down the line of the condemned and watched the first woman slip to the ground. She sank. Her knees buckled and she fell sideways. The smell of gun powder drifted around Svea. It reminded her of sulfur and charred steak.

The SS officer—she didn't even know the name of the man who was going to kill her—stepped behind the next woman. He stiffened his arm.

Svea looked at the wall and started to murmur Julienne's name. Focus on that, she told herself. Julienne had ridden out of camp on a pile of corpses. Svea watched her climb into the wooden cart with the dead and she watched Julienne push her knee down among the cold limbs. She pulled down her cap and ordered the women to push. They juddered towards the entrance slowly, sluggishly, deliberately. The gate groaned open and they turned towards the crematorium. The dead had allowed Julienne to live. And now she was in the Siemens Camp.

There was another crack, which made Svea jump as if she had been bitten by a snake. The woman fell backwards and the SS officer had to dodge out of the way.

The Aufseherin laughed at this.

"Nearly got me," the officer joked.

Svea looked at the amused women in field grey uniforms. They were drinking lemonade and munching blueberries. She looked beyond them and saw a dirt path running toward the Siemens Camp. Somewhere beyond the trees was Julienne. Waves of heat from the crematorium made the path shimmer.

It would have been wonderful to make it out of Ravensbrück alive, she thought. To survive the camp and have it become just a horrible chapter in a long life, well lived, to talk about this wicked place with historians and—she felt tears welling in her eyes at the thought.

The officer moved behind the woman next to Svea. It wasn't right they didn't know each other and Svea reached for the woman's hand. The woman glanced over with wild terror. Her bottom lip trembled and she squeezed Svea's hand.

"Look at the wall," the SS officer barked.

The woman turned to the bricks. There was another sharp crack and a chip of brick hit Svea on the chin. The woman fell. Svea swallowed and tried to control her breathing. Her ears were ringing. How strange, she thought, looking at the blue sky above. The last sound she would hear would be something like a bell.

No. It wouldn't be the last sound.

The officer stepped around the dead woman and moved behind Svea. She steeled her spine. She would not allow herself to shiver. She would not give them the satisfaction of seeing her afraid. She closed her eyes and thought of dancing. She imagined trumpets, and a good beat, and Clärchens Ballhaus, and champagne, and Peter reaching out his hand to give her a twist. She saw her blonde hair flowing out behind her and her feet scuttling over the wooden floor. She watched Peter— good Peter—the best of men—lean in and kiss her. She tried to hold onto this image as she wobbled on one leg. It all could have been so much different, she thought. Peter. The baby. Growing old. She had come to the journey's end. In a few seconds it would all be over.

There wasn't a crack, but a click.

"Damn," came the voice behind her.

She glanced back and felt a spark of hope. Maybe the universe was going to spare her after all?

The officer wasn't handsome, she could see that now. He fiddled with the hammer of the pistol. He removed the magazine of shiny brass bullets.

She turned back to the wall and listened to him fixing the tool that would end her life. While he mumbled and swore, Svea thought about running. Maybe she could push past the Aufseherin and dive into the lake? She was a good swimmer. A strong swimmer. She could glide across the water and hide in the weeds.

She hopped to keep herself upright and almost laughed. Running to the lake? She could barely stand.

At least Julienne might survive, she thought. She would get hot food, clean water, and a bed. Maybe she would survive and return home to France. Maybe she would walk into old age and tell the world about what had been done to thousands of women at Ravensbrück. Maybe she would say Svea's name. But would anyone care about what had happened?

She looked at the sky and marveled at the baby blue. The world was so big and pretty and she wished that she had stopped to enjoy it more. She focused on a fluff of cloud. That, she thought, that cloud would be the last thing she would see before stepping into the unknown. Would it hurt to die? Would the shot echo across the lake? Would some girl in Fürstenberg glance up from playing and wonder what was happening in the women's camp so close by?

The gun was cocked, and she heard him wiggle his boots into the gravel.

She closed her eyes and thought of dancing, of spinning. The ringing in her ears had begun to fade and the SS officer cleared his throat. There was the sound of the crematorium, rumbling.

When it happened, the gunshot echoed across the lake, and rippled into silence.

Author's Note

More than 3,000 women served as Aufseherin in Ravensbrück. For most of them, this camp was a training ground and they were later transferred to such camps as Stutthof, Majdanek, Vaivara, Mauthausen, Bergen-Belsen, and Auschwitz. These women were every bit as brutal as their male counterparts in the SS. Notably, of the thousands of Aufseherin that existed in the camp system, only 77 were brought to trial.

Two of the most infamous Aufseherin were Irma Grese and Dorothea Binz. Grese left school at the age of fifteen and was sent to work on a dairy farm in Fürstenberg. She became an Aufseherin at Ravensbrück in 1942 and was later transferred to Auschwitz-Birkenau where she was promoted to *Rapportführerin*, the second highest rank a female guard could achieve. While at Auschwitz, she beat prisoners with a plaited whip, kicked them mercilessly, and participated in selecting victims for the gas chambers. She led a promiscuous lifestyle at Auschwitz and had a number of lovers—male and female alike. In early 1945, she was sent back to Ravensbrück and then to Bergen-Belsen. She was captured by the British, tried for war crimes, and was hanged at Hamelin prison on December 13, 1945. Known as the "Beautiful Beast," she was unrepentant to the end. During the time that this novel is set, Grese would have already been transferred to Auschwitz. There are, however, a few references to her throughout the narrative.

As for Dorothea Binz, she started at Ravensbrück shortly after the camp was built. Binz worked in the kitchen and was quickly offered a job as an Aufseherin. In a short period of time she established herself as one of the most brutal guards in the camp and her violence was unyielding. She whipped without mercy, she kicked prisoners to death, and she often selected women to be shot. By 1943, she was responsible for training new guards. Binz was reportedly in a relationship with one of the SS officers and they would frequently take long evening strolls around camp to laugh at prisoners who were being flogged. When the war came to an end, she fled but was captured by the British. She was found guilty of war crimes and was hanged on May 2, 1947.

Ravensbrück was a place not just of forced labor, disease, and hunger, it was also home to unrelenting executions. Women were often shot near the crematorium. Today, flowers are arranged near a narrow entrance.

Medical experiments happened at Ravensbrück between July 1942 and September 1943. More specifically, Professor Karl Gebhardt, a leading orthopedic surgeon who taught at the University of Berlin, had wood shavings, dirt, cloth, and bits of glass inserted into legs to mimic battlefield conditions. He sometimes injected disease directly into muscle tissue. Some victims were given sulfanilamides to see if this might slow down rates of infection. In later experiments, bones were transplanted, muscles were severed, and nerves were resected to see if they might regenerate and grow back. More than eighty women were experimented upon in this way and most of them were Polish. They called themselves "Rabbits" because they felt like laboratory animals and the wounds in their legs made it difficult to walk—many of them had to hop. The women of Ravensbrück protected the Rabbits whenever possible and, remarkably, eighteen Rabbits managed to escape Ravensbrück near the end of the war via the Red Cross. They ultimately testified at the Nuremberg Trials. As for Professor Gebhardt, he was found guilty of crimes against humanity and was hanged in Landsberg Prison on June 2, 1948.

Also around this time—between February and April 1942—approximately 1,500 prisoners were taken to Bernberg, just southwest of Berlin, and murdered in a euthanasia center that masqueraded as a sanatorium and mental hospital. This was done under a secret program called 14f13. Nearly half of these victims were Jewish. In the early months of 1942, at least 1,500 Jewish prisoners were rounded up and sent to Auschwitz. This was an attempt to clear all Jews from Ravensbrück, but within a few weeks new prisoners were standing in the Appellplatz. The Jewish population of prisoners would soon swell.

Daily life in Ravensbrück had always been appalling and grotesque, but it quickly became worse as the war came grinding to an end. As the Allies pushed into Germany, and as the borders began to shrink, more prisoners were sent to Ravensbrück and this meant the living conditions became horrifying. With so many women already packed into barracks there was no place for new arrivals. Matters became far worse in late

1944 when Jewish women began arriving from Hungary. An enormous tent was erected and straw was scattered on the ground. As many as 3,000 women were forced to stay in the winter cold with hardly any water or food. They were not allowed to leave the tent and they had to lie in their own filth. Disease swept through these weakened women. We have no idea exactly how many died, especially since the Nazis destroyed much of their paperwork as the Soviets advanced.

A gas chamber was built in Ravensbrück in early 1945, but little is known about it because the SS dynamited it shortly before liberation. An estimated 5,000 women were murdered in this way during the final months of the war. Many of the SS officers who ran this gas chamber had previous experience at Auschwitz. There is additional testimony from former prisoners that railcars were converted into mobile gas chambers and stationed outside of the camp, but we have no definitive proof. The SS is likely to have covered this up. It would be easy, of course, to simply move such killing wagons down the line and into obscurity.

By March 1945, with the Soviets approaching, it was decided that all prisoners able to walk would be marched to Mecklenburg, which is 100 kilometers to the northwest of Fürstenberg. Over 20,000 women were forced to walk on the roads and many died before they could reach their destination.

The camp was finally liberated by the Soviets on April 30, 1945. A Russian tank stands at the entrance of Ravensbrück to this day. Some 132,000 women were imprisoned in the camp and it is estimated that at least 50,000 died, although historians have suggested that this number is almost certainly higher.

As we reflect upon the Holocaust, perhaps it is wise to consider the words of Primo Levi: "It happened, therefore it can happen again."

•

In order to write this novel, and have it be as historically accurate as possible, I am indebted to a number of scholars. I am particularly grateful for the following books, all of which helped me to understand this camp, and female violence in the Third Reich, all the better: Jack G. Morrison's *Ravensbrück: Everyday Life in a Women's Concentration Camp 1939-1945*, Rochelle G. Saidel's *The Jewish Women of Ravensbrück*

Concentration Camp, Wendy Lower's *Hitler's Furies: German Women in the Nazi Killing Fields*, Elissa Mailänder's "The Violence of Female Guards in Nazi Concentration Camps (1939-1945)", Daniel Patrick Brown's *The Camp Women: The Female Auxiliaries Who Assisted the SS in Running the Nazi Concentration Camp System*, Alyn Bessmann and Insa Eschebach's *The Ravensbrück Women's Concentration Camp: History and Memory*, Violette Lecoq's detailed illustrations of her time as a prisoner in Ravensbrück, and Sarah Helm's definitive, *If This is a Woman: Inside Ravensbrück, Hitler's Concentration Camp for Women*.

My deepest thanks and appreciation to Shawn Otto, Janet Blank-Libra, Terri McCargar, Nick Hayes, Jim Reese, Steven Wingate, Lori Walsh, Jon Lauck, David McMahon, Brian Turner, Andria Williams, Amy Weldon, Andrew Erickson, Nicola Sadie, Michael Carson, Lynne Hicks, Jim Hicks, Sean Hicks, Sheila Risacher, Erin Crowder, Jayson Funke, Kevin Linden, Will Swart, the English & Journalism Department at Augustana University, the South Dakota Humanities Council, and the staff at Ravensbrück Concentration Camp and Memorial. I'm especially grateful to the South Dakota Arts Council for the Artist Fellowship Grant that both supported the writing of this novel and also allowed me to visit Berlin and Ravensbrück. This book wouldn't be in the world if it weren't for Kimberly Verhines at Stephen F. Austin State University Press. You're a lucky author indeed when a book you've labored on for years finds the right home.

And lastly, I offer thanks to my amazing, lovely, patient, whip smart, and endlessly supportive wife, Tania. Thank you for immigrating to the United States and making a shared life with me.

About the Author

PATRICK HICKS is the author of *The Collector of Names*, *Adoptable*, and *In the Shadow of Dora*—he also wrote the critically and popularly acclaimed novel, *The Commandant of Lubizec*. He has been published widely in some of the most vital literary journals in North America and his poetry has appeared on NPR, *The PBS NewsHour*, and *American Life in Poetry*. He has been a finalist for an Emmy and he has received grants and fellowships from the Bush Artist Foundation, the Loft Literary Center, and the National Endowment for the Humanities, among others. A dual-citizen of Ireland and America, he is the Writer-in-Residence at Augustana University as well as a faculty member with the MFA program at the University of Nevada Reno at Lake Tahoe. When not writing and teaching, he is the host of the radio show, *Poetry from Studio 47*. He lives in the Midwest with his wife and son.

Printed in the USA
CPSIA information can be obtained
at www.ICGtesting.com
JSHW020805110923
48066JS00005B/22